good things come

by Jodie Beau

I hope you find joy in the journey!

♡,

Jodie Beau

This book is a work of fiction. Names, characters, places, incidents, and lewd encounters are the product of the author's imagination or used in a fictitious manner. Any resemblance to actual persons, places, incidents, or lewd encounters is entirely coincidental.

Copyright © 2018 by Jodie Beau

All rights reserved.

For all the mommies who never got to meet their babies.

Prologue
* Jake *

August 12, 2001
Van's Warped Tour
Phoenix Plaza Amphitheater – Pontiac, Michigan

"I think I want a beer," Krissy says. She pushes herself up off my lap and stands. I see her scan the crowd in front of us, probably estimating how many people she'll have to trip over to get to the nearest beer vendor, and wondering if a beer is even worth the effort. "You want anything?" she asks without looking down at me.

I use my hand to shield my eyes from the sun as I look up at her. The sun streaking through her long blonde curls makes me wish I had my camera. She's gorgeous - not in a girl-next-door kind of way, but in a naughty kind of way. She's a little punk rock mixed with a little girl-genius. With her pierced tongue, cute dimples, and perfect GPA, she'd been making my dick throb since she sat down next to me in Psych 101 in September.

I'm not sure what she sees in me. I'm not a punk rocker or a low-key genius. Shit, I have trouble maintaining a 3.0. I don't have any piercings. I don't play any sports. Maybe it's the tattoos she's digging. For whatever reason, we've been bumping into each other and making out all over campus. It never goes any further than that. Not by choice. She's hot and she's fun, but she tends to drink too much. Contrary to what made-for-TV movies have you believe, most guys don't hook up with chicks who can't walk.

"You sure you wanna leave?" I ask her. "The next act is coming on any minute."

What I really mean is, *Are you sure you want to start drinking this early? I was hoping I wouldn't have to carry you home tonight.*

"Who's up next?" she asks.

I shrug.

"Exactly," she says. "I've never heard of them either. But I wanna be back before Pennywise, so I better get going. You want a beer?"

I shake my head. "I don't wanna fuck with my buzz. But thanks." We smoked a bowl during the last set, and I don't mix weed with alcohol. I like to keep my highs neatly compartmentalized. "You want me to come with you?" I ask. I don't want to, but it's the gentlemanly thing to do.

"No. You stay. They might ID you."

Good point. Krissy is only nineteen, but she has an ID that says she's twenty-one. I don't.

"All right. Be careful."

She blows me a kiss and waves good bye.

I watch her ass as she tiptoes across the blankets and limbs covering the lawn. Everyone is so laid back at this thing. I've never been into punk music, but I'm having fun. Live music, cool people, sunshine. And there's a possibility of sex later. Does summer get better than this? No. I don't think it does.

As soon as I see Krissy's ass disappear into the vendor area, I hear the chords of a guitar letting the crowd know the next act is up. The music starts.

Wait. I know this song. It's a punky cover of Madonna's "Crazy For You." The crowd perks up a little. About as perky as these people get anyway. I see some nodding heads. A few people sit up straighter. I hear a few low whistles and polite claps. Nobody stands up.

Until *she* stands up. She likes this song. Maybe she's even heard this version before. She seems to know what she's dancing to because she doesn't miss a beat. I watch from a few rows behind her as she sways her hips like she doesn't care that she's the only one dancing. She must know everybody is looking at her. She doesn't care. I'm immediately attracted to that kind of confidence. I watch her move her hips back and forth and throw her arms in the air. She has rhythm.

I'm smitten.

Her straight brown hair looks soft to the touch, not filled with product like most of the chicks I hang out with. Her hair is in a sloppy ponytail, held together loosely by a piece of white lace tied into a drooping bow. The lace would ordinarily scream 'pretentious prude,' but it seems out of place in her careless ponytail. A few pieces of her hair have fallen out of the ribbon and hang around her ears. I'm not sure if that happened accidentally, or if she pulled them out. I just know I can't stop looking at her.

Her outfit is nothing special. A tan T-shirt and some short white shorts. Simple. Not tight or revealing. Doesn't scream whore. Doesn't scream desperate for male attention. But she's got it. She's got *all* my attention. That body. Big butt, thick legs. She has just a tiny bit of skin poking past the top of her shorts on the sides. It's barely pinchable. I've heard other girls refer to that as a muffin top. I've also known girls who were dramatic enough to consider a muffin top a reason to cancel all carbs and social plans for two weeks. This girl just does not care.

Suddenly my mind is racing with images of everything that could be. And everything I want. Snapshot after snapshot – so vivid I can practically hear the sounds of a shutter. This girl - bent over in front of me while I slam my dick into her from behind. This girl – on her knees before me while I grab onto a fistful of that messy hair. This girl – and the way she sighs so sweet when I reach my fingers into her panties from behind. Holy fuck. How is this happening? I haven't even seen her face.

The song ends, and the group on stage (I believe they said they're called Me First and the Gimme Gimmes) begins another song. Another cover, this one "Over the Rainbow" from *The Wizard of Oz*. But it's a fun and perky version. This Girl seems to love it because she jumps up and down a few times in excitement. She throws her arms up in the air and her t-shirt rises and exposes that tan spot of soft skin above her shorts. I am legit mesmerized.

I pull my knees up and drape my arms over them, trying my best to look cool and casual, though I'm actually hoping to disguise my hard-on.

This Girl squats down to grab her plastic cup of beer from the ground. When she stands back up, she takes a sip, and then turns to look at her friend. In one second my dick goes from intrigued to rock solid.

It's Roxie. Fucking Roxie and her fucking freckles! My best friend's little sister! Jesus, I've known her since I was six and she was four. Why is my dick hard right now? This is bad. This is not good. This shouldn't be happening. She's barely out of high school for fuck's sake. Oh God. Those images in my head. So bad. So, so bad. Do her parents know she's here? Where did she get that beer? Why is my dick still hard?

I thought I got over this shit months ago when I kissed her at my frat house. I decided then and there that Roxie was off limits. I was crazy about her, but she was the kind of girl I'd want to hang out with in the middle of the afternoon and not just the middle of the night. I'm too young for that kind of seriousness. Besides, she'd be leaving for the University of North Carolina in a few days, and I would be heading back to Central, so trying to start anything with Roxie was a bad idea. Terrible, horrible idea. Try telling that to my dick.

I glance around to see if other guys are looking at her. They are. They *all* are. It's hard not to look at the only girl standing up in a crowd.

I feel protective. I would go over there and tell her to sit, but she's not really doing anything wrong. She's just having fun at a concert. I'm the one doing something wrong. I'm the perverted bastard who just fantasized about sticking my dick in her mouth. Fuck.

And why is my dick still hard? What the fuck? I should be thinking about Krissy's dimples and tongue ring. Not Roxie's freckles. Fuck. Fuck. Fuck.

"Miss me much?" Krissy plops down on the grass in front of me and squeezes herself back between my knees, her plastic cup of beer sloshing a little over the sides.

"Like crazy," I lie.

She leans back into my chest and gives me a quick kiss on the side of my neck. She smells like beer and Victoria's Secret's Love Spell. Not like Roxie. Roxie smells like a pink perfume by BCBG. I close my eyes and inhale Krissy, but still, all I see behind my eyes is Roxie.

"Wow," Krissy says. "I guess you really are excited to see me, huh?"

Great. She can feel my dick through my pants.

"What were you thinking about while I was gone?" she asks.

I grab onto her belt loops and pull her closer to me. "I was thinking about all the things I wish I could do to you after this concert." It's not totally a lie. I *was* thinking about that.

Before I saw Roxie.

"Maybe we shouldn't wait until after the concert." She slides a hand behind her and runs it across my shorts to feel how firm it really is. "I wouldn't wanna waste this. I feel like almost a year of foreplay is plenty, don't you?"

"I don't want you to miss Pennywise. Don't worry about him," I assure her. "He'll show up when we're ready."

She smiles at me and takes another sip of her beer.

"I can't wait."

I can't believe she's saying these things. I've been wanting this chick for months and now she's right here, saying everything I want her to say (and so far, not wasted). But all I can see is Roxie.

Krissy only has two more beers during the concert, so I'm confident this is finally going to happen tonight. When we get to her house, she tells me her parents are out for the night and asks if I want to hang out in her backyard for a bit.

"What do you mean by hang out?" I ask with a grin.

She smiles mischievously. "I believe I was given an IOU earlier."

"And you'd like to collect?"

"I would."

"Okay. Let's go hang out."

So we hung out. And she collected the debt by riding me on a patio chair in front of the fire pit. She bit my neck. She sucked on my bottom lip. She did everything right. But as I came, I could only see Roxie.

I'm going straight to hell.

Chapter One
* Roxie *

June 2017

Thirty years ago, this would have played out like an elementary school game of telephone – whispers from one person to another until the truth was unrecognizable. That's not how rumors work in 2017. News doesn't travel by mouth anymore. There are no quiet whispers or hushed phone calls. Most of us now communicate news via texts, screenshots, snaps, and live feeds. And instead of going from one person to another, it goes from one person to hundreds, to thousands, in seconds.

Today's headline news at the hotel is no exception. It travels from the ballroom to every department of the hotel via Snapchat. I hear the sounds of beeps and vibrations throughout the kitchen, even though we are technically supposed to keep our phones in our lockers during our shifts. I don't enforce that policy though, because I don't want to keep my phone in my locker either.

Speaking of phones, I feel mine vibrating in the pocket of my black apron. I finish slicing the romaine, remove my latex gloves, toss them into the nearest trash can, and pull my phone out to see what the hell is going on. By the time I swipe to unlock the screen, the incident already has its own hashtags. #somebodyisinsomeshit #oristhatactuallyshit #ifthisisntthetimeforpoopemojiidontknowwhatis

A short video plays on my screen. I see the clumpy brown mess and know immediately what has happened. *There is ham glaze in the chocolate fountain.*

Mother effer.

Guests are arriving for a wedding reception – an extravagant and expensive wedding reception – in less than five minutes, and someone accidentally put ham glaze into the chocolate fountain ... instead of chocolate. At least, I *hope* it was an accident, and not a prank. We know too well that there is one person you do not mess with on any day under any circumstances, and that is a bride.

Sunshine looks at her phone and gasps, then looks to me with panic on her face. I don't show my panic. I am a duck. Catastrophes seem to roll right off my back as I appear calm on the surface. But trust me, I'm paddling like hell underneath.

I grab a towel, pull a tray of bacon-wrapped dates from the oven, and set the hot sheet on the counter. I kind of want to laugh, but I know better. It's not good karma to laugh at the misfortune of the catering staff, especially since I used to *be* one of them. Besides, we don't have time for laughing. It's Saturday night. We have shit to do.

A swarm of my teammates surround me and stick fancy toothpicks into the dates while arranging them on silver platters. I leave them to it, knowing as soon as I turn my back the dates will end up in their mouths. It's okay. I made extra.

Weekends are always busy in the hotel's kitchen, but this Saturday night is epic. We have a wedding reception in the Grand Ballroom, a plated dinner for a family reunion on the terrace, an engagement party in the dining room, and a bar filled with pre-gamers drinking craft beer and enjoying the new small plates menu created by yours truly.

The kitchen is a flurry of adrenaline. Bodies move in all directions. The servers hold their trays high, the assistants carry their polishing towels proudly, the prep cooks chop veggies like it's an Olympic sport, and the line cooks plate entrees that should be photographed for magazines. And they do it all with smiles on their faces. Night after night, event after event, ticket after ticket, we generally have a good time in here. My people are happy people. We love our jobs.

And then we hear it – the sound that makes us stop. Smiles turn into scowls. Some freeze in fear. Others scatter and hide like bugs.

I hear the clack of her high heels on the kitchen floor, and I know they are coming for me. As the footsteps get louder, I prepare my eyes to do some dramatic rolling. I look around and see that Sunshine is the only staff member who hasn't disappeared. My faithful Girl Friday stands beside me, all 4 feet 10 inches of her. Not that she'll be any help. Her nickname was never meant to be ironic.

I see the point of Naomi's black patent leather toe come around the corner. She really shouldn't be wearing heels in the kitchen. One of these days she's going to fall on her ass on these greasy, slippery floors. And on that day, I *am* going to laugh. Out loud. In front of everyone. I don't care if it's not very nice. Naomi is not very nice.

A second later, the rest of her body appears before me. I look up from her feet (I would have died for those shoes a few years ago), past her fitted pencil skirt and blazer, to her scowling face. Her hot pink matte lips are pursed in anger and her slanted penciled-in eyebrows look like sperm.

"What can I do for you, Naomi?" I ask, even though I know why she's here. "I sent the servers up with hors d'oeuvres a minute ago."

With her hands on her hips she takes three slow steps forward.

Clack.

Clack.

Clack.

"There is ham glaze in the chocolate fountain," she practically spits out of her hot pink mouth.

What's the deal with the matte lipstick craze? Somebody needs to tell her it looks dreadful. But it probably won't be me.

I open a white bakery box and pull out a cheesecake, keeping up my act of nonchalance while I secretly shake in my slip-resistant clogs. I'm not a fan of confrontations.

"I heard that," I say, as I press a Santoku knife across the cheesecake and slice it in half with a somehow steady hand.

She slams her hands flat on the wooden kitchen island in front of me. I glare at her coral nails and hope she cracked a Shellac.

"Somebody!" she yells. "From this kitchen, *your* kitchen, switched the labels on the ham glaze and the chocolate sauce!"

I give her a sad smile. "That really is unfortunate," I say calmly. "But I'm sure it was an accident."

"UNFORTUNATE?" she repeats in a shriek that nearly makes my ears bleed. "The guests are arriving for cocktail hour. The bride and groom are thirty minutes out. We have an assortment of fruits, crackers, and cookies about to be covered in ham glaze! This is a sixty-thousand-dollar event that has been ruined! And all you can say is that it's *unfortunate*?!"

What I want to say (while pointing my knife at her boobs-by-Bombshell chest) is this: "Listen, fucktard. First, chocolate fountains are so twenty years ago. For sixty grand there should be Nutella somewhere ... or everywhere. Second, my job is to make sure the food is prepared. What happens after the food leaves this kitchen is not my concern. Now, I believe you have a problem that needs fixing, so please try not to fall on your ass as you see your way out of my kitchen. And one more thing, just because the glaze is made *for* ham, doesn't mean it tastes *like* ham. So stick a dick in your mouth and suck it, bitch!"

But I'm not going to get upset and lose my temper. Getting upset is not good for the baby. Instead of lashing out and ending up as the next viral video star, I take a deep breath for six seconds and blow it out for six seconds. It's a calming technique I learned in yoga class.

When I'm ready to speak, what I actually say is

this: "Since the chocolate fountain is part of the dessert buffet, and the guests are only eating hors d'oeuvres now, we have enough time to drain it, clean it, and reassemble it before dessert. If you don't mind it disappearing from the room for at least a half hour. *Or you could leave it in there and see if the guests discover a new favorite treat.*"

I blink my bright blue eyes and smile innocently. It's totally possible that the guests might like ham glaze on their Rice Krispies treats and vanilla wafers. It's made with honey and brown sugar. What's not to like about that?

She doesn't look amused.

"A lot of remarkable things have been discovered by accident," I continue with an innocent shrug. "Penicillin, the microwave, Vernor's, Post-It notes. Wasn't electricity discovered because Ben Franklin accidentally took his kite into a storm? Or am I thinking of the wrong cartoon?"

"I'm glad you think this is a joke."

I set my knife down and sigh. *Peaceful environment.* "If you have a better idea, I'd love to hear it."

"I already have someone working on it. What *I'd* love to hear is how you're going to serve a ham covered in chocolate? Or is that going to be the next accidental discovery?"

"Oh, don't worry about the ham. I made another batch of glaze when I noticed it looked a little funky. I guess this explains it. Anyway, I've got to get these desserts ready for the party in the dining room. If you'll excuse me..." I don't wait for a response. I take my cheesecake and walk away.

I'm so busted. I totally noticed the ham glaze was gone at least four hours ago. I guess I should have done more investigating. I'm blaming it on pregnancy brain. But not out loud. Nobody here knows I'm pregnant. My chef's coat is roomy. I should be good for another month or two. I'm not sure how I'm supposed to announce it. This is one of those times when I feel like, as a grown-up, I should know the proper workplace pregnancy announcement etiquette. But I guess I was absent in class the day that lesson was taught, because I have no clue. All I know is that I don't want to lose my job. I hear stories about workplaces trying to drive out pregnant women so they don't have to deal with the hassle of maternity leave. I don't think my company is that shady, but still, I'd rather not have to worry about it right now.

"Chef, do we have three gluten free plates for the terrace?"

"In the hotbox with the stickers that say, 'Gluten Free.'"

"Chef, have you ordered any to-go boxes lately? I can't find any in dry storage."

"Upper shelf on the left. White box with blue letters."

"Chef, the waffle iron just took a shit. You want me to eighty-six the chicken and waffles?"

"Sunshine, can you grab the spare waffle iron from storage? Gino, I have a few backup waffles in the freezer, can you grab them, please? Terrance, use the frozen for now and give us about ten minutes to get the spare iron hot."

"Sure. Get it hot, Chef Roxie. I'll wait."

Terrance sticks his tongue out at me, and I shake my head. "Watch it before I send you to HR."

I know he's just playing. I have a soft spot for Terrance. He reminds me of Turk from *Scrubs*.

I look at my watch. It's 6:03PM. Three events. Five hours. I take another deep, six-second breath. *Peaceful environment*, I remind myself. Ha. That's kind of an oxymoron. The kitchen of a large, five-star hotel downtown Detroit on a Saturday night in the middle of baseball and wedding season will never, ever be a peaceful environment. I let out my breath. It's just a few hours of madness. We got this.

Chapter Two

I love Mondays. The chaos is over. The hotel is quiet. The weekend guests checked out yesterday. The weekday business guests don't check in until this afternoon. This is the in-between, the day I get to sit in my office and do non-urgent things. Like drink coffee (only one cup of half-caff, pregnancy police - my doctor said it's okay), create recipes, plan menus, work on the kitchen schedule, go over resumes, and put in orders for stock. Most of my Monday work involves me sitting in a chair. Which is really freaking awesome. So, if you're the type of person who likes to shout out "TGIF!" and "It's Fri-Yay," you can take that bitmoji bullshit somewhere else and talk to me on Monday.

"Morning, Boss," I don't know where Sunshine got her nickname. They've been calling her Sunshine since long before I started working here. But it's perfect for her. She gets here so early in the morning that it's not even light out yet, but she walks in as peppy as a high school cheerleader. She's tiny, but she lights up the room with her dark, poofy hair and cherry red lips. It's not uncommon for her to sing to the staff and dance around the kitchen. I've never seen her get mad or lose her patience, and she keeps the staff laughing. She's my lifeline in this place. I don't know what I'd do without her.

"Morning, Sunshine!" I say through a yawn as I walk into my office and set down my bag.

She follows me, grabs my plastic coffee tumbler off my desk, and disappears. It's not that I'm too good to get my own coffee. I swear I'm not one of those people. But it just tastes better when she makes it. I'm too stingy with the sugar, especially now. I don't want to overdo it with carbs and end up with gestational diabetes.

I sit down at my desk and move my mouse to wake up my computer. The screen comes to life, and I see that cute little boy's smiling face in my background photo.

Before I begin work, I pull my planner from my bag. I am aware that I can do this digitally, and that most people do, but I'm a pen-on-paper girl for life. And my planner *is* life.

I open my planner to the current week and lay it on my desk next to the set of pastel pens in my pen holder – because you're never too old for pink and purple pens. And anyone who tells you differently is just being a Pleco in your joy tank. Don't hang out with people like that.

I click open my email folder on my laptop to see that it's empty. I like what I see. A Monday morning with no new emails. No Ham Glaze emails from Naomi with the GM and Executive Chef cc'ed. That's totally something she would do. But it doesn't look like she did ... yet.

I then go to Trip Advisor. I do this every morning to check the hotel's ranking and reviews. While the page loads, I feel my chest constrict with anxiety. This happens every single time. The reviews are mostly pretty good; we've even gone up two rankings since I started working in the kitchen. But my nerves always get the best of me while the page loads.

Sunshine returns with my coffee tumbler and sets it on my desk.

"Half-caff with a shot of decaf espresso and three pumps of hazelnut," she says.

I know she's lying. There's got to be at least five pumps of syrup to taste this good. But I like it too much to call her out on it.

A chef who worked here before me accidentally ordered a whole case of decaf espresso beans (which might be one of the reasons he's no longer working here – but that's none of my business). They've been sitting in storage for years because who the hell orders decaf espresso? Pregnant women. They order decaf espresso. Even so, I'm *pretty* sure Sunshine is oblivious to my secret. I told her I wanted to use up the beans to make some space in storage. I'm sure she bought it.

"Thank you!" I say. "You're a lifesaver."

After she leaves the office, I glance down at the Monday agenda in my planner.

Meat order sent by 8:00.

Produce order sent by 8:20.

Interviews for line cooks at 10:00 and 10:30.

Staff schedule emailed by 1:00.

Leave hotel at 2:00.
Doctor's appointment at 2:30.
Baby announcement photo shoot at 4:00.
What a snooze of a day. I freakin' love Mondays. TGIM!

Chapter Three

I step off the scale beaming. Thirteen weeks pregnant and I've only gained one pound.

The nurse records my weight on the chart and points down the hall. "We're going into exam room four, on the right."

I follow her into the room and hop up onto the exam table where she takes my blood pressure. Perfect. Another victory.

"Go ahead and lie down, and let's listen to this baby," she tells me.

I lie back on the exam table and lower my black pants to the top of my panties. I've only got a teeny bit of a belly, and it might be more pizza than baby, but I'm glad my work pants have an elastic waist.

The nurse spreads some gel along my lower abdomen and presses the doppler onto my belly. She moves it around.

"Your husband didn't come today?" she asks, more out of habit than interest, I'm sure.

We're the only people in the room, but I don't point out the obvious. I try not to be annoyed by her question. I understand she's probably just making conversation, but she really shouldn't use that question for small talk. It may offend someone who isn't married. There are plenty of pregnant women who don't have husbands. There are pregnant women who have wives, pregnant women who have boyfriends, pregnant women who don't know who the baby's father is, pregnant women who are single. I'm genuinely surprised in the age of the easily offended that she would even ask this question. But I don't believe she meant any harm by it, so I let it go.

"I'm not married," I tell her. I don't offer her an explanation, because I don't owe her one. I just want to hear my baby's heart beating already.

"I can't seem to find anything," she says. "Don't panic though," she adds quickly. "The doctor is better at this than I am."

I'm not panicking. I have no reason to panic. I saw Gummy Bear's heart beating a few weeks ago. It's not even an issue.

"Just relax here for a minute, and she'll be in shortly, okay?"

I nod and stare up at the calming cloudy sky painted on the ceiling.

As promised, the doctor arrives in a few minutes and greets me cheerfully, "Hey, Roxie! Let's see what we've got here," she says as she picks up the doppler and presses it into my belly. Left, right. Small circles. Smaller circles. "Sometimes they are stubborn little suckers," she says patiently.

She searches a little longer and still finds nothing.

"You know what?" she asks. "This doppler is ancient. The ultrasound room is empty right now. Let's go in there and find this baby, okay?"

I perk up instantly. I get to see the baby!

I had an ultrasound a month ago, when we saw the heart pulsing on the screen. I was eight weeks pregnant then, and the baby looked like a little gummy bear with nubs for arms and legs.

Insurance will only pay for a few ultrasounds per pregnancy, so I didn't expect to see the baby again until the anatomy scan in two months – which feels like a decade for a pregnant woman.

I am so excited to see my Gummy Bear again and see how much she has grown (I don't know the gender yet, but my mommy instinct says it's a girl). Bonus: I'll have a better picture to use at the announcement photo shoot later. How lucky I am to get a surprise ultrasound!

Her voice sounds confident, and I'm not worried about this at all. Like she said, that doppler is old. I pull my shirt down, hop off the table, and follow her down the hallway to the ultrasound room.

As we walk down the hallway, she asks if I'm here alone. Why does everyone feel like making small talk today?

"Yep. Just me," I tell her. Jeez. It's just a regular prenatal appointment. Do pregnant women usually bring their baby daddies to every appointment? Who has time for that?

When we get inside the room, she flips a switch that turns on the TV monitor mounted to the wall in front of me. I hop onto the exam table, pull up my shirt, and lower my pants for her. She puts more gel on my belly and rubs the transducer probe around.

I watch the screen as the contents of my uterus appear on the wall.

Even though I'd said I wasn't nervous, I feel a sense of relief when I see Gummy Bear up there on the screen. She has grown since my last appointment. She looks like less of a Gummy Bear and more like a miniature baby.

My doctor is quiet. I notice Gummy Bear looks very still. I don't see the pulsing I saw last time.

"I wish you had someone here with you today," she says sadly.

"Why? Is something wrong with the baby? What is it? Down Syndrome? Spina Bifida? Cleft palate?" Every mom-to-be knows there's a possibility of having a less-than-perfect baby. I've imagined it, and prepared for it, because that's what I do. And I already know I will keep my baby and love my baby no matter what. In fact, finding out this early is a good thing because we have more time to learn about the condition and prepare to care for a baby with special needs. I take a deep, calming breath. *It's going to be okay. Whatever it is, we will get through it. I can handle it. I can handle anything.*

"I'm sorry, Roxie," she finally says. "Your baby's heart isn't beating."

Except that.

As dumb as this is, my first thought is How do we get it beating again? Like it's something that can be fixed. *Okay. So Gummy Bear has a heart problem. But there must be a way to fix it. Like maybe they can put those shocker things on my belly and get the heart beating again.*

The doctor takes a few measurements and says, "It looks like the baby's heart stopped beating about a week ago. Maybe less."

It takes several moments before I realize that what she is saying is that my baby has died. My baby is dead. Forever. Not coming back. Not fixable. Gummy Bear isn't going to be the next member of my family.

I don't understand. Why did this happen? What did I do to kill my baby?

As if reading my mind, she quickly adds, "Whatever you do, do *not* blame yourself. These things are usually caused by a chromosomal abnormality, and that is something there's no way you could have prevented."

I can barely even hear what she's saying. This can't be true. We can just wait a few minutes and check again and maybe the heart will be beating. I mean, this never happens. When you get pregnant, you have a baby. That's how it works!

"Are you sure?" I ask.

She nods, looking at me sympathetically. "This is the hardest part about my job. I hate that I have to tell mommies this every day. It is very common, Roxie. Once a woman finds out she's pregnant, there's only a seventy-five to eighty percent chance that she's going to bring a baby home. One in every four women has had, or will have, a miscarriage at least once."

How could that be? I wonder. There's no way that can possibly be true. One out of four? If I know 100 women, that means 25 of them have lost babies. I've never in my life known a single woman who has had a miscarriage, so I know that isn't true. She's just saying that to try to make me feel better, like I'm not a baby killer.

And why are they calling it that anyway? *Miscarriage.* Meaning I miss-carried my baby. I somehow screwed up the carrying of this child.

A miss-carry was when I forgot to double bag my groceries and a glass bottle of balsamic vinaigrette fell out of the bag and shattered all over the sidewalk. That was definitely a bad carry on my part.

I guess this was, too.

The word miscarriage sucks. I don't want to hear that word again. Ever.

"Do you want me to print a picture of your baby, Roxie?"

I nod. I don't know what I'll do with it, but I want something to remember Gummy Bear. I want to have something to show for this. I won't have a baby bump. I won't get to send baby announcements to my friends and family. But I have a baby inside of me who was alive. This baby is a part of my family and a part of my heart. She deserves to be remembered.

She gives me the photo, and I slide off the table with much less hop than I did a few minutes earlier. We walk back down the hallway to the exam room where she explains my options and reiterates that it wasn't my fault. But again, I don't believe her. They wouldn't call it a miscarriage if it wasn't the fault of the carrier.

I stop at the front desk on my way out to make an appointment for my procedure. The doctor said I could wait for my body to realize the baby has died, or she could give me a shot to help my body realize it. She assured me that when that happened, my body would know what to do and I could have my miscarriage at home with no medical intervention. If my body didn't miscarry naturally, or I didn't want to do it on my own, she said she could "surgically remove it."

So, either I can experience the loss of my baby at

home in what I imagine will be very painful and messy, though she didn't mention that part. Or she could put me under and remove Gummy Bear from my body like she was nothing more than a cancerous tumor.

I told them I would need a few days to think about it, but I wanted to schedule the procedure right now, so I could proceed quickly if that was the route we decided to take.

"I'm so sorry, Roxie," the woman at the desk says. But her sympathy lasts exactly one second before she moves on to discuss the business at hand. "Now, the doctor only schedules D & Cs on Fridays. She does have an opening this Friday if you'd like it. You can cancel the appointment if a spontaneous abortion occurs before then."

Spontaneous abortion? How awful! I'll take the word miscarriage back please.

"I work on Fridays," I reply automatically.

"Oh, honey," she says, "I can give you a note. Whichever way you decide, you won't want to go to work. Why don't we write you off for this entire week? You need to heal physically, but also you need to heal your heart."

We're both startled by a loud sound behind me. I turn to see what the commotion is. The door to the exam rooms has been thrown open by a teenage girl. A woman, who I assume is her mother, is walking quickly, trying to catch up. The older woman has a long strip of ultrasound photos dangling from her hand. She got a lot of photos. Probably all different body parts. I only got one picture, and my baby is dead.

"I don't want to see the stupid pictures!" the

teenager spits out as she walks toward the front door. Her blonde hair is striped with lavender, but it looks like she's been stretching the dry shampoo at least two days too long. She flips her hair back and sticks her nose high in the air before telling her mom, "Just throw the stupid things in the trash! I don't want them!"

The mother, who is probably only a few years older than me, looks embarrassed and a little sad as she follows her daughter toward the door. She glances over at the desk and gives the receptionist an apologetic look before following her daughter out of the office. The door closes behind them, leaving the waiting room awkwardly quiet.

I'm not proud of this, but if I'm going to tell this story, I need to be honest about all parts. At that moment I think to myself, *why didn't her baby die instead of mine?* Why couldn't this have happened to someone who didn't want their baby?

I'm a terrible person for thinking it. No wonder my baby was taken from me.

"Okay, Friday, whatever," I say. I just want out of here. Away from all the pregnant bellies in the waiting room, and the mommies whose babies didn't die, and the snotty teenagers who don't realize how blessed they are.

Chapter Four

I walk out of the building feeling like a zombie. One foot in front of the other. One step at a time.

I should call someone. But when I do, it means someone else is going to hurt as much as I do. I don't want anyone else to feel this way. I don't want to break the hearts of the people I love more than anything in this world. I know I need to tell them eventually. But not yet. I want to give them a few extra minutes of happiness.

I make it to my car and get in. I turn the engine on, turn the radio off, and lean my head on the window. I know she said it wasn't my fault, but my mind is spinning with hundreds of different ways I could have killed my baby. I worked too many hours, was too stressed over all the events we've had this summer. I shouldn't have been drinking half-caff. I should have switched to decaf. I shouldn't have gone to the gym. I should have stopped lifting anything heavier than my purse. What was I doing when my baby's heart stopped beating? She said it was about a week ago. Maybe last weekend when we'd had that awful bridezilla arguing over the garnish on the dinner plates? Was that when it'd happened?

A couple of hours ago I was worried that I might lose my job when they found out I was pregnant. I should have worried about losing my baby! Not my job! Maybe that's why this happened to me. Because I worried about the wrong things. They say most of what you worry about never happens. I should have worried more about my baby. But I didn't.

My phone vibrates. I don't answer it. I can't answer it. If I try to speak I will cry. And once I start crying, I don't know if I'll be able to stop.

Why did this happen to us? Our story is supposed to be a romantic comedy, not a tragedy. What did we do to deserve this?

I guess I should probably text Chef my doctor's note and let him know I won't be in for a week. How do I explain it? I can't tell him I lost a baby he didn't even know I was having. Or maybe I don't need to explain it. I can just say I've had a medical emergency. It's not like the hotel pays bereavement for the death of a pregnancy. But why don't they? I just lost a family member. It might have been a family member I've never met, but it's a family member I've loved since I saw those two pink lines eight weeks ago. This baby was everything to us. And now she's just gone with no explanation, and I can't even validate my pain with the rest of the world because no one knew about her to begin with.

We planned to officially announce the pregnancy after twelve weeks, because it's considered taboo and juvenile to announce a pregnancy any earlier. They say you shouldn't announce too early in case something bad happens. But nothing bad ever happens, and everyone announces their pregnancies with their cutesy posts right on schedule. Right?

Or is that wrong? I do a quick Google search on my phone to see if what the doctor just told me is true. It doesn't take long to see that every link I click says the same thing. Google verifies it: 1 out of every 4 known pregnancies ends in a loss. Which means for every three pregnancy announcements I see on Facebook, there's a couple somewhere with broken hearts, with ultrasound photos they never got to share, with onesies that won't be worn, and a bedroom that won't be turned into a nursery. One out of every four couples has suffered. And they've suffered alone.

Well, I guess it's a good thing we *did* wait to announce our pregnancy. If not, we would have to post a public renege, and it doesn't appear like that's allowed since I've never seen one. You cannot renege on an announcement. You cannot mention the loss of a pregnancy. You cannot bother other people with your misfortune. Apparently, if the baby did not make it to twelve weeks, the baby did not exist. So post another silly dog face selfie, and keep your broken hearts to yourself.

Speaking of pregnancy announcements, we were supposed to take our pictures today. I need to get home. I don't want to do it. I wish so badly that I didn't have to do it. But it's time to break some hearts.

I pull into the driveway. They are sitting on the

front porch waiting for me. I see a McDonald's Happy Meal box on the bistro table. We're supposed to walk to the park to take the announcement photos. We ordered a cute banner off Etsy for the pictures – a string of turquoise paper flags with a sign in the middle that says, "Oh, Baby!"

Jake's camera is ready and hanging from his neck with the pink Breast Cancer Awareness strap that he wears for his mom. He stands up and waves when I pull into the driveway. He has no idea anything is wrong. I wish it could stay that way.

My sweet little Sam sits at the bistro table, his tiny legs dangling inches off the ground. It looks like he's just finishing up his McNuggets. He is ready for pictures and looking too cool in his Big Brother T-shirt. With his soft blonde hair falling perfectly across his forehead, he could easily be a model in a Gap Kids ad. I wonder what his sister would have looked like. Would she have had Jake's brown eyes? Or my blue ones? Would she have my freckles? What about her hair? Would she have brown hair like we do? Or would she be an anomaly like her big brother and end up blonde?

This kid has waited so long to be a big brother. How can I tell him he's now the big brother of an angel?

What am I supposed to do with his Big Brother shirt now? Throw it away? Act like it never happened? I mean, that seems to be the normal protocol. I hadn't bought anything for the baby yet, but I guess I can go ahead and delete my Amazon registry. I won't be needing a new Boppy cover or Sophie the Giraffe. There won't be an anatomy scan in August. There won't be a Santa Baby in December. The baby name list can be deleted. I don't know why I bothered with a list this time around because we'd already agreed on naming our Christmas baby Noelle or Noel. But that doesn't matter anymore because you don't name miscarried babies. The reason I know this is because I also looked up this info while I was sitting in my car. Babies don't officially "exist" until twenty weeks gestation. That is when they get names, birth certificates, death certificates, funerals.

And believe me, I realize I am lucky that I don't have to go through that right now. I do realize that other mommies have it worse. Some mommies have to make decisions they should never have to make for their babies, such as when to stop treatment, when to take them off life support, whether to donate their organs, whether they should be cremated or buried, what kind of headstone to put on their graves. I get that. And I will put this into perspective sometime in the future, I'm sure. But what I know right now is that this fucking sucks. And now I have to tell them how badly this fucking sucks.

Again, I wonder why. Why did this happen? Maybe it happened to me because I'm a selfish bitch who'd wished a teenager's baby had died instead of mine. A selfish bitch who'd worried more about losing my job than losing my baby. A selfish bitch who'd only given up caffeine half way. Or maybe the simplest reason for this is that it happened because I'm just not a good mom. Maybe God looked at me and said, "Oh shit. I'm not making that mistake again. Scratch that."

I understand all of that. I accept my punishment.

But why did it happen to Jake? What did he do? And why, someone please tell me why, this has happened to my innocent four-year-old son?

I open the door and get out of the car.

Sam jumps up from the chair. "Mommy!" he yells across the yard. "Can you buh-weave I ate ALL my chicken nuggets AND my Go-gwurt?"

Jake only needs one look at my face to know something is wrong. Sam is oblivious. He runs down the porch steps and into my arms. I lift him, put my arms around him, and squeeze tightly.

"Whoa, Mommy, too tight," he says, trying to squirm away. He stops suddenly and looks worried. "Why are you crying, Mommy?"

Am I crying? I guess I am. The seal has been broken, and there's no going back.

Jake greets us on the sidewalk path that leads from our driveway to our porch.

"Baby?" he asks. "Are you okay?"

I shake my head. "I'm so sorry," I tell them. "The baby didn't make it."

He nods his head. I can see how much it hurts him, but he stays strong for us. "Come on inside," he says.

Sam doesn't seem to understand. "Didn't make what?" he asks. "The baby didn't make what, Mommy?"

Carrying Sam, I follow Jake up the porch steps, past the *Oh Baby* banner on the table, and into the house.

Jake sits down on the couch and puts his arms out for me to sit on his lap. I sit down on his lap, with Sam in my lap, and Jake puts his arms around both of us.

"The baby died," I tell Sam.

I've seen my son burst into tears for things as simple as his sock having a loose thread in the toe. But those are tears of anger or frustration. I have never seen the tears in his eyes that I see now. They are the tears of a broken heart. His heart is broken, and I can't fix it.

I can find the loose threads in his socks and cut them out. I can replace batteries in toys that don't work anymore. I can let him watch whatever he wants to watch on TV when he's not feeling good. I can make him macaroni and cheese when he doesn't like the quinoa salad I made for dinner.

But *this*, I cannot fix.

Jakes holds us both tightly, and the three of us cry together in a heap on the couch until there are so many tears that we don't know whose are whose.

Chapter Five
* Back Then *

September 2012

    I am such a badass. Not only did I select and purchase an over-the-toilet shelving unit to create extra space in our tiny bathroom, but I also put it together by myself. With tools. *Actual tools!* Yep. This girl right here. Totally independent. Except that I'm head-over-heels in love with my hot boyfriend, every minute he is away from me feels like hell, and when it's time for him to leave for work I want to wrap my arms around his feet and beg him not to go. Other than that, though, totally independent.

    Back when I was married, I had to get all purchases for the home, like furniture, appliances, and décor, approved by my husband first. I couldn't so much as buy a three-wick candle from Bath & Body Works without him approving the scent.

Back when I was married... I say it like it was so long ago. It feels like a lifetime ago, but in reality, only a few pages have been turned on the calendar.

I moved out of my marital home less than five months ago, and last week I moved into a teeny tiny studio apartment in The Village with my previously mentioned super hot boyfriend. It may look to others that it happened very quickly. But when you've loved someone as long as we've loved each other, it feels like it happened at just the right time.

P.S. I really like calling him my boyfriend, so please forgive me if I say it too often. We have spent so much time in ambivalence, that I've earned my rights to the word, and I'm going to use it every chance I get.

Can you tell how happy I am? I'm bouncing-off-the-walls giddy. This past summer with Jake, it was sweet, but also frustrating because I was holding back, afraid to admit he was everything. Now that he's officially mine, there's no nagging feelings, no pretending I don't care, no figurative game of tug of war. This time there's no end. We said forever, and I believe he meant it. *I* did.

It's so splendid being with someone who loves me. (Who goes around using words like splendid, you ask? People in love, I guess.) He eats anything and everything I cook, he can kiss me and snuggle me for hours without getting bored, and he trusts me to go to Home Goods by myself and pick out a shelving unit for our bathroom. It's just so ... easy.

After I get the shelves set up, I stand back and proudly admire my hard work (tools, I tell you!). Now that we have storage space in here, it's time to unpack the bathroom box.

I locate the carboard box labeled *bathroom* in our closet underneath a shitload of ridiculously overpriced shoes. I should probably donate them. See, back when I was married, I didn't need to ask my husband's permission to buy things for myself, like clothes, shoes, and makeup. I think maybe because of that, I went a little overboard. Now I have all these shoes that don't feel like me anymore. They were the person I pretended to be for too many years. I don't need them now.

But I'll keep the makeup.

I push several pairs of shoes off the box and try to pick it up, but it's heavier than I remember, so I pull it out instead. *Damn. How much shit do I have in here?*

I push the box across our dull hardwood floor (so vintage!), into the bathroom, and open it up.

How the hell do I still have so many products? Before we moved, I donated a lot of beauty products to a women's shelter in Detroit. I didn't think I had very much left. For the past week I've been living just fine off one makeup bag and basic toiletries. But when I open the box and see all my stuff, that *thing* happens. You know, that *thing* – when you haven't used something in ages but all of a sudden it's your favorite thing in the world and you can't bear to part with it?

My Kiehl's Grapefruit body scrub! My Naked 2 palette! My Smashbox primer! I pull them out and hug them to my chest. How have I been living this long without you, my darlings?

I set them aside and start organizing my new shelves. I roll up towels and washcloths and arrange them on the top shelf. I line up lotions, moisturizers, and face masks on the second shelf.

I pull out a familiar pink box. Tampons. Hmm. Where should they go? They're not something people proudly display in their bathrooms. But we have a pedestal sink, a medicine cabinet that is literally deep enough for pill bottles only, and no linen closet. Maybe I can find a cute makeup bag to hide them in.

Wait a minute.

Tampons?

TAMPONS!

Holy.

Shit.

I close the toilet seat cover and sit down, holding the pink box in my lap. When was the last time I needed these?

I think back and try to remember the past several months. Let's see. I moved in with Jake and Adam in May. I didn't start hooking up with Jake until the end of June, so I had to have had at least one period before that. I was kind of an emotional mess during the time after Caleb, but before Jake. I don't remember a whole lot of it. But I must have had a period.

What about after the end of June? Have I had a single period since we started having sex? I honestly can't remember. What is this? Eighth grade? What twenty-nine-year-old woman doesn't know when her last period was? Seriously.

I grab my phone and open my menstrual cycle app. No data entered since I left New York.

Jake and I haven't been using protection.

When I was younger, before I got married, I was a dedicated birth control enthusiast. I took the pill and used condoms as a backup. Every single time. (Except for that one time when I used too much lube on Jake before I put the condom on and ... well, it was unfortunate.) But anyway, I was real serious about protection. And so was he.

When I married Caleb, we decided we wanted to have a baby. (Did *we* decide? Or did *I* decide? I can't remember now.) We started trying to have a baby and we tried and tried and tried and it didn't work. He didn't want to get any help because he said if it was meant to be, it would be (and he was right). After so many years of negative pregnancy tests, I figured there was something wrong with me. I thought I was infertile.

So when Jake never mentioned condoms, I never mentioned them either. I didn't think we needed them. Oh gosh. What if I'm pregnant and he gets mad because he thought I was on the pill and I wasn't? I mean, he didn't ask, but he probably assumed. What if he thinks I did this on purpose? Is he going to be angry with me? Does he even want to have kids?

We have a history that spans two decades, and are now in a committed relationship, but I don't recall us ever having a conversation about whether we wanted to have kids. I mean, we've only been an official couple for a few weeks. It's pretty early to have such a discussion.

Or is it too late for such a discussion?

I chew on my fingernail. Okay. Calm down. Don't freak out. This doesn't mean I'm pregnant. Periods can be late for a variety of reasons. In the past month I've found an apartment, almost lost my mom to an aneurysm, committed myself to my hot boyfriend, moved in with my hot boyfriend. Tomorrow I am starting school for the first time in seven years. I mean, that's a lot of BIG stuff there. Maybe my body just kind of spazzed out for a second.

I look down at my stomach. Is it any bigger? I guess. A little. But that could be because I'm in love and not obsessing over calories the way I used to.

I wonder how pregnant I am. I remember watching that TV show *I Didn't Know I Was Pregnant* and thinking those women were utter fools. Am I going to be getting my own segment now?

Dude. Chill. I might not even be pregnant. But the way I feel right now, this giddy, I have a feeling I'll be devastated if I'm not.

I stand up and sigh. Have you ever had the kind of adrenaline rush that makes your body shiver from the inside? That's how I feel – like my insides are vibrating. I need to get out of here. There's only one way to answer my question.

I slide my feet into my navy Converse, grab my purse off the kitchen counter, and head out the door into the Manhattan sunshine.

I walk several blocks to the closest Duane Reed while my head spins with … something. Excitement? Apprehension? Fear?

I reach the aisle with the pregnancy tests and feel overwhelmed by the options. Parallel lines, plus signs, digitals. I think a picture of a plus sign would look best in our pregnancy scrapbook. Oh jeez. Back it up, Roxie. There's no pregnancy scrapbook. Take the test first.

I grab a digital because those can't be misunderstood. Then I grab a plus sign … just in case there *is* a scrapbook…

I send Jake a text. He's working the lunch shift at his new job, a bar in the Meat-Packing District. He's supposed to get off at four. I look at my watch. It's 2:25. How the hell can I wait two hours to take these tests?

ME: Hi baby. You're coming straight home from work, right?
JAKE: Yeah. Why? Something planned?
ME: I just miss you like crazy.
JAKE: Miss YOU XOXO

I stop for a coffee on my way back home. I already had a cup this morning, so I get decaf. Just in case.

I'm not sure how I feel about this. I wanted a baby for the longest time. I was married. My husband had an affluent career. We had a condo with an extra bedroom. It just made sense to start a family.

Our current situation couldn't be more different. We're not married. We're not stock traders. We don't even have *one* bedroom. Jake *just* started working at this bar, so, while I'm sure the pay will be fine, it's not exactly what I'd consider stable or reliable. His photography business is our main source of income, and that's not a sure thing either. Right now, he's booking like crazy because everyone wants fall color family shoots. He has booked a lot of holiday shoots as well. But what happens after that? I don't think there's a high demand for photos in the winter.

I'm supposed to start culinary school tomorrow as a fast-track full-time student and hadn't intended on working until I finished. Jake has some money saved, and I have a pretty nice settlement from my divorce. We could financially support a family of three if we needed to. But the bottom line is, we're not in a position at this time to get approved for a car loan. Have we really been approved for a *baby*?

And if so, are we ready for this? As a couple?

I'm not even comfortable enough to poop when he's in the apartment! I live with a perpetual turtle head because I want him to believe I'm a magical poopless creature. He's never seen me unwaxed, unplucked, unshaven. Since we started sleeping together, I've been nothing but my best in front of him. Am I going to be pushing a human being out of my body in front of him in a few months?

Why am I even thinking about this? This is silly. I might not even be pregnant! I mean, I don't feel pregnant, not that I know what feeling pregnant feels like. But I don't feel different at all. No morning sickness. I stab the side of my chest with my finger while I walk. I guess it does feel tender, but I don't know if that means anything. You'd think if I was pregnant enough to not have a period since June, I'd feel something by now. The thought is discouraging.

If I'm completely honest with myself, and with you, I must admit that if this test comes back negative after spending a few hours thinking I was pregnant, I will be crushed. It might not be convenient, but thinking I might have Jake's baby growing inside me makes me realize how much I would love to have Jake's baby growing inside me. Because if there's one thing I've learned lately, it's that sometimes life is better unplanned.

I get back to the apartment and chew off the fingernails that had finally started growing back after my mom's surgery. I pace the few feet of empty space we have. I look out the window and count cabs. I Google pregnancy symptoms. I try to guess what my due date would be.

Omigod! Stop! Just stop!

I finally hear footsteps coming up the stairs to our walk-up. I run to the door and pull it open. There he is, standing on the other side – my maybe Baby Daddy, looking sexy as hell as he smiles at me and pulls his ear buds out.

"What's up, baby? Everything okay? You look a little ... unsteady?"

He means it in only the most endearing way, so I forgive him for his smartass comment, grab onto the Los Pollos Hermanos T-shirt I bought him for his birthday, pull him into my chest, and kiss his lips.

"I missed you," I whisper.

He puts his hands on the small of my back and lifts the back of my shirt to place his hands on my bare skin. "I missed you, too."

I turn, take his hand in mine, and walk toward the bathroom. I pull him inside and turn to face him.

"Do you remember that time we used a condom?" I ask.

He touches a finger to his chin like he's thinking deeply about it. Then he shrugs. "No, I really don't." He looks confused.

"Me either," I say quietly. I bite my lip nervously as I wait for his reaction.

It happens slowly. I watch his face express confusion, suspicion, and in the end, maybe a little bit of hope? His mouth turns up slightly on one side, like an almost smile. "What are you saying?"

I pull the boxes from the back of the toilet where I set them, and hold them up.

His eyes get wide. His mouth opens. "Oh," he says.

I can't tell if it's an *Oh, yay!* Or an *Oh, fuck!*

"I wanted to wait until you got home to take it."

He is apparently speechless, because he stands there with his mouth still open in an O.

I gently push his shoulder from the bathroom doorway and close the door. No peeing in front of boys. Hope taught me well.

I pee in a tiny cup and dip the plus sign test first. I set the cup in the medicine cabinet and close the door, then I lay the test flat on the edge of the sink.

I open the bathroom door to find Jake in the same position with the same expression. I take his hand and pull him into the bathroom with me while we both stare at the plastic test on the sink. First, a horizontal line appears. Then, as it starts to dry, a vertical line shows through it. It's a plus sign.

I look at him nervously. He squeezes my hand and meets my eyes. I can't tell what he's thinking just yet.

"What do you think?" I ask him.

He is careful to choose his words. I give him time.

When he's ready, he says, "I think this is ... I think it's ineffable."

Ineffable. It means it's too great to be put into words, our special word to be used when all adjectives fail to express how we feel.

"You're not mad?" I ask him apprehensively.

"Mad? No." He kisses me on my temple.

I pull the digital out and dip it into the cup. "I just want to make sure it's right," I tell him.

We watch that test as the dotted lines blink and blink and blink ... and after approximately twenty-five years it finally spells out the word. Pregnant.

"I don't think there's any mistaking that," he says.

"What does this mean?" I ask.

"Are you in shock or something? It means you're pregnant."

"I know. But, I mean, what do we do now?"

He shrugs. "I don't know. I've never done this before. Have you?"

I shake my head.

"You should probably make a doctor's appointment. And then we get ready to have a baby!" He squats a little and picks me up, lifting me by the backs of my thighs. He presses my back into the bathroom door to keep us steady. My legs dangle at his sides as I rest my elbows on his shoulders. I love the way he makes me feel like I'm a lightweight and not a size 10. "We're going to have a baby, baby. I better hold you like this while I still can. Before your stomach is huge and I can't lift you anymore."

I snort a little and he laughs, too. Then he kisses me softly on the lips.

"Are you sure you want to have a baby with me?" I ask. I don't know why I get so insecure around him sometimes. He's never given me a reason to doubt his devotion. I guess I just sometimes question whether I deserve it.

"There's no one else I'd rather have babies with, you noodle!"

I laugh again at his choice of insult. "But it is kind of soon, don't you think?"

"Rox, it's not like babies knock on the door and ask if this is an appropriate time. It doesn't matter if it's too soon. We'll make it work."

He walks us over to the bed. It's a short walk. Usually he would throw me at this point, because I love it when he gets rough with me and tosses me around. But he hesitates.

"I guess this means I can't throw you around anymore, huh? Don't want to hurt the baby."

"Maybe not right now. I'll ask my doctor when I see him."

Jake laughs again. "That's great. Make a spreadsheet of all the questions you need to ask. Can my boyfriend throw me around the bed? Can he pull my hair? Can he spank me?"

"I'm right on top of that, Rose."

"Great. Now get on top of *me*."

He turns so his back is toward the foot of the bed and falls back. I land on top of him and kiss him.

"I love you, Rox."

"I love *you*, Boyfriend."

Chapter Six

October 2012

"Today you are twelve weeks pregnant."

I must have had a period or two over the summer because I was only eight weeks pregnant when I took those tests last month. At my first prenatal appointment two weeks later, they did an ultrasound to date my pregnancy since I couldn't remember my last period. We got to see our little ten-week munchkin, the same size as a Lego minifigure.

Whew. Not knowing you're pregnant until your period is only a month late is *much* better than being one of those people having a baby in their pants on *I Didn't Know I Was Pregnant*.

"Good morning," I say, wiping the sleepiness from

my eyes like a child. I hear a car honking from outside the single window of our apartment. I love waking up to the sounds of Manhattan traffic. But even more, I love waking up next to him.

Jake lies next to me on his stomach, propped up on his elbows and reading a pregnancy book he checked out from the New York Public Library. I've only just opened my eyes and already I want him. Pregnancy hormones are insane, but I don't think they can take all the blame. In case I haven't mentioned this, my boyfriend is smokin' hot. His messy hair, his brown eyes, that chest, those arms...

Back in the day, I used to run from this because the more you love, the more you lose. The higher you are, the harder you fall. I used to be the girl who stayed as close to the ground as possible. Now, I've let myself climb all the way to the top, and as I look over the edge all I can do is give it all I've got and love every second of it. Me, Jake, and this baby growing in my belly. We might not have it all forever. But we have it all right now.

Jake has taken to his pending fatherhood better than I imagined he would. Not that I expected him to be an absent dad. Feeling unloved and abandoned so many times by his own father, Jake would never abandon his child. I like to think he'd never abandon me either, but it's hard sometimes to know for sure. I guess having a high school boyfriend hook up with a skank behind your back, a college boyfriend withhold the fact he has a pregnant girlfriend at home, and your husband living a secret life where he likes to suck fake penises while dressed in drag ... well, can you blame me?

Jake didn't run out the door, but he *has* been doing

a lot of running. He ran to the library, ran up the stairs past those infamous lions, and checked out as many pregnancy and parenting books he could fit in his book bag – yes, a guy with a book bag. Swoon.

He ran to Duane Reed to get me ginger ale when my stomach was upset.

He ran to the market to get me oranges at one in the morning when the chicken I cooked for dinner turned against me and I was hit with a desperate need for citrus.

But he didn't run away. Consider me hashtag blessed.

In the beginning I tried reading the books he brought home. *What to Expect When You're Expecting.* What a train wreck. A more appropriate title would be *Ten Thousand Things That Can Go Wrong When You're Expecting.* That shit should come with a warning label. I made him return it. The internet is bad enough. I don't need a whole book of things that can kill my baby sitting on my end table.

Now Jake does the reading on his own, sifts the info through his special will-my-girlfriend-lose-her-shit-over-this filter, and tells me only the facts I need to know.

"Our baby is now the size of a wine cork," Jake says while looking at the open book laying across his pillow.

"Wow. So much bigger than a Lego minifigure already!"

"Yep. Baby's grown a lot the last few weeks. Pretty much all organs and systems have been formed. The hard part of development is over."

He closes the book and sets it on the nightstand. Then he brushes the sheet down past my chest and belly button to say good morning to the baby. I don't have an actual baby bump because – let's be honest here – my stomach has always been a little … we'll say poofy. Now it is a firmer poofy rather than a mushy poofy.

He runs a finger along my little bump, and I wish his hand would keep going. He kisses me just under my belly button, and I wish his lips would keep moving. I've only just opened my eyes and I'm already wet. I push his hand farther down. He reaches into my panties and slides a finger across my slippery clit.

"Jeez, baby," he says, pretending to be exasperated. "It's like that? We haven't even had coffee yet."

"Coffee's overrated," I whisper.

"I'll remind you next time you're buying a six-dollar drink at Starbucks," he replies as he presses his finger into my clit. "Is this what you want?"

I shake my head.

He pushes the blanket off, scoots himself down a little lower, and puts my leg around his neck.

"Is this what you want?"

I nod.

He slips down lower, pulls my panties down just a little, and dips his tongue into me quickly.

I gasp. I feel like an addict lately.

He runs his tongue over my clit slowly. Sometimes he barely taps it. He's such a tease. I lift my hips against him eagerly to let him know I'm ready for more pressure, but he continues to tease me with light and slow touches.

When I can barely handle the tease anymore, he flips over so I'm on top of him. I hold onto the headboard as I move my hips and rub myself over his tongue just the way I want it.

"Fuck, Jake," I pant from above as I grip the headboard so hard my knuckles turn white.

He keeps his tongue moving. At just the right moment he sucks my whole clit into his mouth. He wraps his lips tightly around it and sucks while licking.

"Fuck!" I yell again as I start shivering and come on his face.

He tries to keep going because he likes to torture me, but I roll off him gasping for breath. I look at the clock. I opened my eyes six minutes ago. I have high-power vibrators that don't work that quickly.

"You know," he says, leaning against the headboard, "the baby will start hearing sounds at eighteen weeks. That means you have six weeks before you have to stop swearing."

I hit his chest with a pillow before I crawl toward him and place myself between his legs. I pull his boxers down. He's already hard.

I look up and meet his eyes while putting my mouth around him. With just the tip inside my mouth, I flick my tongue at the underside of the head and then run my tongue around the rim. I come up for air, lick the little bit of come from the tip, and then go back down. This time I go all the way down and I look up to see him bite his lip. This won't take long at all.

I put my hands around the shaft and move up and down while my mouth sucks the tip. Moments later when he comes into my mouth, I swallow everything until I'm sure it's done. Then I suck a little to make sure.

I look at the clock again. Three minutes.

He gives me a high-five and leans against the headboard to catch his breath. Once he recovers and can form words, he says, "I'm glad we're so good at this. When we have a little one running around, we're gonna have to be quick. Especially in this place. We might be having a lot of bathroom sex, huh?"

Jake and I are no strangers to sneaking around. We've become very good at it. I don't think we're going to have a problem having sex once the baby is here.

"Now that we're twelve weeks, that means we can start telling people, right?" he asks. "I've been working on some ideas for the announcement."

Oh. Dear.

I sit up on the foot of the bed and cross my legs Indian style. I am prepared for battle.

"I think we should wait a little longer," I say meekly. I *did* originally say we would start telling people at twelve weeks. I thought we would. I thought I'd be ready. I'm not.

"I like this," I explain when he gives me a look from across the bed. "I like this bubble of happiness we live in. I don't want anyone trying to pop it with their negativity."

"I get it, babe. It's been nice to have a few weeks to get used to this on our own. No unsolicited advice. No side-eyes. No explanations needed. I understand. I do. But keeping it a secret for too much longer is not fair to our families. This is the first grandchild, and first niece or nephew for both families. They deserve a chance to be excited about this baby, too."

"But *will* they be excited?" I ask.

"What do you mean? Of course they will!"

I'm not so sure. How do we tell my family that the kid who is like a son to them has impregnated their daughter while living together unmarried with no plans to get married anytime soon, or ever? I don't think it's going to go over too well.

And a big announcement on social media? How will that look? I still have my ex-husband's last name, and I'm pregnant with someone else's baby. My signature on the divorce papers is probably still wet, and I'm already twelve weeks pregnant. Jake and I only changed our relationship status and became "Facebook official" six weeks ago. Yet we are having a baby in six months. People can do the math. They will know I technically got pregnant while still technically married if they want to get technical about it.

I shouldn't care what people think. But I do. We are creating a family and I don't want my family tarnished with rumors and eye rolls. We're just two people in love and having a baby. It doesn't need to be added to the list of things the internet blew out of proportion this year.

I bite my lip. "I don't know."

It's a stare down. Him. Me. A pile of crumbled blankets between us. He takes an arm and sweeps the blankets off the bed. At first, I think he's pissed. Then he reaches across the bed, grabs one of my legs in each hand, and pulls me toward him. God, I love the way he manhandles me. He wraps my legs around his waist and puts his finger under my chin, so I can't look down.

"Tell me what you're afraid of," he says patiently. "And let me tell you why you don't need to be."

That's my boyfriend. No bullshit. Tell me the problem and let me fix it.

"Isn't it obvious?" I ask.

"Not to me."

"Getting pregnant by accident? I mean, that's something teenagers do."

"It wasn't an accident." He says this so surely.

"What do you mean?"

"Accidents are when condoms break. Or when they fall off because you used too much flavored lube before you put it on. That was a legitimate accident."

I cover my mouth and giggle, remembering one of the best clips on our blooper reel. "But it wouldn't have resulted in a pregnancy," I reminded him, "because I was on the pill just in case something like that happened. I was on birth control pills as a *backup*. I was hardcore responsible."

"We both were. Because we knew we did not want a baby at that time."

"I think I was more worried about STDs than babies. But a baby would not have been ideal either."

"Exactly. So, we took measures to make sure that didn't happen. What measures did we take to prevent a pregnancy this time?"

This is the part that makes me cringe every time I think about it. I know how bad it looks. "None."

"Right. So how is that an accident?"

"It wasn't intentional. I hope you don't think that."

"I don't think that."

"It has to be one or the other. If it wasn't an accident, then it was intentional."

"It doesn't have to be one or the other. We didn't actively prevent it, and we didn't actively intend it."

"NTNP!" I say quickly. "It's called NTNP. Not trying, not preventing."

I learned that back in my TTC (trying to conceive) days.

He smiles and nods. "Okay. How do you describe those couples? Why are they NTNP?"

"Um, it's kind of like, let's just have fun and live

our lives. If it happens it happens, and if it doesn't it doesn't. Maybe we'll try harder one day, but for now we are happy to leave it up to chance."

"See? That sounds so much better than calling this an accident. We were NTNP! We never talked about it. I never asked you. But I was there, too, and I didn't bring up birth control either."

This was the perfect time for me to ask him something I'd been wondering a long time. *Why didn't he?* I know why *I* didn't bring it up. I didn't even think of it as a possibility anymore. For so many months, getting pregnant was *all* I'd thought about. It was nice to *not* be thinking of it for a change. And for sex to be fun again. The idea that I could get pregnant with Jake honestly never crossed my mind as anything other than an ironic joke, like, oh hey, wouldn't that be hilarious?

"Why didn't you?" I finally get to ask. "Did you think I was on the pill?"

"I don't know, Rox. The first time it happened it was fast and unexpected. I *should* have put on a condom. I felt bad after because I didn't. You know you're the only person I've ever not worn a condom with?"

"No," I say shocked. "I didn't."

I feel bad that I can't say the same for him. Sometimes I wish I could erase the last seven years. So many times, I've wished it could have been us this whole time, since we were kids. But I know I can't dwell on that. It's a waste of negative energy. He's mine now. And if we had stayed together many years ago, who knows, maybe we would have grown apart by now, and I would have divorced him this summer instead.

"Yeah. The first time I felt bad for it, but after the first time ... you didn't mention it. And I knew from before how important that was to you. I figured you weren't worried about it. And if *you* weren't worried about it, then *I* wasn't worried about it."

"When you say you weren't worried about it, was it because you thought I had it covered? Or do you mean you weren't worried if you got me pregnant?"

"Mostly, I thought you had it covered. But do *not* feel guilty about that!" he adds quickly. "There was a time when I considered the possibility of you not being on birth control, and, to tell you the truth, I didn't hate the idea."

"What did you think about the idea then?"

He shrugs. "I guess I thought like the NTNP people. I thought, if it happens, we'll figure it out."

"Really." I say it more like a statement than a question. Almost like I'm testing his answer, like I don't totally believe it.

"Yeah. I mean, I'm already in my thirties. I'm not anywhere close to settling down with anyone –"

Ouch.

" – And suddenly you come back into my life, and I didn't know if you'd stay or take off. But I knew there was no one else I'd rather have a baby with. Ever. If a baby came along and we were together ... great. Perfect. If a baby came along, and you decided you didn't want to be with me, then I'd still get to co-parent with my favorite person. And I'd also have a new favorite person that I might not have ever had otherwise. It didn't seem like a bad idea. Hey, don't cry, baby. Why are you crying? I'm trying to make you feel *better* here. Not worse."

I laugh and sniffle at the same time. "Fucking

hormones."

"These are happy tears?"

I nod.

"Good. I don't want you carrying around any shame about this, okay? We are adults. We were careful when we needed to be. And we stopped being careful when we were ready. How or why we became pregnant is nobody's business. Maybe we *did* plan it. How do they know?"

"That's the other thing bothering me."

"What?"

"This came really soon after my divorce. I don't think anyone would believe we planned it that way."

"For one, fuck them. For two, who the fuck cares what anyone thinks?"

"You do realize who you're talking to, right?"

He gives me a sad smile. "It must be so hard to be you, babe."

"Only when you're not around to talk me off the ledge. Also, you do realize you're going to have to stop swearing in six weeks, right?"

"Ha. Yes. I'm working on it. Now can we work on our announcement?"

I bite my lip. I don't know if I'm quite there yet. I'm feeling a ton better than I was before we talked about it, but I'm still not ready to break the internet with an announcement. "I agree with you that it's not fair to keep our families from celebrating our baby. But I'm not on board with social media yet. I think I need a few more weeks for the public announcement."

He nods. "That's fair. I'm gonna make some coffee, and we can think about how to tell them."

"I'll make breakfast."

Thirty minutes later we are back in bed, warm plates on our laps. We don't have room for a couch or a dining table. Our place really is that small.

Jake turns on the TV and pushes play on a recorded episode of MTV's *Teen Mom*. Jake acts like he hates it, but he's the one holding the remote.

"You think we should get married?" he asks, right in the middle of a Farrah meltdown.

I nearly spit out my coffee. (My doctor says I'm allowed one cup a day.) I look over at him, his face curious and somewhat shaken. I can tell this isn't a spontaneous question. It isn't something he blurted out without thought. Knowing that, kind of makes it worse. Come on, Jake, that's the best you could come up with? The guy who always knows the right thing to say just royally fucked up this proposal. If I can even call it a proposal. I like to think I've become much more low-maintenance than I'd been in my past. I didn't need an airplane spelling out the proposal in the sky, or a video proposal at a major sporting event. But this? Really, Jake? Really?

Ever since we'd seen that positive test, the idea of marriage had been lingering in the air, heavy but unspoken. I was hoping it would remain unspoken. The idea that he was asking me to marry him because he thought he was supposed to, and not because he wanted to, was worse than the awkward avoidance of the topic. I liked the elephant in the room much better than this. A few minutes ago, I felt lucky in love. One stupid question later, and I feel like a charity case.

"Wow," I said, smiling dreamily at him. "You really know how to make a girl swoon, huh? That was so bad I almost want to cry. And they wouldn't be happy tears this time."

He stabs his fork into his quiche gently and then absentmindedly does it again ... and again. Stab. Stab. "I could have come up with something better," he admits with another stab. "But I didn't want to plan an elaborate proposal if you were gonna say no." Stab. "And I'm pretty sure you're gonna say no."

Of course I'm going to say no. What the hell is happening right now?

"Then why are you asking?" I ask. I don't try to hide my annoyance with sarcasm this time. I hate this fake shit.

Stab. Shrug. "I thought maybe you'd feel more comfortable telling people about the baby if we were engaged. I feel like it's going to be a question people ask us. And I'd like to know how to answer them when they do. I would rather ask you, and get turned down, than not ask and have you secretly mad or hurt about it."

"Wait. Lemme make sure I got this. What you're saying is that you're asking me to marry you, and hoping I'll say no? So that *I* look like the bad guy when people ask when we're getting married?"

Shrug. Stab. Sigh. "No, Roxie. Jeez. When you say it like that I sound like a dick. I'm just trying to do the right thing. If you say you want to get married, we'll get married. I'm fine with it either way. I just want this conversation over with."

"Wow. This just keeps getting better," I say after a short laugh.

He shakes his head at me, pretending to be angry. He probably wants to walk away and slam a door or something, just to make a point. But there's nowhere for him to go. I'm still not sure if that's a good thing or a bad thing. It's too early to tell. They say love grows best in little houses, right?

I could make a big deal about this. I could get hormonal and cry over that God-awful proposal that should have been special. I could get angry and tell him he's totally ruined the romance of any proposal in the future and we should probably just break up now because this relationship is obviously doomed. But I practice the *choose your battles wisely* relationship plan.

It was shitty, but I know his intentions were good. I let him off the hook with a gentle punch to his shoulder. "Relax, baby. We have enough going on right now. I am not getting married before this baby is born. I am not getting married just because we have a baby. And if you ever decide you do want to marry me, you better hope you have something better than this. Or you'll be meeting the same fate as that quiche."

He breathes out and leans back on the bed. "Thank God."

He presses play, and Farrah's meltdown resumes.

I grab the remote from his hand and press pause.

"Seriously, Jake?"

"I mean, thank God we don't have the added stress of planning a wedding while getting ready for the baby. Not thank God I don't have to marry you."

"I hope that's what you meant." Now I'm unsure. This is so weird.

"I did. I would marry you in a second. I can't wait for you to get rid of that guy's last name and take mine. But I'm excited about having this baby, and I want to put everything I have into it. The best announcement, the best nursery-"

"You mean the best corner of the studio that can fit a bassinet?"

"Yes. We'll take parenting classes and labor classes,

and I just want to do everything right for this baby. And everything that's right for us. I honestly don't think getting married right now is right for us, and I'm glad you feel the same way. That's all I'm saying. Can we please resume *Teen Mom*? Or should we have sex? I think it's been like an hour since your last orgasm. You must be feigning."

"Yeah, I kind of am. Just let me finish my breakfast."

♥

"Okay," Jake says when he gets out of the shower later. "Here's what we're gonna do."

"What?" I ask, without looking up from painting my big toe purple.

"First, we go through our phones and look for pictures of the two of us that we've taken since you got pregnant."

"Okay."

"Then I'll put them together in a slideshow and add text to make it look like a mockommercial."

I look up from my toes and scrunch my face. "A what?"

"A mockommercial. Like a mockumentary. It will look like it's a commercial, but it'll really be a baby announcement."

"Is mockommercial a real thing? Or did you make that word up?"

"It's a real thing. Are you cool with it?"

"Okay," I say, unsure what he means, but willing to trust him. Jake tends to be good at what he does. Except when it comes to marriage proposals, but I'm trying to forget about that.

"Then we'll call everyone on Skype and tell them we just emailed them a funny video and ask them to watch it while we're on Skype. That way we can sort of be there with them when they find out."

"That's a great idea!"

"Cool. Text me some pics while your nails dry, and I can work on it while you're in the shower."

Jake has our mockommercial (I Googled the word and it came up in my search results, so I guess it's a real thing) ready by the time I'm done blow-drying my hair. I cry when I watch it the first time. I cry when I watch it the second time. I'm going to need some waterproof eyeliner and mascara if I'm going to make it through the next six months. This hormone shit is insane.

"Does this mean you like it?" he asks laughing.

"It means I love it! Now stop playing it, so I can compose myself before we Skype."

"Who first? Your parents?"

I nod. I'm surprised to realize this ball of nerves in my belly is from excitement rather than dread. For four weeks now, I've felt sick to my stomach when I thought about telling my parents I'd gotten pregnant by accident. Or maybe that was morning sickness. But either way, I wasn't looking forward to that conversation with them. I imagined my embarrassment, their disappointment, the shame. But all of that went away after talking with Jake this morning. He was right. It wasn't an accident. If we were really against the idea of a baby, we would have used protection. We're not dumb. We know how babies get made. Whether we consciously acknowledged it or not, we accepted that idea when we chose not to prevent it. For the first time in weeks, I feel nothing but excitement.

We sit down on our bed, because, other than the toilet, it's the only place to sit. Jake pulls the laptop in front of us and dials my parents on Skype.

My dad answers. "Hello, love!" he says in a fake British accent.

"Hi, Dad!"

"How's school?"

"Oh, it's going great! I can make crème brulee now. And I know what fennel is. Oh, And I learned how to make this awesome pasta. I call it kickbutternut squash ravioli."

"Kickbutternut? That's great. Can't wait to try some. Hey, Jake!"

Jake waves.

"Is Mom home?" I ask.

"Yeah, she's reading on the back porch."

"Can you get her to the computer, so we can see you both at the same time? We're gonna email you a video we made."

"Oh. Okay."

He yells for my mom. Jake emails the video while we wait. My mom's pretty face appears on our monitor, and she waves.

"Hi, Mommy!"

"Hi, guys!"

"Dad, Jake just sent you an email. Can you open it and watch it? We made a cool video about living in New York, and we want you to see it."

I see my dad typing on the computer. I hear the mouse click. "Got it. Opening it now."

Jake plays our video in the corner of the screen, so we can watch it at the same time.

A picture of Jake and me at Top of the Rock fills the screen. Text appears on the left side of the photo: *Tickets to Top of the Rock - $68.*

Another photo appears. It's a picture Hope took of us in a subway terminal. It's one of my favorite pictures of us, because we didn't know she was taking it, and we are looking at each other and laughing. That picture needs to be on canvas someday. It was an excellent choice for our mockommercial. Text appears on the left side of the photo.

Monthly MetroCards - $224

That picture fades and another appears. This one is Jake and me eating hot dogs in Central Park.

Hot Dogs from a street cart - $6

The fourth picture is the two of us sitting on the steps at the Met.

Realizing there are three of us in these photos – Priceless.

The photo lingers a few moments to give people a chance to catch on.

The last image is an ultrasound photo of our little Lego munchkin taken at ten weeks. The text under the pictures says *Baby Odom can't wait to meet you this spring.*

I hear screaming. I see open mouths. It's not terror and disgust.

It's joy.

"Oh my God!" my mom screams and touches her hands to her heart, which hopefully means she's very happy, and not having another aneurysm. "I've been waiting for this for so long!"

My parents hug.

"Congratulations, you two," Dad says. "I couldn't have picked a better dad for my grandchildren if I'd chosen him myself."

Oh jeez. I'm crying again. Seriously. Come on, hormones! Give me a break!

We tell them we need to make it short because we have others to call, but we'll talk more later.

We call Jake's mom next. Then Adam. Then Jake's dad, stepmom, and brother and sister. It's joy all around.

When all the announcements are made for the night, and I've had to reapply my mascara and concealer four times, Jake removes the laptop from our bed, and then promptly removes my clothes. It *has* been like seven hours after all.

Chapter Seven

December 2012

"Today you are twenty weeks pregnant."

Jake worked until 3AM. How is he awake before me?

I sit up in bed, wipe the sleep from my eyes, and accept the mug of hazelnut half-caff he hands me. He's already showered. He's been counting down the days to this ultrasound. If this was a musical, he would totally be dancing around the apartment and singing to birds on the windowsill.

"Today's the day we find out the sex," he says. He drops his towel in front of the closet and I admire his butt from the bed.

"Wrong!" I say firmly, after I sip my coffee. "Today

is the day *most* people find out the sex. Not us. Team Green. You know this."

We've had this conversation at least a dozen times. I don't know why he still thinks I'm going to change my mind. I want that moment in the delivery room where the doctor makes the big announcement. I want Jake to have that moment to run out into the waiting room and tell the family whether we had a boy or girl. So much of a pregnancy is about the mom. That moment for him to announce the sex to our family, it's kind of all the glory he gets, and I want him to have it.

Plus, I love the idea of gender neutral baby gear that can be used for future babies.

Look. This is how pregnancies work these days. Couples announce the pregnancy on social media, usually between eight and thirteen weeks, with some cute photo or video. At twenty weeks, they announce the gender, and usually the baby's name, with another cute photo or video. People congratulate them. And as far as everyone else is concerned, that baby now exists. The baby will now be referred to by name for the remainder of the pregnancy, even added onto greeting cards as part of the family. Its name will be embroidered on no less than a dozen blankets and bibs, and probably the diaper bag. The name will also be put on the wall over the crib in the nursery. The name will be used so much that people will forget that the baby is not *actually* here yet. And by the time the baby *is* born, *twenty weeks later*, no one cares anymore. It's old news. That baby's been around for five months already. And that's fine for everyone else. They can do whatever makes them happy. For me, I am not announcing the gender, or the name, until the baby is born. I don't want an anticlimactic birth. I want my baby to be celebrated once the baby is *here*. Jake doesn't understand any of this. I've given up trying to explain it to him.

"I'm going to ask the tech to put it in an envelope in case you change your mind," he says. "Then we can open it together, or we can do a gender reveal photo shoot. I've done some cute ones lately. You wanna see em?"

"I've seen them, Jake. Don't you know? I'm a devoted follower of yours on social media. They're very cute. I just don't want *us* to do a gender reveal. I want to do a *baby* reveal. Once the baby is here, you can do any kind of announcement you want. I promise you that."

"But you're gonna let me take maternity photos, right?"

"I didn't intend on having maternity photos taken."

"Rox, whether you like it or not, you got knocked up by a photographer. And I will respect your wishes about when to reveal things. But when it comes to pictures, you're gonna shut your mouth and let me snap my shutter whenever and wherever I want."

Oh damn. I kind of like it when he puts me in my place like that.

"I give you so much control over our lives," he continues. "When it comes to pictures, that's *my* control. Got it?"

Got it. Please fuck me now.

"Got it. But I get to choose the wardrobe. There will be no bare belly shots of me in a pair of unbuttoned jeans with baby blocks across my stomach."

"You can dress up as the marshmallow man from

The Ghostbusters for all I care."

I gasp. "Are you saying I look like the marshmallow man?"

He shrugs and smirks at me. "Well, I mean, you *are* kind of white."

I toss a pillow at him. He's lucky he's cute.

I finish my coffee and set the empty mug on the nightstand.

I get out of bed, take his shirt off him, and push his boxers down to the floor.

"Say it again," I whisper. "Tell me to shut my mouth and fuck me the way you want to."

♥

Christmas Time – 2012

"McDonald's Coke?" Jake asks, as he adjusts the rearview mirror of our rental car.

I verify that there are indeed two McDonald's Cokes in the cup holders of the Toyota. "Check."

"Gummi bears?"

I verify there are two bags of Gummi bears in the side panel of the passenger door.

"Check. Check."

"Road trip playlist consisting of no more than thirty percent songs that were once played on TRL?"

I give him an innocent shrug. "It might be more like thirty-five percent."

"God, I love you," he says, and pulls me over for a kiss. I almost don't reach him now that this belly is popping.

I stretch over to meet his lips. I swear every time he says he loves me it's like I'm hearing it for the first time. Every time our lips touch I feel like I'm falling out of an airplane.

"I don't care if it's ninety-percent boy bands and Britney," he says. "As long as I'm with you."

Dude. I should be rolling my eyes at this nonsense. I'm not.

We chose to drive to Michigan for Christmas instead of flying. For two reasons: 1. I love being trapped in small places with him, and eight hours in a car is better than two hours on a plane. 2. To save on miles. Jake is flying to Michigan twice a month for photo shoots, and I want to make sure he can continue to do that without breaking the bank. Every month we stay above water means more money to spend on baby stuff. I racked up tons and tons of miles during my shopaholic days, and they have proven to be useful. I guess all those shoes had a purpose after all.

This is our first Christmas as a couple. We spent Thanksgiving in New York with my parents, so this is also our first holiday as a couple where we'll be navigating several families in two days. Jake has always been around for holidays with my family, so that is normal for us. But now we also have his mom, as well as his father's family to visit. I'm looking forward to watching it all unfold seamlessly (also known as wishful thinking).

Everything flows pretty seamlessly. We have Christmas Eve dinner at Jake's Dad and stepmom's house. His brother and sister each invite their boyfriends, and even surprise us with gifts for Baby Odom. I feel like I fit right in and it's easy to imagine being a part of their family.

Christmas is another wonderful day. We invite

Jake's mom to spend the day with us and everyone gathers at Adam's first thing in the morning for breakfast (this amazing steel-cut oatmeal I'd put in the crock pot the night before). Then we hang out, watch *It's a Wonderful Life* and *Miracle on 34th Street* while munching on cheese, crackers, and sweet baby gherkins until dinner. (Just because I'm halfway through a high-end culinary education doesn't mean I'm too good for gherkins.)

We get a bit of a surprise when Adam sets an extra plate at dinner for his girlfriend! Emelia is another doctor at the hospital. She is fun, and hilarious, and I do what I do best by getting ahead of myself. I imagine her as the sister I never had. We can go shopping together. Have lunch dates. I can be a bridesmaid in their wedding. And Godmother to their babies... Hey, a girl's gotta have dreams.

The holiday flows seamlessly. In fact, our "new" family seems so perfect that I find myself wondering if it's too good to be true. I start to look around wondering which shoe is going to drop first. I need to stop that shit.

When we get to bed on Christmas evening, Jake relaxes under the covers with his iPad, probably checking his business pages on Facebook and Instagram.

We are staying at Adam's house in Jake's old room. Since my bed was brand new, we took that one to New York with us when we moved. A lot of Jake's stuff was left here. It's convenient because he stays here twice a month when he comes home for photo shoots. I won't lie. At times I have wondered if he's ever brought any women back to his room when he was home. Maybe

Lifetime movies have me a little extra paranoid about how easily Jake could be living a double life. But those fires are always snuffed out almost as fast as they are started. I am slowly becoming more confident that his love and loyalty are real. I feel my insecurities fading more each day. I now spend more time thinking about how lucky I am to be his forever girl. We just celebrated Christmas with his family. His mom gave me a Christmas gift. That's about as real as it gets.

While he's scrolling through Facebook, I step into the walk-in closet and put on the pink cashmere cami and panty set that I wore in the boudoir pictures he took of me last summer. I look in the full-length mirror on the closet door to check out my body. The shirt stops before my naval, pushed up by my round belly. I touch my bump. I can finally feel the baby moving around in there from the inside, but I can't feel anything from the outside yet. It's a nice belly. I got the basketball, not the watermelon.

"Damn!" Jake says, when I step out. "What's the occasion? Is this one of my Christmas presents?"

"No. I just wanted to see if it still fit. But I thought maybe, if you wanted to –"

"I want to. Whatever it is, I want to."

"-take some pictures. I thought this outfit would be nice to wear, just for pictures for us to have later. So we can remember what my body looked liked pregnant. Just for us, Jake. Not going on the internet."

"You look perfect. I'll set up my lights."

"I didn't mean right now. I was just making sure the outfit fits. I'd need professional hair and makeup first."

"Can you just humor me tonight, and we'll do a real shoot later? I like to do maternity shoots around week thirty. You have time to schedule hair and makeup appointments. But can I take pictures of you now, just for fun?"

I reach over and put my finger on his lips. "No, boyfriend. That's not how this works, remember? When it comes to photos, you're in charge. Don't ask me. Tell me."

"Okay, girlfriend. Get yourself some heels, and get your fine ass on this bed. Now."

I reach down to the bottom of the closet to grab a pair of high heels from my suitcase.

Jake jumps out of bed and quickly sets up some lights. I try to recreate the boudoir poses from over the summer.

"Do you know how badly I wanted to touch you during that shoot?" he asks, while he snaps some photos of me standing by the window. Hopefully none of the neighbors are looking. Nah, who cares?

I glance back at him. "Do you know how badly I wanted you to touch me?"

"You did?"

"Yeah. I was hoping after all those years that you were still attracted to me. But you acted so nonchalant about it."

"I had a hard-on the whole time. Just like I do now."

"Good thing you're allowed to touch me whenever you want now."

"True dat." He comes up behind me and kisses my bare shoulder. I feel goosebumps pop out all over, like someone just hit my power button.

I sigh.

This is the best life ever.

"Don't mind if I do," he says, pulling down the

strap of my cami with his teeth, while he pushes his hand into the front of my panties.

It's probably best to close the curtains now.

Later, when we're cuddled in bed, I switch on the lamp on the nightstand again.

"What's the matter?" he asks.

"I forgot. I do have one more Christmas present for you."

"You mean the surprise lingerie photo shoot wasn't it?"

"Nope. I have something better than that."

"Nonsense. There's nothing better than that."

I open the drawer of the nightstand and pull out the gift. It's small, flat, and wrapped in blue baby snowmen paper.

He opens it up to find an envelope. Once he opens the envelope, he pulls out a pink and blue gender reveal card. "What's this?" he asks.

"You know I don't want to find out the baby's sex until he or she is born. But I know that you do. And I don't want to take that away from you, because this is your experience, too, not just mine. Go ahead and open it and find out if your baby is a boy or a girl."

"And not tell you?"

"Can you keep a secret, Jake Odom?"

He shakes his head. "Not from you I can't. I do want to know. But I want us to find out together."

"If I can't find out in the delivery room, the next best thing is finding out from you. Just see how long you can keep it a secret. And when you can't take it anymore, I'll let you tell me."

He nods in agreement. "Deal."

"Go ahead, open the card."

He opens it and pulls out the ultrasound photo that I had put into the envelope while my eyes were closed. The tech had given it to us at our last appointment, just in case we changed our minds about finding out the sex.

He looks at it, puts it back in the envelope, puts the envelope back in the bubble mailer. I see no change of expression.

It feels a little weird to know that he knows this huge thing about our lives that I don't know yet. But I'm okay with it.

I watch him, waiting for a reaction, but he remains poker-faced. I'd asked him before if he wanted a boy or a girl and he'd said that was a silly question. He wanted *our* baby, no matter what.

He leans over the bed and kisses me on the lips.

"Are you happy?" I ask quietly.

He smiles. "More than I've ever been in my whole life."

Chapter Eight

January 2013

"You okay, baby?" Jake asks.

I'm sitting on the bed folding clothes. I've been living in yoga pants and giant hoodies. I finally admitted defeat and bought some maternity clothes. I thought I'd be excited about it, but something doesn't feel right to me. Something is off.

I put some of the folded clothes into our suitcase. We are headed home again for our baby shower. I'm only twenty-eight weeks, but Mom and Allison are having it a little early so we don't have to travel too late into the pregnancy.

"You're packing for our baby shower," he says, like I don't know, "but you look like you're packing for a funeral. What's going on, babe? Is it the winter blues? Or something else?"

I frown and shrug. "I don't know, Jake. I really don't. I just don't feel right about something."

He sits down next to me, looking alarmed. "You mean something with your body doesn't feel right?"

I shake my head. "No, no. Everything feels right with the baby. It's something else."

"Are you nervous about the drive?"

I shake my head again. "No. I'm looking forward to it. I already got the playlist ready." I give him a sad smile.

"Hmm." He puts a finger on his forehead while he thinks. "Are you nervous about the shower? Are you afraid something will go wrong?"

"No. I'm excited to see all the cute baby stuff. I don't know where we'll put it all, but I'm excited to see it."

"Is that what's wrong? Are you feeling bad about us not having any room for baby stuff?"

I close my eyes and imagine it. I imagine driving home with Jake, my favorite songs on the radio, my hand in his. That's great.

I imagine the baby shower. My parents in from Florida, a few dozen people who love us, a bunch of cute baby clothes, maybe a Boppy pillow or jumparoo. It feels good.

Then I imagine us loading as much of it as we can fit into the rented SUV, bringing it back here to Manhattan, trying to cram the boxes into any empty space we can find, hanging little onesies in our only closet next to our own clothes, keeping the crib and dresser in the box because there's no room for them, taking the glider back to the store because the only place I'll be rocking this baby to sleep is the same place we eat dinner and the same place we watch TV.

Suddenly I understand what's wrong. It's not *going* home – it's coming *back*. As much as I loved this city as a wife and shopaholic, it doesn't feel right to me as a mom. I take a minute to imagine the baby shower differently, with us loading up our own SUV, driving to a cute brick house in a subdivision, decorating a nursery in grey and turquoise, setting up a crib, dresser, changing table, and gliding rocking chair, hanging the baby's clothes in their very own closet, arranging their books on their own bookshelf, with lots of room for them to grow and play. That is when I start to feel better.

"What is it?" Jake asks.

"What?"

"You were thinking of something and you were smiling. What were you thinking about?"

"Oh, nothing," I say quickly. Jake uprooted his entire life for me. Because *I* wanted to live here. How can I expect him to move again? He's going to think I'm some nutcase chick who is never satisfied. I can't keep changing my mind about huge things, like which state we live in. It's bad enough I've changed the name of our baby four times already.

"Baby, come on. Tell me what's going on."

"I was just thinking how nice it would be to be able to decorate a nursery like everyone else does when they're having a baby. That's all. No big deal."

"Hmm. Okay."

The rental is crammed with everything from newborn through six months. The stuff we won't need until later, like the high chair and exersaucer, have been stored in Adam's basement until we make our next trip.

    I have seven weeks of school left, and nine to twelve weeks of pregnancy. My externship in a hotel's kitchen has been great so far. I'm supposed to start looking for a career position. The idea of working for a popular restaurant in New York makes me so excited, and if I was the same person I was a year ago, I would be applying to the best places in Manhattan and getting ready to kick some ass out there as a job hunter. But things are different now. This baby is now my number one. And my baby deserves better than a studio apartment with no room to play. We can't afford anything bigger in Manhattan. I've secretly looked at some places in Brooklyn and Queens, and the prices are astronomical there as well. Then there's the cost of childcare to think about. Jake is a bartender. I'm a chef. Both of us will need to work evenings. We would have to find an evening daycare or nanny and the prices on those are insane. We could probably work ourselves into the ground and pay for it, but at what cost?

    Back home, Jake's business is successful enough that he might only have to tend bar a few nights a week, and he could do that on my nights off. We could possibly get by without childcare. If not, we have Adam, Jake's family, Allison. Add that to the lower cost of living, and I feel like it's the right thing to do to move back. Our money would go further, our baby would be with family when not with us, we'd have a support system. I tried making a pros and cons list to staying in NY, but the pros side was empty. It's so obviously the best thing for us.

    I haven't talked to Jake about it. He's been asking me if I've looked for jobs in New York, and I just keep blowing him off, telling him there's no point looking for work while I'm obviously pregnant, that I'll start after the baby is born. But he doesn't want to work on building his business in New York until I've found a permanent position. We're kind of in an awkward limbo right now. I'm waiting (and hoping and praying) for him to mention it first. So far, he hasn't.

Jake closes the door of the trunk and turns to me. "You ready to go back home, beautiful?"

I give him a fake smile and nod. "I don't care if we only have five hundred square feet, as long as I'm with you."

"Ha. Right on."

He hugs me and lifts me off the ground a little without squishing the belly. He's very talented. "Did I tell you how beautiful you look today?" he whispers.

"About three times," I whisper back.

"Just making sure," he says as he sets my feet back on the wet, slushy road.

He takes my hand. "Come on. We have one place to stop before we hit the road."

"Where are we going?" I ask curiously, as I follow him to the passenger seat.

He opens the door for me and waits until I'm sitting and buckled before he closes it.

He walks around the front of the SUV and gets in the driver's seat.

I look at him curiously as he starts the engine.

"It's a surprise," he says with a mischievous grin. "I really love your belly right now. It's, like, the perfect size. Big enough that you're obviously pregnant, but not so huge that you look like you're going to topple over."

A ha. We're going to do our maternity shoot today. That must be what the surprise is. He took some great pics of me in the pink cashmere on Christmas, but I bet he's arranged a shoot with both of us in it. I don't think it's necessary, but it's very difficult to explain to a photographer why you don't need pictures of everything all the time.

He drives a few miles from the restaurant where the shower was held before he stops in front of a charming home in a subdivision.

Yep. It's a photo shoot. I wonder if Jake packed us some nicer clothes to wear for this. My shower dress is cute. And at least I'm not wearing a pair of jeans held together with a ponytail holder, so it could be worse.

We get out of the rental as a man gets out of a Chevy Malibu in the driveway. He must be the photographer.

I look at Jake and smile. I'm not mad about it. Jake deserves to have some photos with him in them, too. It is his baby after all.

"Jake? Nice to see you again," the man says, shaking Jake's hand. "And you must be Roxie," he says as he shakes mine. "I'm Reese. Nice to meet you."

Reese opens the front door of the home and we step into an empty living room. Completely empty. No furniture, no paintings or photos on the walls, not even a lamp. The photo studio must be in another room. We can't take pics without professional lighting. Jake would never allow it.

"This is the living room," Reese says as he waves an arm across the room. "Hardwood floors, fireplace, ceiling fan, fresh paint, windows only three years old."

Um, okay. Does he think I'm blind? Why do I care how old the windows are?

Maybe my pregnancy brain is slowing me down a little. It takes a good minute, maybe two, before I realize this man's not trying to take our pictures. He's trying to sell us a house.

He shows us the kitchen, dining room, three bedrooms, two bathrooms, and the large, green backyard. Every step of the way I imagine our little one there. From learning to walk in the living room, to doing homework in the dining room, to inviting friends over for BBQs in the backyard. This isn't just a place to raise our baby, but a place to raise our family. Me, Jake, this baby, and hopefully a few more little ones in the future. This house is the real thing. I love it. It's everything I wanted for us.

"I didn't even see a For Sale sign out front," I finally say quietly.

"Ah," Reese explains. "It's not out there yet. It just went on the market, and it seemed to be exactly what Jake was looking for, so I called him right away."

"You've been working with Jake awhile?" I ask.

Reese nervously runs a hand across his chin. "Ah, um, a few weeks, yes. Maybe I should give you guys some time alone to discuss it."

Reese goes into the backyard via the sliding glass door in the dining room.

Jake looks at me nervously once we're alone.

"How many weeks?" I ask.

"I don't know? Ten? Twelve, maybe?"

"You've been looking for a house in Ann Arbor for three months without telling me?"

"Yeah," he admits sheepishly. Then he places a hand on each of my arms to look me straight in the eyes. "Listen, I know you had your heart set on a life in New York, and you know I will live there the rest of my life with you if that's what you want. But I also know you are stubborn as hell and have a tough time admitting when you might have made the wrong decision. I spent too many years of my life without you because you were too proud to admit you were wrong. I just wanted you to see this house and know that if you want to move back and raise our family here, I support that one hundred percent."

And what do I do? Cry.

"How did you know?" I ask him once I'm somewhat composed.

He puts a hand under my chin and tilts my face up a little. "Because I know you. Rox, please do not be afraid to talk to me. I don't care how many times you change your mind about where we live, where you work, what we're having for dinner, or what we're going to name this baby."

I nod, feeling more grateful for him and more in love with him than ever.

"We've been preapproved for our mortgage based on my W2s and our savings accounts, but with us only having one steady income right now, we're going to need a larger down payment. I hate the idea of you using any of your divorce settlement because I hate the fact that you were ever married to begin with, but this is a buyer's market right now and things can change quickly, and we can-"

I kiss his lips to shut him up. I also hate it that I was married to someone who didn't love me. I hate it very much. But I can't change it. I think of my divorce settlement as payment for work. I took care of that man for years. *Here. Sorry our marriage didn't work. I like to dress up as a woman and have someone dressed up as a wild animal put rubber penises into my anus. I'm sorry I never told you. But here, take this money in exchange for your years of arduous work in our home, and try to have a good life.*

"Shh," I tell him. "This is exactly how I want to use that money. I don't even need to see any other houses. Let's raise our family here, Jake."

"You got it, baby."

Finally, for the first time in many months, everything is right. I'll finish school. We'll wait for baby to arrive. I'll pay off my lease in NYC, maybe sublet. And then the three of us will start our life together. No more living in limbo, no more uncertainty. Just us. Forever.

Chapter Nine

March 2013

Thirty-six weeks. Gawd. I have never complained about this pregnancy. I took the morning sickness, headaches, heartburn, and exhaustion like a champ. After so many years of wanting to be pregnant, I truly understood what a blessing it was, and I took every symptom with a smile.

Until now. You know that feeling you get after Thanksgiving dinner when you eat too much, and your pants feel tight and you can't wait to get home and unbutton them? Imagine feeling that way, then looking down and realizing you're not even wearing pants. *That's* what this feels like.

Every step feels like there's a bowling ball pressing into my bladder. I even feel like the space between my legs is getting wider from the pressure.

I have one week of my externship left, and then I'm done with school.

This is Jake's last trip to Michigan for photo shoots before the baby comes. He flies back to New York tomorrow. The next time he leaves, we leave together. The *three* of us. It's still such a weird feeling to think we are going to have a baby here in a few weeks.

I know what you're thinking. It's scary for me to be alone right now, this close. But my doctor assured me there's nothing going on yet. Statistically, most first babies are late. I probably have four to five weeks left of this darling bowling ball baby whose sex and name remain unknown (to me anyway). My mommy instinct says it's a boy and it's been saying that from the very beginning. It's so strong, in fact, that if the doctor told me it was a girl, I'd tell him he was lying. Jake has been very careful not to use any gender specific pronouns, and I know he hasn't told anyone in the family because both of our mothers have been begging to find out the sex of their grandbaby.

"How do I know what color burp cloths to buy?" Jake's mom asked.

"It doesn't matter what color they are," I insisted. "They're used to clean spit-up. It's not like they need to be pretty."

"But there are hardly any gender-neutral clothes out there," my mom complained.

"Great!" I replied. "That means we get to go shopping when the baby gets here!"

As far as names go, we haven't decided on anything for sure. We have a few picked out, but we aren't deciding on anything until we meet him (or her - but I'm sure it's a him).

Good Things Come

If you know anything about me, you know I most likely had a baby name spreadsheet created before the urine had a chance to dry on that pregnancy test. I'm pretty sure a wise person once said, "A girl can never have too many spreadsheets." (It was me. I was the one who said that.)

Our name list is edited pretty much daily. Adding, removing, changing spellings, changing first and middle name sets. I put a lot of thought into the list. Not only because my baby's name is important and something he or she will live with until the end of time, but also because the list is my haven. It keeps me from doing dangerous things, like Googling every teeny tiny twinge, and interacting with other pregnant bullies (I mean, um, women) on The Bump forums.

I'm not tech-savvy enough to edit Excel documents on my phone. I still use a laptop. The laptop doesn't comfortably fit on my lap anymore. In all honesty, nothing is comfortable currently. My doctor said being on my left side is best, so I'm now lounging on my left side, my head propped up with my hand, and the laptop on the bed beside me. This position would not work well for writing a memoir, but it works fine for editing names on a spreadsheet.

I hear a siren outside. Police, ambulance, or fire truck? I guess ambulance, but I don't get up to look out the window and see if I'm right. Jake and I like to place bets - usually for oral sex. He's gotten very good at distinguishing the different sounds of the rescue vehicles. We should probably stop this little game of ours before his dick gets conditioned like Pavlov's dogs and automatically gets hard at the sound of a siren.

I miss him tonight, but I'm also kind of enjoying some alone time. I can take up as much of the bed as I need ... which is all of it.

I can dip my potato chips directly into the dip container, instead of putting the dip into a bowl first, like Jake insists. Seriously, *why*?

When Jake's not here, I can also watch anything I want on TV – even the Kardashians. It's not my fault really. It started a couple weeks ago. The TV was on, but I wasn't watching it. It was just background noise while I stood at the stove, perfecting my hollandaise sauce. Then I found myself glancing at the screen occasionally. At one point I grabbed the remote to rewind something I couldn't hear. Before I knew what was happening, Khloe was cracking me up, and I was on the edge of my seat waiting to see if Kourtney and Scott were going to work it out. I now have the series recording on my DVR. And approximately seventeen hours to watch them all before Jake gets home. And this may be a silent plea for help. SOS.

I stare at my spreadsheet while Kourtney overenunciates her words. Let's see. Laine above Avery and Abigail? Cody before Sam? Or just under Sam? I still really like Reed. Maybe we should delete Cody all together.

I see the Skype alerting me to a call on the laptop. It's Jake!

I press pause on the TV before I answer. Shh... Don't want him to catch me in the act.

"Hi, baby!" I say cheerfully.

He smiles and waves. "Hey, Little Girl. Whatcha doin?"

"I was just going over our name list."

"You add any new ones?"

"I'm liking Reed today. And not liking Cody."

"I still like Sam."

"But would we do just Sam? Or Samuel?"

"I think Samuel would be better when he's an adult. And then he can decide if he wants to be called Sam or Samuel. But we might be having a girl and this conversation is irrelevant."

(But we're not.)

I bite my lip. I love Sam. But Samuel I'm not crazy about. All I think when I hear that name is Samuel Jackson in *Pulp Fiction*. SAY WHAT AGAIN! Just thinking of the tension in that scene gives me anxiety. I fear that naming my kid Samuel might have me feeling that adrenaline and tension every time I say his name.

"I miss you," Jake says.

"I miss you, too, baby. You won't believe what else I'm doing tonight."

"What's that?"

"I'm dipping chips directly into the dip container!"

He fakes surprise. "No!"

"'Fraid so."

"I better not find any broken pieces of chips in there when I get home."

"Don't worry. I don't think there will be any left when you get home. How did your shoots go today? Just babies and families this week, right?"

"Yep. And I met with a bride, too. She's the sister of one of my clients and wants me to do her wedding."

"But you don't do weddings."

"No," he says. "I don't do weddings *now*. But I'm thinking of trying it. She's pretty high profile in Detroit – a DJ – and she thinks she can get me featured on some bridal websites."

"Hmm," I say. Not sure how I feel about that. Brides are crazy. So much drama. So much stress. That's why he didn't want to do weddings.

"Yeah. I've been thinking," he says, "with you not having work lined up, I could start taking bigger jobs. I don't want you to have to rush right into the work force. It's pretty late in the game to hit wedding season this year, but even getting a few could help us out. If it turns out to be something that works, I can start booking for next year, maybe go to some wedding conventions to meet some brides and pass out business cards."

"Hmm," I say again. I like it that he's thinking about what's best for his family. Weddings could be huge. Especially if he gets featured in magazines and websites. He could quit tending bar completely and be a full-time wedding photographer.

"The hours would be great, ya know?" he says. "Mostly Saturdays, a few Fridays. The rest of the week editing and printing from home. I think it could work."

"Then I'm excited for you, and I hope you book the job."

"I have another surprise for you," he says.

"What's that?"

"Can you tell where I am right now?"

He moves the screen, so I can see the room behind him. There's a fireplace with a wooden J and R on the mantle. Wait. Is that our fireplace at the new house? "Are you at our new house? Did you decorate it?"

"I did a little bit," he says from offscreen as he walks me up the stairs and down the hallway. He opens the door to our bedroom, and I see it's all set up. The curtains I had on my Amazon Wish List! The custom headboard Allison made for us as an early housewarming gift!

"I love it!"

"And …," he says, moving the screen toward the

door of the baby's room. "Drum roll please."

I wait to see what's behind the door.

"Drum roll," he repeats.

Oh, he was serious.

I try to mimic the sounds of a drum roll, and it comes out sounding more like an episode of *Law & Order*.

He turns the iPad around to show his face. "Are you kidding me, Rox? That was the worst drum roll I've ever heard. You're gonna need to do better than that if you want me to open this door."

I try again. "Bah dump ching."

He raises an eyebrow and grins. "Honey, that's not a drum roll. That's a rimshot. It's the sound you hear when someone tells a bad joke. Try again."

I swallow and try to retain my patience. I'm going to kill him.

"Do you even know what a drum roll sounds like?" he finally asks.

I don't speak. I breathe a certain way, and he knows I'm getting annoyed.

He sets the iPad down for a second and I hear him bang on the wall a few times in quick successions. When he picks up the tablet again, and I see his face, he says, "I got you." He turns it away from his face again to show the door of the nursery. "Now, I present to you…"

He pushes the door open, and I see that the gifts we received at our shower have been put into place. I see a lot of the nursery décor from our registry that hadn't been purchased yet. That sneaky, sneaky man. Before me, on my laptop screen, is the nursery of my dreams. Light grey-and-white-striped walls with turquoise accents. There's even a picture frame on the bookcase showing off Baby Odom's most recent ultrasound photo.

I put my hands over my face to hide my cries because I'm sure he must be sick of seeing my tears.

"You're not mad, are you?" he asks timidly.

I shake my head.

"I know you probably wanted to do this yourself, but I didn't want to put any added stress on you. A newborn baby and a big move at the same time are gonna be hard enough without having to set up an entire house. I thought this way you'd be able to relax for the next few weeks. Plus, you know Allison has a good eye for decorating, so I thought our house was in good hands. If there's anything you don't like we can redo it or-"

"Jake!" I interrupt him while dabbing a tissue to my eyes (I've learned to keep the tissues close for the last, say, seven months). "I'm not mad. I love it."

He breathes a sigh of relief and smiles. "Okay. Good. Now I got some work to finish up before bed, so I'm gonna let you get back to your Kardashians."

I look behind me and see I paused the TV on a perfect Kim scowl. Busted.

I blow him a kiss goodbye and close the Skype window right before I hear a knock on the door. I'm a little alarmed because I wasn't expecting anyone, and I heard that homicide is the leading cause of death to pregnant women...

I manage to get off the bed and waddle over to the door with only minor difficulty. I look through the peephole and see a gigantic eyeball staring back at me. I hear my New York best friend, Hope, laughing from the other side.

"Greetings!" she says when I open the door. She

walks in and takes a good look at me. I wish I'd known I was expecting company. I would have dressed in something nicer than yoga pants and a Yankees T-shirt. Ha ha. Just kidding. No, I wouldn't have.

But I might have taken a flat iron to my hair instead of this messy top knot. Ha ha. Nope. Wrong again. I apologize in advance to all who come to my door these next few weeks, but I'm in the zero fucks given stage of pregnancy.

"You look great!" she says, and I'm kind of confused, because Hope does not tell lies. "You've totally got that glow going on."

"Thanks," I say. She drops some bags onto the tiny counter space, and then gives me a hug and a kiss on the cheek.

"I hope you don't mind me dropping by, but when you said Jake was out of town I thought you might like some company. And if not," she points to the bags on the counter, "you're sure to like pad Thai and curry."

Thai food is not something I have learned how to make on my own yet. So yes, I'm sure to like it. And, of course, I'm happy to see my friend, too. Especially since we're leaving the city soon and I don't know when I'll see her again.

Hope opens the cupboards and starts pulling out plates and glasses like she lives here.

"Make yourself at home," I say, though she already has.

She smirks at me and pours us each a glass of root beer. Ever since I've been pregnant, I've been obsessed with root beer. I'm sure my friend would rather have a margarita or a glass of wine.

"You could have brought some drinks if you wanted. I can resist."

"Hey," she says handing me a glass, "solidarity, girl."

I take a sip of the frothy drink and it feels like little bursts of heaven in my mouth.

She nods at the TV. "Is that the Kardashians?"

"It is," I admit, expecting reprimand for my brain-cell-killing trash-TV habit.

"Awesome," she says, taking a seat on the bed with her plate of takeout. "This must be Pre-Kanye. Look how little Kylie was." She sighs dramatically. "Those days were the best."

I can't believe this. My friend has never mentioned a Kardashian around me before. Now she knows all their names, and their kid's names, too. It kind of makes me wonder ... are there others like us? Keeping their *Keeping Up...* addictions secret?

"We can watch *Teen Mom* next if you want," I say.

She's quiet for a few moments while she finishes chewing. "I'm gonna miss you, ya know?"

Thud.

"No, no," she quickly adds. "Do not cry. I didn't come here to upset you."

I blink back my tears and take a big bite of pad Thai so I can concentrate on my food instead of my feelings.

"The real reason I came over tonight is because this is probably the last time we'll spend together, just the two of us, and I wanted to give you something."

I sit up straighter, instantly intrigued. When Hope says she's going to give you something, you seriously never know what you're going to get.

She pulls something out of the back pocket of her jeans. It's a piece of notebook paper folded up and tucked in to itself like she is about to pass a note across homeroom in junior high. With a quick flick of her wrist, she tosses it into my lap.

"I hope this is a list," I say, smiling again.

She shrugs. "You know I'm not big on committed relationships, but you and Jake are the real thing. Keep this list around and look at it when you start to feel bored, or comfortable, or start taking each other for granted. It'll keep you on your toes."

"Should I read it now? Or wait until I get bored?" Gosh, I hope I never get bored of Jake. I can't even imagine something so dreadful.

"You can read it now. And start following some of these rules right away."

"Oh, there are relationship rules here? From a single person?" I grin, so she'll know I'm joking. She might be single, but she knows what she's doing in life. I'd take relationship advice from her before I took it from my own mother, and she's been married thirty-five years.

I open it up. I love the title.

The Swoon Life List

1. Number one rule, above all others, is do not use the bathroom in front of him. No boys in the bathroom!
2. Don't ever go to bed with hairy legs. Shave, pluck, and wax… everything … always. Act as if you're going on your third date, every day.
3. Always make sure your toenails are painted.
4. Put on perfume, even if you're not leaving the house.
5. Wear sexy underwear always. Even when

you're on your period.
6. Go on a family date at least once a week. It's important that you get out of the house, away from bills, and chores, and stress, and have fun together.
7. Go on a date without baby at least once a month, more if babysitters are available. This baby will become your everything. You need to remember that at one time, you two were everything.
8. Kiss him on the lips every day.
9. Make a list of everything you love about him, everything you find sexy about him, and some of the sweetest things he's ever done or said. Don't let yourself forget about those times. Read the list often. Add to it when you can.
10. Remember to be kind. Do a chore that he usually does. Leave little love notes around. Record his favorite movies on the DVR. Buy his favorite snacks at the grocery store. Little things are sometimes the biggest things.
11. Hold hands when you're walking together.
12. Show appreciation. Say thank you. When you see he's done something you asked, or even something you didn't, let him know you noticed. Don't be a constant nag.
13. Nostalgia is powerful. Take time to remember where you came from. Look at old photos. Put pictures of special memories on the walls to help you remember.
14. Don't say "I love you" every time you hang up the phone, or "I love you" will become a euphemism for "goodbye." It will lose its

power.
15. Sleep in the same bed together every night. Try to go to bed at the same time when at all possible.
16. No TV in the bedroom.
17. Don't fart in front of each other.
18. Don't forget to spend time with your friends sometimes, too. And do some things on your own. It's good to miss each other.

I fold the note back up and tuck the corner into the pocket. I really hope there's not a day when I need this list to remind me to be good to Jake, but I'm glad I have it just in case.

After a few episodes of reality TV, Hope hugs me goodbye.

"You got this, girl," she whispers on her way out.

♥

When Jake arrives home the next evening, he kneels on the floor and kisses my belly.

"I missed you, Little One," he tells the baby.

I've already accepted that I'm now in second place, and I'm okay with that.

He kisses me next. "Missed you, too."

"I made dinner," I say. Sweet potato Shepherd's Pie. I needed some comfort food after spending a good part of the day watching birth videos on YouTube. Ugh. The screaming. The ripping. I shudder. It's terrifying.

"I've been thinking..." I tell Jake as we sit down in bed for dinner.

"I figured," he says.

"And I think I'm ready."
His eyes open wide. "Ready for the baby?"
"Oh no. Not that. I'm ready to find out the sex."
He looks up from his plate again, startled.
"You don't want to wait for the delivery room?"

I don't tell him what I've been watching or the horrors I've seen. I simply shrug. "I was just thinking, and I think I want us to have one more special moment between the two of us before (my vagina is ripped in half) our lives are changed forever. And I don't think that moment is going to come in the delivery room (while my vagina is being ripped in half). I've thought a lot about it, and I'm ready to find out in a calm, non-painful, no screaming, sweating, and panting kind of way."

"Gotcha," he says. "Then I'll make sure I find a calm, non-painful, no screaming and panting kind of way to tell you."

Chapter Ten

Easter Sunday, 2013

One day, in the future, I imagine we'll spend our holidays as one big happy extended family. I can see us drinking hot chocolate with our parents while someone plays Christmas carols on the piano. (Nobody in my family plays the piano, and no one owns a piano either, but that doesn't mean someone won't pick up the habit one day.)

I can see big Thanksgiving dinners with my brother and his future wife, Jake's siblings and their future spouses. We'll play football in the backyard while the leaves fall around us like confetti.

On Easter, our future kids and future nieces and nephews, will run through our yard carrying their baskets looking for plastic eggs filled with candy and coins.

I imagine our future as an episode of *Parenthood*, with all of us eating dinner in the backyard under a canopy of stringed lights, with the raspy, comforting laughter of Mae Whitman filling the yard. (Okay, so Mae Whitman isn't *actually* a part of my family and won't be having dinner with us now, or ever. But you get the idea.)

The future is going to rock.

But right now, for this holiday, it's just us, and Manhattan – for the last time.

It has been a week since I told him I was ready to find out the sex of our baby. He hasn't found a way to tell me yet, and I haven't brought it up to him again. I'm sure he's working on something special. Or maybe waiting for something special, like today, or maybe my 30th birthday coming up in a few days. I trust him to tell me at the right time, in the right way. And I really like not knowing when it's coming. That way it's still a surprise.

I have discovered, through books, internet articles, and classes, that hardly anything about pregnancy comes as a surprise. I heard that only 15% of women have their water break spontaneously before they go into labor. It's not like in the movies when you're just walking through Target, and it bursts out of you like a popped water balloon.

About 90% find out the gender early, nowadays as early as ten weeks. With C-section rates being over 30% in some hospitals, and inductions being around 25%, going into labor unexpectedly, unplanned, and unmedicated is a rarity these days.

I feel robbed, like everything I've learned in the

movies has been a lie.

After I put on my Easter best, I stand in front of the mirror before we leave for church. I ordered the cutest baby blue maternity dress from an independent clothing boutique I saw on Instagram. It looked way better on the tanned model in the photograph than it does on me and my pale winter skin. I should stay away from pastels. Most people probably should. "Ew," I say under my breath.

"You look gorgeous," Jake lies. I appreciate it.

"I should change," I say.

"No, no, no," he insists. "You're not changing. I bought this tie just to coordinate with your dress. If you change, *I* have to change, and I don't want to change." He holds out his hand. "You're beautiful. Everyone will be looking at that huge belly and your pregnancy glow. Not your dress. Come on."

"I'm not worried about the dress. I like the dress. It's my white skin I'm worried about."

"You're right. I bet everyone at church will be wondering why that pregnant lady hasn't been hitting up the tanning salon." He rolls his eyes. "Come on!"

I take one more look in the mirror and then another look at Jake to see if he appears to have enough patience for me to undress and give myself a quick spray of instant bronzer. Nope. His face looks about as patient as a typical millennial. I have zero chance of another trip to the bathroom.

"Fine. Let's go," I surrender.

After church, Jake surprises me with brunch reservations at Jack's Wife Freda. Sunday Brunch isn't as big of a thing in the Midwest as it is here, so I'm glad I got to try one more brunch place before we move. It really is the perfect Easter surprise.

"Isn't it crazy to think that next Easter we'll have an almost-one-year-old with us at Easter brunch?" I ask as I look around at the impeccably dressed families of the Soho bistro. The little boys in bowties, the little girls with flowers in their hair.

"We might even be working on baby number two by that time," he says with a mischievous grin.

I look up from my eggs benny. We hadn't discussed future children yet. I figured we'd get the first one out of the womb before I brought up the topic … but if he wants to talk about it …

"You intend to have more than one kid?" I ask. "With *me*?"

He shakes his head playfully. "What do you mean *with you*? Yes, I'd prefer to have all my kids with the same woman. I'm a photographer, not a professional athlete."

I shrug. "It just seems like that's what most people are doing these days, having babies with multiple people."

He laughs. "I think you've been watching too much *Teen Mom*." He pauses and takes a sip of his coffee. Then he leans back in his chair and stares at me curiously for a moment. He looks like he's going to say something important, so I lean forward, anxious to hear it. "Tell me," he says. "Would you still ask questions like this if we were married?"

I take a bite of my potatoes, to give me time to think about my answer while I'm chewing. Would I wonder these kinds of things if we were married? I realize that the answer is no, I would not. If we were married, I would assume that we were together forever, and obviously if we wanted more kids, we'd have them together.

"No," I say honestly. "I wouldn't. But that doesn't mean we should get married," I quickly add.

"Do *you* intend on having a second baby with *me*?" he asks.

It seems silly to me when he asks questions like this. Like I'd ever want to be with anyone but him. I feel like he should know that, without a shadow of a doubt. But then shouldn't I know the same about him? Why don't I? He doesn't do anything to make me question him, but I constantly do anyway. I wish I could shake my annoying sense of insecurity, but it seems like it's a permanent fixture. I just might be ruined. Damaged goods.

"If I have a second baby, and I hope I do, I wouldn't imagine it being with anyone else," I say.

The server drops the check off and Jake slips his card into the black book.

"Okay. Good," he says. "I'm glad we got that cleared up. But we can talk more about baby number two after baby number one gets here."

"Deal," I agree.

"You think you're okay to walk home?" he asks as we step out onto Carmine Street.

It's not that far, only like eight blocks. But he may be concerned that I'm overdoing it since we already walked to church that morning, and then walked to the restaurant after.

"I'm good," I say to reassure him. Walking is supposed to help with labor later. Or so I heard. That could be a lie, too. Who knows anymore?

We slowly begin our walk back to our apartment. Slowly, because I'm gigantic, but also because I want to savor every moment I have left here in this city, especially when the sun is shining.

We've only gone a few steps when I see a baby blue plastic egg sitting at the base of a tree.

"Aww, look," I say as I point out the egg, "there's an egg right next to that little leprechaun. Someone's having an Easter egg hunt."

"Honey. That's a garden gnome. Not a leprechaun." He bends down and picks it up.

"Jake! You can't take someone else's egg. It's probably for a little kid," I tell him.

"It's not," he says, smiling. "It's for you."

He holds it out in the palm of his hand for me to get a closer look.

Sure enough. The egg says Roxie on it in grey marker. Huh. Cute. He must have come here last night and left this egg. I'm surprised no one stole it.

"Open it," he tells me.

I take it from his hand and handle the egg tenderly. This must be it! The big reveal must be inside this egg. This blue egg. If the egg is blue, it must be a boy. I stare at it, now questioning whether I want to know after all. Once I find out, there's no going back.

"Go on," he says.

I press the crease in the middle of the egg and it pops open, revealing a mini Reese's egg. No reveal.

There's a slip of paper folded up inside. I open it and read it. It says *Happy Easter, Roxie.*

Well then. That was anticlimactic.

I stick the egg in my purse, and we keep walking. I see a pink egg in a flower box outside of a window. "Is that one mine, too?"

He nods.

This one I can pick up on my own because it's higher up. Eggs on the ground (or anything on the ground, really) must stay on the ground. Because I will squat for nothing at this point.

I look at the pink egg and see my name written in marker again. He's using pink to throw me off this time. Clever.

I open it and find another Reese's egg and a note that says, *You're going to be a great mom.*

I smile and stick it in my purse with the other.

I find another egg two storefronts down, on a window ledge. I still can't believe no one took them before I found them. This one is yellow with another Reese's egg that I decide to eat right away. Even though I'm full after brunch, I've always got room for a Reese's egg. The note in this one says, *If you like pina coladas...*

I laugh out loud. Neither of us can think about pina coladas without remembering the infamous lubrication situation of 2005.

The next one is pink again. Another Reese's egg. *I've loved you since I was nine years old.*

And I was hoping I wasn't going to cry today...

A few more blocks, a few more eggs.

You're my favorite radio station.

Would you like a screaming orgasm?

High-five, baby!

As we get closer and closer to Washington Square, I keep trying to go in different directions to avoid it. I know where we are headed, and it makes my stomach clench with nerves. I was sitting in Washington Square when my dad called to tell me about my mom's aneurysm. I sat on a bench thinking I'd just said goodbye to my mom forever. It was the worst feeling I've ever had, and I've not been able to go back to that park since.

Whenever I try to take a different route, Jake keeps

nudging me toward it.

"We have to stay on the route of the eggs," he insists.

"But Jake..." I whine. Doesn't he know how I feel about that place?

Yes. He does. That's why he's forcing me to go there.

When we arrive, I see an egg sitting on the very bench I was sitting on when I got that phone call. This egg is big, like a dinosaur egg. It's yellow, and it says "Mommy" on it in the grey marker. I blink back tears as I gently pick it up. Maybe what he's doing is trying to turn a bad place back into a good one.

I press the center line on the egg to crack it open. This is it. No going back.

I pull out a soft piece of grey cotton. It's a V-neck T-shirt.

I hold it up and read the print on the front of the shirt.

It says #boymom in white letters.

I knew all along my baby was a boy. But now it's confirmed. I put my face in the T-shirt to hide my tears, then I hug the shirt to my chest. His trick worked. I don't feel dreadful standing here anymore. I feel peaceful. This guy kills me sometimes with his perfection. If it wasn't for his awful marriage proposal, I'd think he was too good to exist in real life.

"Congrats, Boymom," he says and gives me a kiss.

I hug him and hold him extra tight for a few moments longer than most hugs last. Then I press my forehead to his. "Congrats, Boydad," I whisper.

I hear the click of a shutter.

I look over and see Hope holding Jake's camera in front of us.

She gives me a sneaky smile. Of course, he had help to set the eggs out and make sure no one stole them. She was probably only a few steps ahead of us this whole walk.

She takes a few more pictures of the two of us with the shirt and my giant belly under the arch.

Once my eyes are dry, she hands me the camera, and I press buttons to scroll through the pictures she took of me opening the egg. Somehow Jake managed a gender reveal and an impromptu journalistic-style maternity shoot all in one. I'm supposed to be the hardcore planner of the two of us, but he just showed me up big time. And I'm okay with it.

The pictures are perfect. Even with my pasty skin.

"You're the best thing that's ever happened to me," I whisper to him, as I take his hand and we head for home. "Until our little boy gets here anyway."

Chapter Eleven

April 2013

"We have *your* hospital bag, *my* hospital bag, the diaper bag, the Boppy pillow," Jake says as he surveys the mass of bags hanging from his forearm.

"Checkcheckcheckcheck," I say through quick bursts of breath.

"I have extra batteries for the camera," he mutters to himself. "Phone chargers, Kindle charger, iPad charger, keys."

"Come the fuck on!" I manage to scream out.

"And an angry girlfriend."

"It fucking hurts! And don't you dare tell me to stop fucking swearing because I swear to God, Jake!"

Everything I read on Google and The Bump (when I wasn't distracting myself with baby names) said that first time pregnancies were notorious for ending in very long labors. They all agreed that it's better to labor at home where you're comfortable, instead of in a hospital room.

I realize now that I didn't quite think this one through. I took their advice and labored at home as long as possible. But I had no idea – Omigod! – that it would hurt this bad. And now I have – Holy shit! – to waddle down three flights of stairs, and take a cab to the hospital. And pray there's not too much traffic, or I'll end up on the 11 o'clock news.

"Oh shit. What if I waited too long for an epidural?" I ask as I make my way sideways down the stairs. I can't walk down the stairs straight anymore because I feel like I'm going to topple over. Either way it's scary because I can't see the stairs I'm trying to step on. Jake leads the way and takes my hand, reassuring me each time I put my foot down that there is indeed a step there.

"What happened to a natural, drug-free delivery?" he asks innocently.

I can tell he's not trying to be a smartass. But still. He's lucky I don't push him down the stairs.

"I didn't know (gasp) it would (gasp) hurt this bad."

By the time we make it to the street, it's taking every ounce of self-preservation to keep from screaming like a wild animal.

This can't be right. Something must be wrong with the baby. Nothing should hurt this bad. Ever. I used to think a toothache was the worst pain imaginable. That was before I felt like my body was being turned inside out.

Luckily Jake finds a cab relatively quickly. We

don't need to tell the driver to hurry. The poor guy wants to deliver a baby in the back of his taxi even less than we do. The driver quickly gets our bags in the trunk while Jake helps me into the backseat. Once we're buckled in (always a safety girl), the cab takes off. Despite my pain, I manage to take a picture of the driver's ID sign posted in front of us. I want to remember this later. His name is Raoul.

He takes off, flying through the streets of Manhattan in a race against time. I pant in the backseat and hold on for dear life. It's exhilarating. The pain, the urgency, the city lights flashing past my window in a bright smudge. Between the bursts of agony that make me feel like I'm being ripped in half, I take a deep breath and a long look at Jake. He's giddy. One hand in mine, one on his camera. I think he has the pregnancy glow that I was supposed to get. I lean in closer to him.

"Selfie," I say.

Jake takes my phone from me because his arms are longer. We both smile for the camera. But as soon as the selfie is snapped, I find myself looking away and blinking back tears. Is that our last picture together before our lives change forever?

I make a point to look around and take mental pictures of everything I see. I sniff my wrist to smell my perfume. Calvin Klein Euphoria. I want to remember this moment forever. I want to smell that perfume one day, five, ten, twenty years from now, and remember this exact feeling, this exact moment. Pain, fear, curiosity, hope. My life will now be divided into two parts: before I became a mom and after I became a mom. This cab ride across Manhattan is the line between them.

It's the end of our short-term life in New York City

before we move to suburbia. More significantly, it's the end of just us. It's not going to be about us anymore. Will we be okay? What will it be like to love someone more than him? What will it be like for him to love someone more than me? Will there be enough love to go around? Or will our relationship die a long, painful death from malnourishment? Will we get so wrapped up in taking care of our little one that we'll forget to take care of each other? Will I find myself years from now a nagging baby mama and him a resentful, underappreciated dad? Will I be a good mom? Will he be proud of me? Will we agree on parenting and disciplining? There's so many questions and no answers.

Suddenly I start to think this is a bad idea. I'm not ready. We're not ready. I didn't read those books Jake brought home from the library. All I know is the five Ss of soothing. That's not enough. I need more time. Wait.

Screaming like a dramatic pregnant woman in the back of a cab?

Check.

This baby doesn't care if we are ready.

When we left the apartment, I was worried that I would be too late for an epidural. As much pain as I was in, I thought the baby was ready to fall out right there. I can't believe it when they examine me at the hospital and tell me I'm only dilated to a six! If this is six, what do nine and ten feel like? I never wish to find out. I don't care how big that needle is for the epidural. I will take it again and again and again to make sure I never feel another contraction.

Once the epidural is working its magic, I'm totally fine. My parents flew in a few days ago, on my due date, so they arrive quickly from their hotel room. The four of us chill out in the room for a few hours, playing Euchre and Uno. We can see my contractions happening on the monitor, but luckily, I can't feel them.

Nurse Jaime is a perky brunette with a high ponytail who looks young enough that I would card her if she tried to order a drink from me. She comes in to check my cervix again and Mom and Dad step aside. Jaime pulls the curtain around my bed before shoving her hand up there to check it out. I find it funny that I'm not comfortable pooping when my boyfriend is home, but during the last several months I've had so many hands up my vagina that it doesn't even faze me anymore. We could be sitting around eating pizza and watching movies as normal as it feels to have everything wide open and on display for strangers.

Jaime nods and pulls off her glove with gusto, "Ten! Dr. Lehman should be here in about fifteen minutes. He was just finishing up at the office when I talked to him."

I gasp and look at Jake. This baby is coming. Like now. Ready or not, here I come.

"You're gonna feel some pressure, and you're going to want to push. Don't push until he comes in, okay? I also suggest that anyone who is not going to be here for the birth start saying their goodbyes and head to the waiting room."

Mom and Dad get the message. When the nurse pulls the curtain back and leaves the room, Mom and Dad stand up and come over to the bed to say goodbye.

"We'll be outside if you need us," Dad says. "Mom's gonna get Adam on Skype," he says to me, "and I'm gonna get your mom on Facetime," he says to Jake. "The four of us will be in the waiting room to hear if we have a baby boy or baby girl in the family."

"Bye, Daddy," I tell him, after he kisses my cheek. "Listen for the baby song."

Mom comes over, and I swear she must know exactly what I've been feeling, because she leans down and whispers, "I promise you'll never look back, baby girl."

It feels kind of, well, *grown up*, for the two of us to be here in this room, doing this *huge thing* without adults around. I mean, except for us. I forget that we're adults sometimes. I realize I'm thirty, but I still don't feel qualified to be responsible for a human life. I feel like I should have to take test before I'm allowed to do this. I can't even get a driver's license until I can prove to someone that I know how to safely maneuver a car through the streets. It seems weird that they'll let me have a baby and take it home without proving my capability.

Jake sits next to me on the bed. Even if I do feel unprepared for this, and even though I might have a small yearning to call the nurse and have her bring my mommy and daddy back, I am glad we are doing this on our own. People like to make the joke that your parents and friends weren't there when you made the baby, therefore they shouldn't be in the room when the baby is born. But it's not even about that for me. I think it's important for us to start our family alone before we invite others in. I want some time with just the three of us first, because no matter how close we are with our families, these two are my priorities now.

"I'm gonna miss your belly," he says as he touches it for what might be the last time before our baby is here.

"You never know. It might decide to hang around for a few years."

"That's fine. We're just gonna be putting more babies in it anyway."

It's a relief to hear he's not expecting me to be at the gym working this gut off right away. And that he thinks I'm going to be the mother of his future children as well. Even though we talked about it, there can never be enough reassurance. (I know. I'm so annoying.)

"What are you thinking?" he asks.

"That I'm not sure if I'm qualified for this," I whisper honestly. "Have you wondered that? If we are going to know how to do this?"

"Nope. Not at all. That's why they're called maternal instincts. We're gonna be fine, baby. I have no doubt. We got this."

I hear a tap on the door and Jake stands up. Dr. Lehman pokes his head in before entering the room.

"Howdy," he says, walking into the room in his scrubs. He looks prepared and confident, which makes me feel a little better about this next step. He washes his hands at the sink first. Then grabs some gloves from the box on the shelf, and puts them on both hands. There's a stool ready for him at the bottom of the bed. He plops down on it. "We ready to have this baby?"

Am I allowed to say no?

Thirty-nine minutes later, the two of us become a family of three. I never knew a sound so precious until I heard my baby cry for the first time. They place that little body on my chest, and I am overwhelmed by the amount of love I feel for this tiny, wrinkled, purple, screaming creature. After some skin-to-skin contact with Mommy, I pass him over to Jake for some skin-to-skin contact with Daddy, too. I've heard people use an expression about their hearts beating outside of their bodies, and that was the moment I totally understood what they'd meant.

They let us press the button to play the baby music out of the hospital's loud speakers. I know my family is out there in the waiting room on the edge of their seats, so I tell Jake it's time for him to have his moment, the moment I insisted he have.

"Go on, baby. Go tell my parents to come back and meet our little boy."

Our little boy.

If our life was a movie, this would be a great time in the storyline to insert a montage over a nice piece of music, maybe *What a Wonderful World*. It would show videos of us in the past; holding hands under a table as children, playing in the autumn leaves as teenagers, doing shots together as college kids, touring the Met together as adults, and now introducing the world to our little boy.

Sam.

Chapter Twelve

April 2013

"I think the three of us should walk home from the hospital," I say to Jake as I stand and look out the window of our hospital room. It looks like a bright, sunny spring day -- a perfect opportunity to use the gigantic travel system we bought on Allison's insistence. What I'd really wanted was a little umbrella stroller, something that could easily be folded up and tossed over a shoulder. Not my shoulder though. Screw that. Maybe Jake's?

"Umbrella strollers are shit!" my Michigan best friend, Allison, had told me, insisting I add an expensive travel system to my gift registry. "Just use your completion discount on it at the end. It's worth it. Trust me. It's like the difference between driving a car and driving a golf cart. You could take a golf cart to the end of the block, but would you take a golf cart on a road trip? No. An umbrella stroller is good for nothing but back pain and sidewalk rage. The reason they are light enough to throw around is because after using one for longer than fifteen minutes, you will *want* to throw one. Into a street. And run it over with a car. And once you run it over with your car, you'll want to back up and run it over again."

"No umbrella strollers. Got it."

I figured I should probably listen to her. She's done this three times. She probably knows what she's talking about more than the first-time-mom bloggers who use affiliated links to make money. So I took her advice, and used my completion coupon to buy an expensive enormous stroller/car seat combo.

Many years ago, when I was a snooty twenty-something who thought I knew better, I made a list of all the things I swore I would never do once I had kids. I'm pretty sure that having a stroller the size of a minivan was on the list. Allison told me back then that I would be crossing things off that list as soon as my first baby was born. Turns out I crossed one off the list before he even got here. Now I am going to be the mom taking up the entire pathway at the park with my giant stroller. And I can't wait.

I look over at Sam's little crib where Jake is dressing him in his "going home" outfit: a onesie with the infamous I Heart NY print, and the teeniest, tiniest black cotton pants. He's only going to be a New York resident for a few days, but I want him to see the pictures of his homecoming one day and remember where he came from.

"I feel like you're being a little too ambitious, hun,"

Jake says. "You just gave birth yesterday. We'll go home and get comfortable for a little while, and then we can take him for a walk if you want, maybe get some coffee and go to Bryant Park."

"That sounds amazing! Yes! Yes! Yes!" I practically squeal. It just dawned on me that I can finally drink as much coffee as I want! The thought makes me want to jump in the air and pump up my fist, but I *did* just have a baby yesterday, so maybe I should take it easy.

"I thought you would like that idea," he says while he scoots those tiny pants up Sam's itty-bitty thighs. "I scheduled KidCar to pick us up at eleven-thirty, so hopefully they'll have us ready to go by then. They said about two hours."

Kid Car. It's a car service that picks you up with the car seat of your choice already installed safely in the backseat. It seems safer to me than putting an infant carrier into the back of a cab. I know, a car is a car, but, well, you know… cabs…

When the car service arrives, a nurse walks us down to the exit. After a brief lesson on car seat safety, she has me fasten Sam into the infant carrier myself before she checks the straps to make sure he is in there safely. She checks the position of the chest clip, and pinches the straps to make sure they're not too tight or too loose. Good to go! Okay, so at least they gave me *one* lesson before just tossing me out into the world with this helpless baby and hoping for the best.

I sit in the backseat with Sam. Jake gets up front with the driver. As we drive past familiar sites, I mention them to Sam. He'll never remember this. It's hard to imagine that a city that means so much to me will never know my little boy. I'm sure we'll bring him here on vacations someday, when he's old enough to remember. But he's not going to be raised as a New Yorker. I know it's for the best. I absolutely believe that. But that doesn't mean I'm not going to show him as much of this place as I can before we leave.

The KidCar pulls up in front of our building. I get Sam out of the car seat as Jake steps around back to help us out. Once the driver takes off, we stand there in front of our building and I give Sam a quick look around at his first home.

I love spring. I love New York. I love Jake. I just gave birth to the sweetest, softest little baby boy who showed me how much more love I was capable of feeling. My heart feels huge as we enter the building and begin our slow climb up the stairs.

When we get to our floor, I peek at Sam's scrunched up face. The little white bumps across his tiny nose. Those cute, kissable lips with the perfect Cupid's bow. Even in my arms, he's too far away. I look at Jake and swoon a little inside. We created this. And it's perfect. All of it. Just the way it is.

This is it, my happy ending. Let the credits roll.

And isn't it when we are happiest that we have the most to fear? Isn't it when we have it all, that we have it all to lose?

When I open the door to our apartment, my perfect little bubble of happiness pops like shattered glass.

I push my way through the baby blue streamers that hang from the door frame. Jake must have decorated when he came home yesterday to shower. I think it's sweet until I see what else he has decorated the apartment with. There's a banner taped across the wall above the TV. No, it's not an Intervention banner like last summer. It's much worse.

Roxie, please marry me. (This time I mean it.)

My heart sinks. I set Sam down in the Rock 'n Play next to our bed. I would curl into a fetal position myself, but my belly is still a little larger than usual, so I sit cross-legged on the bed. I rock back and forth with my head in my hands. And I cry. I'm overwhelmed with feelings, so much that I feel raw and exposed, like a peeled veggie. I feel a joy like no other. I am bubbling over with happiness. That's great! Right? I mean, it's supposed to be. It *should* be.

And it *would* be, except that I'm feeling so many other things all on top of that. It feels like I'm being smothered in emotions and about to suffocate.

Along with joy and love, I feel a fear like I've never known before. I didn't worry about the baby very much when he was inside of me. There were a few things that could go wrong in there, but none that concerned me too much. Now that he's on the outside, all I can think of is hundreds of different ways this cruel world can hurt him or take him from me. And I've never been so scared of losing something before in my life.

I also feel doubt. Did I really do anything to deserve him?

I feel apprehension. What did I get myself into? Moms always make it seem like the first few months are absolute hell. It seems fine so far, but he's only been here a day. What if I can't handle the crying? What if I can't handle the lack of sleep? What if I end up a massive disappointment to both of them?

I even feel a little sad because Sam isn't in my belly anymore. I had gotten so used to feeling him swimming around in there, and now my belly is still and it feels, well, empty. And that makes me sad. It's stupid, I know. There are mommies whose babies don't get to come home from the hospital at all. And other babies who must stay a very long time after Mommy has been allowed to leave. My baby is perfectly healthy and home beside me, and I'm over here whining because he isn't in my belly anymore. I am rotten!

And then there's shame. What kind of mom thinks these things? I should be nothing but happy right now. Am I completely losing my mind? Is this the beginning of postpartum psychosis?

Now there's anger, too. Why would Jake do this to me right now? All those pregnancy books he read. Did they not teach him anything? Did they not warn him that I'd be an unstable train wreck for a few days after the baby was born?

And the disappointment. Another marriage proposal to turn down. I'm going to hurt his feelings, and I don't want that.

I continue to cry. It's too much. Too soon. I can't think about this right now. I just can't.

I haven't looked at him. He hasn't said anything yet. He's probably alarmed by this outburst and might even have his hand on his phone in case he needs to call 911 to get me committed.

I hear the banner crinkle a little as the tape gives out and it falls to the floor. I hear it crumbling like Jake is smashing it up. Then I hear him lift the lid to the garbage can.

After a few minutes, my sobs turn to whimpers and sniffles. I wipe my eyes with my shirt, but I don't look up. I am afraid to look at him. He's going to hate me. He'll think I've lost my mind.

It's crazy how fast things can change. Everything was so perfect. And now this. The air is heavy. The silence is painful.

When I finally do hear a sound, it isn't the sound I'm expecting. It's laughter. Jake is laughing.

I finally look up at him with my swollen, red eyes. He's leaning on the kitchen counter with his arms across his chest, shaking his head and laughing.

"That," he says, "was the absolute worst response to a proposal ever. If I had recorded that, it could have gotten us on *Ellen*. You wanna do an encore, and I'll get out my phone?"

I just stare at him. I don't speak. I don't even know what to say. Until he smiles at me. And just like that, I know everything is going to be okay.

"It's too much right now," I say, looking down at my feet and realizing I'm still wearing my Converse ... shoes on the bed ... obviously distraught. "We need time to be a family first. I feel like you're trying to *change* us before we even have a chance to *be* us."

He's quiet for a moment before he relents. "You're right."

I sneak a look at his face. "I'm sorry," I whisper.

He comes and joins me on the bed, pulling me down beside him. He rests his elbow on the bed next to my head and props his face up with his hand.

"No. *I'm* sorry," he says, mindlessly twirling a piece of my hair around his finger. "On Easter, you said you'd feel more secure about us if we were married. And I don't want you feeling insecure about us. I don't want you to question if I'm coming home from work every day, or constantly wondering when I'm going to leave you. I just want *you* to know that *I* am all-in. With *us*. I thought if I asked you to marry me again after Sam was born, you'd know I really meant it. So forget I asked. Let's just pretend instead that I told you I love you and I'm looking forward to spending the rest of our lives together with this little guy, married or not. Okay? Can you do that?"

I wipe a tear off my cheek and nod. He might be a really bad proposer, but damn if he doesn't recover quickly. "I swear I don't deserve you," I whisper.

"No? You don't think so?" He's still mindlessly twirling my hair and not even looking at me. "What if I told you a story about a little boy who felt unwanted in his own home? There was this little girl who knew it, the only one who knew how hard he cried sometimes. And this girl, not only did she comfort him when he felt unloved, but she set a plate for him at her own family's dinner table almost every night, to make sure he knew he was wanted somewhere. She laughed at his jokes, even when they weren't that funny. He wasn't super smart like her or her brother, and he struggled with his grades, but she insisted he was the best speller and the bravest person she knew. When other people looked at him, all they saw was everything he *wasn't*. But this girl, she only saw him as everything he *was*. And what if I told you a story about that same little boy who was ashamed to order his free lunch in the cafeteria at school because he was afraid his friends would make fun of him? Would you believe that little girl brought him a lunch so he wouldn't have to? What if I told you this girl kept secrets for him to make sure her parents didn't unwelcome him at the dinner table? Like when he skipped school and smoked too much weed?"

"And had sex with their daughter?" I interrupted.

"Yeah. That. And what if I told you that this girl loved this boy and believed in him, even after he dropped out of college to work as a bartender and start a photography business that no one else thought would ever turn into shit?" He finally drops the piece of my hair and looks me straight in the eyes. "What would you think of her? Would you say she deserved him?"

I can't even say anything. There's nothing to say. It's the first time I've ever been able to see myself the way he sees me. And forgive me if I sound like a 13-year-old girl right now ... but ... I. Can't. Even.

How is this real? How is this my life? How did I get so fucking lucky?

"What would I say about her?" I repeat the question. "I would say the only person luckier than her is the little boy who gets to call him Daddy."

"See? How could I not love the shit out of you?"

"Are you even real?" I ask him. "You're too perfect."

He laughs again and sits up. "I'm pretty sure I just made you cry and rock back and forth like you were in *The Exorcist*, so..."

"But you made up for it ... perfectly."

I wrap the hem of his t-shirt around my finger and pull him back down.

"Hey. Speaking of loving the shit out of me. Did I poop while Sam was coming out?"

He laughs so hard he almost chokes. "Baby, there was so much stuff coming out of you that I have no idea what was what. I didn't specifically see poop if that makes you feel better." He pauses. "Rox?"

"Hmm?"

"Promise this is just because you're overwhelmed right now, and not because you're unsure you want to be with me."

"I promise!" I say with certainty. "You and me

forever. That's never going to change. I'm just not sure about getting married. Last time I got married I found out my husband liked to put rubber penises in his mouth. I don't know if I'll ever be ready to go back to that."

"Okay, well, first, I have no desire to put rubber penises anywhere. And second, is 'penises' really the plural of penis? I thought it would be something weird, like peni or peen."

"Peen?" I repeat before laughing. "I don't know. We'll have to Google it sometime."

"Or how about we don't Google it? You don't need to know the plural of penis. You're only going to need one for the rest of your life, right?"

"Right. One penis. Yours. Forever. Deal."

He lies back, and mocks defeat and disappointment. "I guess this means I need to cancel those monogrammed towels I ordered."

Chapter Thirteen
One Year Later

April 2014

Being a parent is like living inside a comic strip. The turbulence follows me from little square to little square, while people point and laugh at me over their morning coffee.

After cleaning up the remnants of Sam's first birthday party, I sit down in the recliner with our laptop and a bottle of wine to finish the photo book I'd been creating on Shutterfly. I start back at the beginning of Sam's first year and realize it's basically page after page of mishaps and disasters. Booboos and messy faces for Sam. Dry shampoo and messy faces for me. Jake, he always looks good. Really, *really* good.

As I arrange the gorgeous photographs from Sam's

birthday shoot into the book, I know two things for sure:
1. I am beyond lucky to have a boyfriend who is both a photographer *and* a bartender – I mean, can anything beat that?
2. The first year of Sam's life was absolutely the best year of mine.

When I'm satisfied with my creation, I hit the save button, finish my glass of wine, and get up to go find my boyfriend.

"Baby?" I stand in the doorway of Jake's office wearing a flirty nightie that I picked up at Target earlier. Now that wedding season has begun, we've both been busier this week than we've been in months. Because of the extra hours at work, we haven't had sex in four days. I thought this cute nightie might help get us out of our drought. I'm not sure if four days is enough to be considered a drought, and it probably wouldn't be to a married couple. But since we're not married, I hold us to a higher standard. And four days is three days too long.

He's at his computer with his back to me. Wearing an old T-shirt and a pair of gym shorts, he leans back in his chair with his hands clasped behind his head. On the monitor is a photo he took at a wedding last weekend at The Colony Club.

"Yeah?" He doesn't turn to look my way. He's concentrating hard on the photo.

I walk into the room and get a closer look at the screen. The couple is gorgeous, as most are on their wedding days, but the venue behind them is the real showstopper. Black and white checkered floors, crystal chandeliers, an indoor balcony that looks like a king and queen would stand there to greet their guests. I've seen it before, but it's gorgeous enough to appreciate again.

I look away from the computer monitor and lean back, my butt resting on Jake's desk. "I finished my photo book," I tell him.

He moves his eyes to look at me, but I notice his gaze changes slightly. The photo was interesting to him. But he looks at me like he's mesmerized. God, I love the way he still looks at me like he wants to attack me. I hope it never goes away.

I squeeze my fingers around the ruffled hem of my nightie where it hits me right at the hip. I act like I'm about to lift it up. But I don't.

He tilts his head, intrigued.

"Do you want to see it?" I ask innocently.

"I'm sure it's perfect," he says of the photo book. "I'd rather see what's under that little nightie." He remains in his laid back, hands behind the head position. Something about the vulnerability of his hands behind his head, and the low-key T-shirt and gym shorts look, it really gets me hot. I remember many, many years ago during *The Summer of Jake and Roxie*, when I saw him sitting that way on the patio behind The Bar. We were just friends at that time, but seeing him like that, my first instinct was to climb on top of him. I used to be afraid that once I'd gotten what I'd wanted (him), that the desire to climb on top of him would go away. I can say with certainty that it has not. He's every bit as sexy at thirty-three as he was at twenty-three. In fact, I think he's even sex*ier*, because he has ten more years of wisdom behind his eyes. Ten years of beautiful women everywhere, and he still chooses me every day.

Good Things Come

When he was twenty-three, he was my brother's best friend. I was his best-friend's little sister. Of course we wanted each other back then. We were forbidden fruits. Everyone wants what they aren't supposed to have.

But we're not forbidden anymore. I'm no longer that twenty-one-year-old with the perkiest chest, looking hot in a bikini at the pool. I'm the mother of his child with a little bit of a baby pouch that won't seem to go away no matter how many mountain climbers and leg raises I do at the gym. But the way he looks at me hasn't changed in ten years, and for that I am thankful.

I pull the fabric of my nightie up a few inches.

He doesn't even blink.

I pull the pink cotton up slowly, up above my tiny bikini panties, past my waist, over my bare chest, and over my head. I pull it off and let it drop to the floor of his office. Then I lean back on the desk again with my shoulders back, mostly so my boobs don't look too saggy.

He sits up straight and brings his hands from behind his head. He motions with his finger for me to come closer, but I shake my head. I've been working hard getting this baby weight off. I need him to spend some time appreciating it from afar before he gets to touch it.

I push my hand down my body across my stomach and to my panties. Once my fingers reach the lacy edge of my panties, I push them down an inch or two with my thumb. I saw that pose on the cover of a men's magazine once and thought it was cute. I guess he likes it, too, because the wheels of his office chair move quickly across the hardwood floor. Before I have time to stop him, he's sitting in front of me with his mouth on my nipple and his hand on my ass. Shit. So much for playing hard to get tonight.

I lean my head back and sigh. Okay. Fine. I guess he can appreciate it from afar another time.

I push my panties down to the floor and straddle him on his swivel chair. He sucks on my neck while I pull his shorts down and lower myself onto him, slowly because it feels good to have him back inside me after four long days. Then faster as he grabs onto my hips and starts pulling me down hard on top of him. I guess the days have been long for him, too.

He puts his thumb in just the right spot so that it hits my clit while I ride up and down.

"Get up," he orders me once I've come all over him and stopped shivering.

Knowing what he wants, I get up, turn around, and bend over slightly, resting the palms of my hands on his desk. He stands behind me and pulls my ponytail back while he whispers in my ear, "You want me to fuck you now, huh?"

"You know I do."

"Say it."

"I want you to fuck me, Jake."

It doesn't take him long. It never does once I start swearing. There's something about seeing his good girlfriend turn bad that pushes him over the edge every time.

He pulls his shorts up and sits back down in the office chair with a sigh. "God, you're fucking amazing," he tells me. "And your ass has never looked better. Bible."

I laugh at the reference from my favorite TV show. "Thanks," I say. And I mean it. Compliments from

Jake, even though they come often, never get old. I can say the same about our sex life. Pun intended.

I sit on his lap and wrap my arms around his neck. "I love you."

"I love you, too," he says, and kisses my cheek.

"I really do want to show you the photo book," I tell him after a few minutes of recovery. I get up off his lap and stand with my back to him, so he can appreciate all the plies I've been doing in barre class. I put my night shirt back over my head and pull up my underwear. "Will you come look at it with me?"

He stands up and follows me into the living room. He lies back in the recliner and I sit on his lap with the laptop across my knees. While I open the file, he twirls a piece of my hair from behind.

"Here he is at two weeks," I say, pointing at a picture of my scrawny, barely six pounds baby. "And here's him at three weeks. Look what a difference it made once we started feeding him formula."

I'd been devastated when Sam's pediatrician had told me he was losing too much weight, and I would need to start feeding him formula. I don't know why my body wouldn't produce enough milk for him. I'd pumped around the clock. I'd had two home visits with a lactation specialist. I'd taken all the recommended supplements. It just didn't work out. I can still remember the shame I'd felt as we stood in line at the grocery store that day with a gigantic container of formula on the belt. I remember looking around us, to see if there were any other moms near the checkout lanes who might see the formula, fearing their judgements and my failures. I realize now I was being too hard on myself. When the next baby comes around, I'll know better. Babies need to eat *something*, period.

I flip to another page and show Jake our three-month-old with his bottom lip sticking out in a dramatic pout. "He was so miserable with his first cold," I remind Jake.

I'd spent that whole night staring at him, making sure he was breathing, sucking boogers out of his nose, touching his forehead to check for fever, worrying that maybe it wasn't just a cold, but meningitis or pneumonia. When the next baby comes, I hope to worry a lot less.

"Remember what you said to me that morning?" I ask Jake.

"I'm pretty sure I made you an Irish Coffee and told you to get some sleep."

"Yep. You gave me a drink, took the baby, and said, 'I got this.' So, I went to bed."

Jake has known exactly what I've needed this past year. It makes me wonder if I give him enough of what he needs as well. Blow jobs count, right?

I turn the page to show Jake the spread of our first family vacation. "Here's Chicago," I say, looking at pictures of us in front of The Bean and on The Skydeck at Willis Tower. "Remember how we started to call it Pee-cago, because every one of the subway elevators smelled like pee?"

I feel like pinching my nose just from the memory alone. I'd never spent any time in subway elevators before, because I'd always taken the steps. Having a baby in a stroller, you have to take the elevators. And they can be pretty horrifying. Imagine a firefighter trying to put out a fire using a giant hose filled with urine, and you can get a pretty good idea of the living nightmare that is subway elevators.

"Rox," he says, suspiciously narrowing his eyes at

me. "Please tell me you didn't put a picture of a stinky subway elevator in this book."

"Ha. Nope. But here we are at The Bean right before Sam's blowout."

Our hotel had been all the way at the end of the Blue Line, by the airport, and was almost an hour train ride into the city. I figured we would need a lot of diaper changes while navigating the city by foot all day. Thinking I was so smart and such a prepared mom, I'd packed a separate tote bag with *just* diapers -- about twenty of them, you know, just in case we were delayed by a zombie outbreak or something. I mean, I was prepared!

Imagine the horror when Sam had a blowout in Millennium Park that went all the way up his back and into his hair. That's a yucky situation to begin with. Now imagine how worse it got when I realized I'd brought the diaper bag, with no diapers in it, and left the tote bag full of diapers at the hotel.

Jake was, as always, the Champion of Equanimity. While my first instinct had been to throw my head in my hands and give up on life all together, Jake's first instinct had been to laugh hysterically before he ran to Walgreens for diapers. Jake kept a clear head and got us through the disaster one step at a time. Then we both had a beer for lunch.

"Oh, and here I am dressed up for my first day at work," I say when I flip the page to a picture of the three of us that Jake took with his tripod and timer before I left for work that morning. When I'd seen the ad for a hotel in downtown Detroit looking for a catering manager, I couldn't *not* apply. I'd really enjoyed my externship working at a hotel in NYC. Even though this wasn't a chef job, it was still a job where I could utilize my skills. Helping plan parties? I mean, hello, perfect for me.

It was the first time I'd ever had a job that required me to dress nicely, and I'd gone all-in with a new wardrobe to celebrate (some things never change). I'd looked cute in my striped pencil skirt, but I'd felt so sad that day. I was glad that Jake and Sam were now going to have lots of time alone together for daddy and son bonding. And I knew it was important for me to have a purpose in life outside of being a mom. Important for my mental health, and for our bank account. But boy was I ever sad.

Who would want to leave those cute chubby cheeks? I didn't even like being away from Sam while he was napping. How could I be away from him for eight hours a day? The night before my first day, I'd cried.

"I think I made you your favorite fall drink when you got home from your first day."

"You did. Apple cider mimosas with a cinnamon sugar rim."

I also remember how seamless it was to go from stay-at-home-mom to career mom. I was only sad the first day. After that I realized how blessed I was to be able to work outside the home. When I was at work, I got a break from home that I wasn't even aware I needed. Missing my family all day made me appreciate them more when I got home. And being able to contribute to our household finances made me feel like I had more value as a mom. Being a working mom might not be for everyone, but I realized right away that it was right for me.

I click over to the next page and see a picture of 10-month-old Sam with a bruise on his forehead. He'd been walking along the couch and fell into an end table.

"His first boo-boo," Jake said. "You were hysterical."

I was. I took him to the emergency room, where the doctor patiently explained to me that babies hit their heads all the time, that their skulls are more flexible than ours, and that they are much closer to the ground than adults. Their simple falls and bumps are unlikely to cause any brain damage. "Just keep an eye on him for the next 24 hours for any alarming signs or symptoms," she'd said.

But the problem with that was that Sam was just starting to creep around the house, and started walking shortly after. We would watch him for 24 hours, but before the 24 hours were up, he'd bump his head again. It was a non-stop worry cycle. I'd gone through a lot of beer these last few months.

No, I do not have a drinking problem. But Momming is rough.

I flip the page and it's time to show off Sam's wonderful 1st birthday party. Pinterest Moms everywhere would bow their heads in respect. The theme was *The Very Hungry Caterpillar* by Eric Carle, and I *nailed it*. The whole family was here this afternoon. Even my parents came in from Florida. Sam loved opening his gifts and eating his birthday cake. He had the widest smile on his face all day long.

"I've never seen him happier," Jake said, proudly. Then he elbows me gently. "And never seen you so miserable."

He's right. Sam's first year is over. Just gone. Forever. I'll never get my baby back. I used to have a baby. Now I don't. Now I have a toddler who walks and says "Mumma" and "Day." He's a completely different person. So yes, I had been wiping tears from my eyes most of the day.

I set the laptop on the end table and lean back into his chest. "You know what the worst part is?" I ask him.

"What?"

"Never knowing when the last time is. Like, we used to hold him horizontally. You know? And last night, I was getting ready to put him in his crib, and I realized I was holding him vertically. I wondered, when was the last time I held him horizontally? And I realized that there *was* a last time, there had to have been, but I didn't remember it. Because I had no idea at the time that it *was* the last time. I didn't realize I needed to spend extra attention on that moment, take a selfie, post it on Facebook so it would come up on my memories every year, record it in his baby book. I didn't do any of that. Because I didn't know. And now I'm wondering if this is how it's always going to be? Will I know when I've carried him to bed for the last time? What about the last time he falls asleep in my arms? Will I even realize it? To think that one day I won't hold him anymore, it hurts. I wonder at what age does it start to be weird that your kid is sitting on your lap?"

It's a rhetorical question, and he seems to know that because he doesn't offer an answer.

He puts his arms around me from behind and kisses the back of my neck. "I know it's tough sometimes. But think of the bright side. Life is getting easier now. He's sleeping through the night. *We're* sleeping through the night. We have more time for sex," he adds with a grin.

Good Things Come

I sit up straighter. "Oh, that reminds me." I stand up. "Wait here," I tell him. "I have to show you what I bought for Sam."

I quickly make my way to the foyer where I left the Target bag. When I return to the living room, I stand in front of Jake, holding up the tiny size 12 Months T-shirt. It says Big Brother on the front.

He looks confused, then a little excited. "Are you trying to tell me something?"

Oh shoot. Oops. "No! Sorry. I didn't even think of that. But that would have been a cute idea to put the shirt on Sam and see if you noticed." I decide right then that once I get pregnant, I'm putting this shirt on Sam, and I'm going to see how long it takes Jake to notice. I can even do our pregnancy announcement that way at our next family get-together. Maybe the Fourth of July.

Wait. I'm getting a little ahead of myself here.

"You're not pregnant?" he asks to confirm.

"No." I sit back down in his lap holding the tiny T-shirt in my hands. "I saw it at the store, and it made me realize that I'm ready to make Sam a big brother. Like you said, life is easier now. I think that means we're ready for baby two. What about you? Do you think you're ready?"

"I got really excited when I thought this was a pregnancy announcement. But we're not married yet. I thought we'd be married before we had another baby."

I nearly choke. Poor Jake. "I swear, if you were an actor on *Saturday Night Live*, you'd have your own marriage proposal DVD on the shelves by now."

"Baby, nobody buys DVDs anymore. I'd have a 'best of' compilation video on YouTube. Why don't you just stop being difficult and marry me?"

I nod in approval. "That was your best one yet. In fact, we can put that quote on our Save the Dates."

"Come on. All jokes aside. When are we going to get married?"

I groan.

Being a catering manager, I deal with weddings and wedding planning every day of the week. Even on my days off I get emails and phone calls from brides-to-be. As a wedding photographer, Jake also deals with weddings every day of the week. It never goes away. Like a flower pot that's been overwatered, we have weddings overflowing from the top and leaking out the bottom. There's something about working behind the scenes that ruins the magic for you. The truth is, I hate weddings. I know, they're supposed to be romantic and sweet and all about love and happy-ever-afters. But let me tell you, they're not.

Weddings are about one thing: impressing people. If you have money, you can impress people by buying a $6000 wedding gown and making sure every one of your Twitter and Instagram followers know that it cost $6000. You can get an amazing venue that can't be touched for less than a hundred grand, along with having an LA-based floral designer who is popular among celebrity weddings fly in some arrangements for your special day.

If you don't have a lot of money to flash around, you can impress people with your ingenious creativity. You can have your wedding somewhere unexpected, like a cider mill. You can serve food you don't usually see at weddings, like a make-your-own pizza station. You can pick a color theme that's never been seen before, like red and turquoise. You can wrap everything in burlap because no one in the history of weddings has ever wrapped anything in burlap. (Shh... yes, they have. But don't ruin it for them).

If you don't have a lot of money, and you're lacking in the creativity department, don't fret. There is another way you can impress your followers. You need to hit that gym and hit it hard. Nothing but two-a-days until you achieve the absolute best physical appearance of your life. You must look so good on your wedding day that fifteen years from now your kids will look through the wedding album and ask who these people are.

I don't think it was always this way. I bet there was a time, like a long, *long* time ago, probably shortly after the dinosaurs met their maker, when weddings were magical. There are people today who still believe in the magic, who still feel the fairy-tale-like aura. I watch them sit there at the ceremony and dab at their eyes and gush over the bride in the receiving line. Either they're excellent actors, or they just don't know any better. I honestly envy their naivete.

Me, I know better. I stand in the back of the hotel's ballroom watching these theatrics, and I don't gush over how gorgeous the bride is, or swoon over how in love they are. Instead I find myself wondering if the seam of her dress will rip open when the two of them kneel to light their stupid unity candle. I wonder how long it will be before she finds her groom with his mouth around a strap-on.

Some may think my opinion of weddings, and marriage in general, has been skewed from the loveless marriage and subsequent divorce of my past. That may have a little to do with it. But I think the biggest problem here is I've gotten too close to the situation to see it as anything more than what it really is: a very expensive joke.

"Why?" I ask, once I finish groaning. "What does being married have to do with anything? Kourtney Kardashian and Scott Disick have two kids together, and they aren't married."

"You're the mother of my child, Roxie. Now you're talking about more than one. I'd like to call the mother of my children something other than my 'girlfriend.'"

"You could call me Baby Mama."

He scowls at me.

"What's wrong with using boyfriend and girlfriend? I like calling you my boyfriend. It's sexy. Why do you think stores sell boyfriend jeans and boyfriend sweaters? Because they're more desirable to women. No one sells husband jeans, right? Husbands are the guys who mow the lawn while the wives fold the laundry and pretend they don't see those yucky skid marks in his underwear."

Jake laughs behind me.

"Boyfriends and girlfriends," I continue, "are romantic and sexy. They go out on dates. They go ice skating, have picnics, take sporadic trips to the mountains. They sleep in on Saturdays before they head to Home Goods to look at curtains, or the farmer's markets to sample homemade jams and salsas. You wanna know what married people do, Jake? They poop in front of each other. They wear sweatpants at home, and in *public*. They spend their nights balancing their checkbook or strolling the grocery store arguing over whether they should buy the store brand or the generic. It's a sad, sad life."

He snorts. "This argument is completely irrelevant. For one thing, we both work on Saturdays, and we will most likely always work on Saturdays. And if we both have a Saturday off, we have a child that will wake us up by 8AM regardless. So, this fantasy you have in your head of this cute couple on a lazy Saturday morning browsing farmer's markets together in the best fall fashions is long-gone and over, never going to happen."

I scrunch my nose at him. *How did he know we were wearing the best fall fashions in my fantasy?*

"Second," he continues, "we already live together. We still comb our hair, shower and shave regularly, and don't poop in front of each other. I think it's safe to say that a piece of paper isn't going to turn us into an eighties sitcom overnight."

I give him my death stare. *How does he do this? How does he know one of my worst nightmares is turning into Pam Bundy?*

"And third," he says, "we don't even have a checkbook. Nobody has a checkbook anymore. This isn't 1994."

"Are you sure about that?" I ask. "Maybe we *do* have a checkbook, but you won't find out about it until we're married. Maybe I'm protecting you from a certain kind of hell. You ever think about that, huh?"

He raises an eyebrow. "*Do* we have a checkbook?"

I cross my arms and pout because I know he's right. "No. I was just using it as an example."

"For the sake of your arguments, try using examples from this century."

I shrug and take a deep breath. I dig my toe into the carpet and drag it back and forth in a half circle. "I just feel like our time has passed, Jake. If we were going to get married, we should have done it already."

"Uh, I tried that. Several times. Enough for my own bad proposal DVD apparently."

"I know! I mean, we did things differently than most couples by having a baby first. I think we should just stick it out and keep going. To get married now would seem redundant. Things are working for us. If it's not broken, don't fix it."

"I disagree that we did things differently than most people. I think a lot of couples have kids before they're married. I'm telling you, at least half the couples I photograph these days have children already. Sometimes they do this cute thing at the ceremony where the bride and groom and all the kids have a different color sand and they pour all the sand into the same vase to symbolize that they're a unit. Oh, and when the parents dance with the kids, it gets more tears from the guests than any other moment at the wedding."

Why is he telling me this? I know all about the sand ceremonies and the first dances. "That's sweet, Jake. But those are probably kids from previous relationships."

"Sometimes. Not always. Look, I get what you're saying about not fixing something that's not broken. And believe me, I know all about your disdain for weddings, and I understand it. I just wish you could have the same last name as us. When Sam starts school, it might be weird for him that he has a different last name than his mom. And I wish we had an anniversary to celebrate. We've been living together almost two years and never celebrated an anniversary. I mean, what *is* our anniversary?"

"You want an anniversary? Pick one. Let's see ... There's September 26th, 1999, when you kissed me for the first time while walking home from school. There's January 31st, 2002, when you kissed me for the second time at your frat house. June 11th, 2005 was the first time we had sex. Wait. No. It was the 12th because it was after midnight. June 29th, 2012, was the time you fucked me up against my bedroom door after I kissed you in the rain. August 3rd was the first time you told me you were in love with me. August 21st was the day we agreed to forever, when we were in Florida. Pick one, Jake. Fuck it, let's celebrate them all. We don't need a wedding anniversary as an excuse to celebrate us."

"You remember all those dates? Just on the top of your head like that?"

"Of course I do. I remember the best days of my life. And you've been a part of every single one. I don't need a day of the year to appreciate you and tell everyone on Facebook how madly in love with you I am. Because I feel like I show you appreciation every day. And I feel like you do the same." I pick up his phone from his lap and start swiping furiously.

"What are you doing? Setting a daily alarm to remind me that you love me in place of a wedding band?"

Ouch. I look up from the phone, crushed. That hurt. At the end of our first summer together, we set alarms in our phones to go off at the same time every day to remind us that we were thinking of each other, even though we didn't talk.

I hate it when he brings up that alarm, because I know every time he thinks about it, he remembers that it didn't stop me from forgetting about him. It didn't stop me from falling in love with someone else. It didn't stop me from planning a ridiculous wedding to another man. It didn't even stop me from marrying someone else. Yes, the brides I roll my eyes at on the daily, I used to be one of them. I'm not proud.

I try not to think about those days. I understand all that bullshit about our past being responsible for turning us into the people we are now, but I'd rather just forget about it.

"No," I say, ignoring his comment about the alarms because that's something I don't want to talk about, ever. "I'm putting our anniversaries in your calendar, so you don't forget to spoil me with gifts and fancy nights out."

I move through the year on the calendar, setting anniversary alarms for the exact same time Jake set ours for ten years ago: 4:20. He didn't choose that time because he smokes weed, he hasn't done that since college, but because it was after my classes, but before he started his work shifts.

"Okay, fine," he relents. "We have plenty of anniversaries to celebrate. We can leave this conversation alone for a year or two until I get up the courage to ask again, *if* I ever do. But I would like to know, are you saying that you're not ready to marry me *now*? Or that you won't be ready to marry me *ever*?"

I pick at my fingernails while I take some time to think about it. Poor Jake. *If he ever gets the courage to ask again.* Why does he need to ask? I guess I just don't get it. I thought guys only got married because of pressure from their girlfriends. You'd think he'd be happy that I've let him off the hook.

"I'm absolutely opposed to a wedding," I finally say carefully, "and I don't think that will ever change."

He nods his head patiently. "Okay. Although I would love to stand at an altar and see you walking down the aisle toward me, wearing a beautiful dress, with Sam holding your hand ... I respect your feelings. I don't like them, but I respect them. What about a marriage?"

I take another moment to think. "I'm not totally opposed to being married to you," I eventually say.

"Hey, if I get a 'best of bad proposals' video, you should definitely have a 'best of backhanded compliments' segment."

I laugh out loud. "I'm not *totally* opposed," I repeat, "because I am confident that I will love you forever. That much I know is true."

"And there's a but coming."

"But I *do* like being unmarried. I like knowing that you come home every day because you love us. I love it that we make it through every argument and rough patch because we are crazy about each other, and not just because attorneys are expensive."

"I see."

"But most of all, Jake, I'm scared. I'm scared things will change. That we'll get too complacent, too comfortable. We'll stop trying. Remember when I first came home from school after my junior year, and you took me to that diner, and you were explaining why flings are so great? Because people are only showing their best selves in the beginning? And after that they turn into zombies?"

"Yes. I remember."

"I guess I'm afraid of turning into a married zombie. I feel like right now, after almost two years of living together, we are still showing our best cards. And I don't want that to change. But I'm not saying no to a marriage permanently. I'm just saying no right now."

"Got ya. We're gonna make a baby then?"

"Yes. Let's make a baby."
"Is it too soon to start right now?"

Chapter Fourteen
One Year Later

April 2015

I see the word on my medical chart and flinch.

Infertility.

It doesn't come as a huge surprise, because it has been an entire year of baby-making without any actual babies being made. As the months went by, I had no choice but to think of the possibility, and try to get used to the diagnosis. But when I see it in bold print like that, I put my head in my hands and rub my forehead like the subject of a meme. *How can this be? I have a child. I can't be infertile.*

"A couple is considered infertile after one year of

unprotected sex without achieving pregnancy," my OBGYN explains. "The good news is that now that you've made it a year, it's time for you to see a reproductive endocrinologist."

She says it like it's a victory. We made it a year. Now we get a specialist. Yippee!

She hands me the business card of a recommended RE and sends me on my way.

Wow. Thank you for absolutely nothing. My insurance company wouldn't pay for me to see an RE until after one year of trying, and my OBGYN has been useless these past twelve months.

"You're probably having sex on the wrong days," she'd suggested.

"We have sex nearly every day," I'd argued.

"You must be having too much sex then. Try every other day, or every third day. The sperm might need time to mature."

Every three days? Dude. Please. I'm not going to refrain from sex to get pregnant. That makes zero sense. (But we tried it anyway for two months. It didn't work.) We also tried pineapple core, pomegranate juice, fuzzy socks, and fertili-tea.

I call the RE and set up an appointment from the parking lot as soon as I get to my car.

We got pregnant with Sam so fast. We weren't even trying. I guess I just assumed that when we decided we were ready for baby number two, baby number two would come along – just like that. I thought babies were something people could *decide* to have. I mean, we know how things work. We know how babies are made. We just don't know why we haven't been able to make one. On purpose. People get pregnant by accident all the time (ahem). Why can't we get pregnant on purpose?

I planned to have my babies two years apart. Adam and I were two years apart and it seemed like the perfect age gap. Month after month after month I got further and further away from that goal. Baby number two should *be* here already. Now my baby, my only baby, is two years old with no siblings and no explanations. I've had to let go of my idea of a perfect family, and it hasn't been easy.

I've tried telling myself that it's okay, that a three-year difference is still doable. But now I'm starting to realize it's not even likely at this point that Sam will have a sibling before he's three, and it kills me. Every month I get more fed up, more frustrated, more impatient. So impatient that I make doctor's appointments from parking lots.

I swear, the not knowing *why* is the most frustrating part. I wish someone could just tell me, "Look, you were meant to have one child and one child only. Stop wasting your time." But instead of giving up, being told no only makes me want to try harder. So harder we will try.

When I finish up my call with the doctor's office, I open Facebook for a quick second to check my notifications. What's the first thing I see on my newsfeed? A photo that pushes the knife in even deeper. It's an ultrasound photo.

A couple months ago, a former coworker of mine announced on Facebook that she was ready to try for another baby (Who puts that on social media?). People went nuts on her post, telling her that it was probably too soon since she'd just been released from prison, that maybe she should try to stay sober and out of trouble for a little while, and maybe try to get custody of the kids she already has before she decides to have another. It was a Michael-Jackson-eating-popcorn kind of status update.

I remember talking about it with another former coworker, like is this chick for real? She is an admitted drug addict whose two kids were taken away from her by the state. Surely she won't be able to get pregnant again. Is she even allowed to get pregnant again?

Guess who just posted an ultrasound photo…

One word. Unfollow.

Seven more words. You've got to be fucking kidding me.

This is the *why* I'm talking about. Why her? Why not us? I don't understand.

I throw my phone into the passenger seat and put the car into drive.

When I get home, Sam yells from upstairs. He must have heard the door open.

"Mommy! Come wook! Come see Daddy."

"What's Daddy doing, bud?" I yell up there.

"I show you," he says. "Come up."

I set my purse on the end table, leave my shoes on the door mat, and walk up the carpeted steps.

Sam greets me on the landing in his favorite Bubble Guppies shirt and takes my hand.

"Wook, Mommy," he says, leading me down the hall to his room.

I peek into the room and see Jake on his knees, taking apart Sam's crib.

"Hi, babe," he says, turning to look at me for a second before he gets back to work.

I knew this was coming, but it still hurts. No more

crib. No more baby. I always thought we'd get Sam into a big boy bed when he had a little sibling who needed that crib. We were supposed to have a baby to put in that crib. Now where is it going? Into the basement so I can see it every day when I do laundry. Like I need another reminder that I'm a failure as a woman.

I put an excited smile on my face for Sam's sake.

I pick him up and kiss his forehead. "You get to have a big boy bed now!" I tell him. "Are you excited?"

He smiles big and nods. I set him down and he sits at the foot of the crib next to his wooden Melissa & Doug tool set.

He watches Jake pick up a screwdriver from the real tool set.

Jake holds it up, so Sam can see the tool better. "Screwdriver," Jake tells him.

Sam nods and selects his wooden screwdriver from his box. "Skoodiver."

I watch my boys for a minute as they "unscrew" together on opposite sides of the crib.

"Nice job, bud," Jake says.

"I'm gonna go get dinner ready," I tell them. I blow them kisses and head downstairs.

I try to get my mind off my lack of baby by chopping up peppers for the stir-fry. I know I need to concentrate on what I do have and not what I don't. I do know that. But sometimes it just hurts.

I really have no reason to complain. This past year was way less emotional than the one before. Once Sam turned a year old, he didn't grow *as fast*. His month-by-month photos didn't show a huge change every month the way they did the year before. He's also not completely helpless anymore, so my job as a parent is less all-consuming than that first year.

By all counts this year should have gotten an A+, and it would have, if not for one thing – twelve things – twelve months of failed pregnancy attempts. In all fairness, that means our year was maybe an A-. But some days it hurts like a D.

After dinner we begin the bedtime dance. Bath, jammies, bedtime story, cuddles, bed. We stand in the doorway of Sam's room, staring at our two-year-old who has finally fallen asleep in his big boy bed for the first time. I feel my bottom lip quiver. Jake takes my hand and squeezes it. He knows what time it is.

I swear people are going to think all moms ever do is cry and drink alcohol.

We turn to walk away when he suddenly stops in the hallway, turns to me, and gently pushes me into the wall by my shoulders. He presses his body into mine to keep me where he wants me. He puts his forearm on the wall above me and touches his forehead to mine, his lips too far to touch mine, but close enough that I can feel his breath. His eyes gaze into mine and I remember the first time he did this very thing. It was the first time we hooked up, right after we got into his apartment. I remember the excitement, the anticipation, the throbbing all over. I wanted him so bad that night that I swore I'd never want anything as badly in my life. I find myself starting to throb again, and I'm happy to realize this move still makes me as hot as it did then. He moves his free hand to my lower back and pulls me closer to him. He never breaks eye contact and I feel like the wait for his kiss lasts an eternity. When his lips finally touch mine, my bottom lip isn't the only thing quivering.

"What's it gonna be tonight?" he asks quietly when he pulls his mouth from mine. "I bought that tequila you like. How 'bout rough sex and margaritas?"

I think that sounds perfect. I need it after that stupid doctor's appointment and watching my baby's crib go into the basement.

"Fuck the margaritas," I say. "Let's just do shots."

"Nice."

We take the bottle, salt shaker, and lime wedges to the bedroom because you're never too old to do body shots, right? Just kidding. We are too old for body shots in public. But no one needs to know that we act like coeds at a frat party when we're alone, right?

Having sex with salt, limes, and tequila is fun, but messy. By the time we are finished, we need showers and new sheets. Once everything is cleaned up and we're back in bed, Jake sits up, grabs his glasses from the nightstand, and leans against the headboard with his laptop on his legs. I sit next to him and grab my own glasses and a paperback from my nightstand. Before I begin reading, I glance over at the laptop monitor and see he's editing a woman's boudoir shoot. I see a photo of a thin blonde standing tall in a pair of hipster panties and stilettos, her hair hangs loosely over her shoulders, thinly covering her nipples. I look over at Jake's face to see if his expression changes at all while he scrolls through the pics.

It doesn't. He remains unaffected. He could be looking at wallpaper samples for all the emotion he expresses.

My friends have asked me before if it's hard for me to deal with Jake getting so close to his female clients. Sometimes a woman has her own ideas for a boudoir shoot, but most of the time Jake helps them. He decides on poses and sometimes even helps her select clothes and props. I remember the sexual tension I felt during our boudoir shoot a few years ago, before we were an official couple. It was hot enough that we often have our own personal boudoir sessions here at home, but I still don't worry for a second that he's into anyone else while he's working. I feel incredibly blessed to be with a man who has never once made me question his loyalty to me. I imagine this kind of career might be hard for a lot of couples, but the jealousy and mistrust has been kept at bay with us. (Knock on wood.)

"How'd the appointment go?" he asks.

"As expected," I tell him. "She officially marked us as infertile, so the insurance would cover the specialist. We have to wait three weeks for our appointment though."

He touches my bare thigh under the covers to comfort me.

"It'll be okay, baby. I'm not worried about this at all. So maybe we need a little help. We can obviously have children because we already have one."

"I know," I say quietly. I wish I could be as confident.

Chapter Fifteen

June 2015

Once we are diagnosed as infertile, the first step is to find the reason. If we find the reason, we could find the cure (maybe). At our first appointment, our doctor warned us that a reason for infertility is only found about half the time. The other half is considered "unexplained." She warned us to prepare for the fact that we may never know why.

We undergo several tests and procedures, including over a dozen vials of blood, a balloon being inflated in my uterus, and Jake having to jerk-off into a cup. Lovely, lovely stuff. The results are as follows:

Jake: Sperm perfect. Large quantity, swimming in the right direction, 12% perfectly formed (which sounds low, but is normal). No chromosomal issues discovered.

Me: Tubes open. No chromosomal abnormalities present. All hormones normal, except progesterone. Diagnosis: Anovulation. For reasons unknown, I am not ovulating, I have probably not been ovulating for some time, something that could have been detected over a year ago with one simple blood test if my OBGYN wasn't such a twat. What this means, in case you weren't paying attention, is that our infertility is *my* infertility. It is 100% my body causing the issues, i.e.: my fault.

"What do we do now?" I ask him the night after our follow-up appointment, after Sam's asleep and we're in bed, lying face to face under the covers. "We're still young enough that we can wait and see if things change. Obviously, I ovulated once in my life, so it's possible I can do it again. We should have at least two years left before my egg quality goes to shit, maybe three or four even."

"Or?" he asks. "What's the other option?"

"The other option is seeing if we can get my body to ovulate with medications."

"Did she say what your chances were?"

"She said if a couple is going to be helped with oral meds, it usually happens within three months."

"Hmm. Three months to get pregnant. Three months after that and we can announce. That means we could be making a pregnancy announcement by Christmas!"

"Yeah. If it works."

"Think positive. It'll work. And we'll be able to put a Santa hat on an ultrasound photo."

Oh my God. He is adorable.

"We're gonna do this then?" I ask.

"Sure. If we can afford the meds, then why not?

Wouldn't you rather we tried and failed, than always wonder if it would have worked?"

"Yes. Of course. I just never thought this would be us, ya know? That it would come this far."

"Well, no, you wouldn't have. I've never heard a little girl say, 'When I grow up, I'm going to fall in love, get married, then take medication to make my ovaries do their jobs.' All they know is that when they grow up, they're going to have a family. Somehow, someway. If this is what we need to do, then we'll do it. As long as we are both satisfied with Sam, and we see having another child as just a bonus, then we really can't lose, right?"

"Right."

Chapter Sixteen

April 2016

Oral fertility medications are gateway drugs. They suck you in. They're cheap and easy to swallow. You take them for a couple months and maybe grow some great looking follicles. Even when the drugs fail, you feel better – because you are *doing* something. The drugs give you the (false) sense that you have some control of your fertility. You're not just a woman who cries to herself in the bathroom anymore. You're a go-getter now. You're a warrior.

When it doesn't work after a few months, your doctor thinks it's time to "get more aggressive." By aggressive, she means inject yourself with very, *very* expensive drugs. Seven months ago, you would have thought shooting yourself up with synthetic hormones was some whack shit you wanted no part of. But now you figure, *hell, we've come this far...*

You get your drugs in the mail, overnighted in a Styrofoam cooler with ice packs. And you watch the tutorials on YouTube. And you try to stab your stomach with the needle, but your hands are shaking so bad that your boyfriend takes the needle and sticks it in for you.

The next day you manage to stick the needle in on your own while your boyfriend stands by for moral support.

By the third day you're doing it alone and you consider buying yourself an Infertility Warrior T-shirt. Because you are a fucking badass.

Days four and five go by like a breeze. Just pinch and stab, no big deal. The ultrasound wands stuck up my vagina several times this week ain't no thing anymore either. I got this.

After a few more days it's time for all those eggs you've been growing to be released from your ovaries. It's ovulation day! Give yourself a huge pat on the back because you rock, girl. If this was a Snapchat story, you'd add an arm flex emoji.

Now your man needs to go into the clinic and masturbate into a cup. After the clinic has removed everything from the sample besides the sperm, they'll put all that goodness directly into your uterus to be ready and waiting for those eggs.

The day after ovulation (1dpo) is when the dreaded two-week-wait (TWW) begins. This is the fourteen-day stretch in which you try (and fail) to not completely lose your shit. You've basically done all you can do. Now you wait to see if it worked.

And wait.

Wait some more.
Still waiting...

A normal TWW looks like this:

1dpo: Google pictures of what a fertilized egg looks like at 1dpo.

2dpo: Check the due date calendar to see when your baby's due date would be if you get pregnant this month. (And why wouldn't you get pregnant this month with all those good-looking eggs and that perfect lining and high sperm count?)

3dpo: Feel really optimistic. In fact, the longer this journey takes, the closer you are to the outcome you desire. Right? RIGHT?!?

4dpo: Google informative charts of the blastocyst's journey through the tube to the uterus. Those eggs should be almost there.

5dpo: Today's the day the blastocyst should arrive in the uterus. Meditate to make your womb more welcoming. Analyze every twinge. Send subliminal messages to the blastocysts. Hatch and attach, little babies.

6dpo: Dude. Seriously? I'm only on day six? Are you kidding me?

7dpo: Time for your progesterone check. Go to the lab for your blood draw. The phlebotomists know your name by now, and they know to poke you right under that freckle for the perfect draw.

8dpo: Beginning at 7am, refresh your medical chart every 15-30 minutes to see if your test results are in yet. When they finally show up in your chart after 1pm like every month, you Google to see how many women on random internet forums got pregnant with the same progesterone level.

9dpo: We're in the home stretch. Symptom spot like a mo-fo. Was that a little wave of nausea? Do you feel more tired than usual? Keep poking yourself in the chest to see if your breasts are more tender than they were last month on this day. Promise yourself you aren't going to test until 13dpo. You want a clear, concise line. Not an ambiguous test that gives you more questions than answers. People who test too early are ridiculous. You're never going to be one of those people.

10dpo: Take a test even though you swore you wouldn't. You *are* one of those people. It looks white as fuck, but you hold it at thirty-seven different angles to see if there's the faintest hint of a line. When you don't see anything, you hold a flashlight behind it to see if anything is visible then. Nope. Nothing. You throw it in the trash. Two hours later you go back to the bathroom and take it out of the trash to look at it again. It's still negative. Cover it up with toilet paper in the trashcan so no one sees it and finds out how dumb you are for testing this early. Go back and pull it out of the trash one more time before bed.

11dpo: Feel discouraged because of the negative

test. Feel ashamed for testing so early. Be extra hard on yourself for being stupid. Open your fertility app on your phone sixteen times because you think it might tell you if you're pregnant or not.

12dpo: Test again. Still no line at any angle and in any light. Maybe it's too early? Hit up Google again to read stories of women who got negative tests on 12dpo and positive tests later. Check your heart rate at least 90 times throughout the day. Don't give up hope. These last few days are the only moments of hope you feel every month. Hold onto them.

13dpo: Tell yourself this spotting is implantation bleeding and not an impending period. Google the difference between implantation spotting and period, just in case the criteria has somehow changed since last month. Take the quiz. Because an internet quiz will be able to tell you, with complete accuracy, what is going on in your body.

14dpo: Another negative test. More spotting. Google how many pregnancies don't show up until after 14dpo (it's like 2%, but that's enough to keep you holding on).

15dpo: Call it CD1 and order a pizza. Drink a glass of wine. Or a bottle. Definitely a bottle.

Oh, and don't forget during these two weeks of torture that you also have a child who needs to be, like, fed and bathed and stuff. Meals to cook, dishes to wash, floors to mop, groceries to buy, Pinterest-inspired birthday parties to plan.

You also have a boyfriend who claims to want this just as badly as you do, but has no idea which day of your cycle you are on, and no idea just how far down this rabbit hole you've fallen. Oh, and don't forget you have a job that requires you to do some shitty stuff, like plan baby showers.

Except this isn't about you. It's about me. And this is my life for the last two years. Two fucking years. My kid is three and still nothing. I can't believe I thought we'd be making an announcement by Christmas. We've passed Christmas, Valentine's Day, *and* Easter. Is my kid going to have a sibling before he's four? At which point do we throw in the towel?

Eat your pizza. Drink your wine. Bang your head on the wall. I mean, *my* head.

This sucks. It really, really does.

♥

"Mommy," Sam says, pointing to the picnic table at the playground where two women and their children have stopped for a mid-playdate snack. "I'm hungry. And firstee."

I look in my bag and a little piece of me dies inside. I have half a bottle of water. No snacks.

When Sam was a baby, my diaper bag was always well-stocked (Except that one time in Chicago). Now that Sam is potty-trained (halle-fucking-lujah on that one), I've loosened the reins on the diaper bag. Meaning I carry a purse now. And while I *did* think to bring sunblock and baby wipes in case of emergency, I did not bring a charcuterie board of designer cheeses, nuts, and deli meats like the Better Moms at the picnic table over there.

I sneak a glance and am instantly intimidated by them. They look like grown-ups, like the kind of people who know how to pronounce the word 'acai' correctly. The kind of people who make me feel dumb, which I realize is more my problem than theirs.

I hand him the water bottle and he shakes his head. "I want juice!" he says, pointing to the table again where those four darling children are enjoying their organic juice boxes.

"You must not be very thirsty if you don't want the water," I tell him quietly as I take his hand and try to lead him back to the playscape where the Better Moms won't be disturbed (ie: where they won't hear that I forgot to bring snacks to the playground).

"But Mommy! I want juice!" He is louder this time. I can feel the eyes on me from the picnic table. I feel the imaginary spotlight shining on us as the audience judges from their seats and wonders what I'm going to do next. *How will she handle this*, they're thinking as they nibble their nuts.

"Okay, buddy, we can leave if you're hungry. We can go to McDonald's or we can go home. But once we leave the playground, we are not coming back. Did you want to drink some water and play a little longer? Or do you want to go get something to eat now?"

He points to the table again. "I WANT VAT!"

"Okay. We'll go get a snack now then."

I take his hand to lead him back to the car. Once his hand is in mine, he tries to drop to the ground dramatically, accidentally swinging himself into the side of the slide and bumping his head.

Really?

He screams. "Mommy! You hurt me!" Then the whining-tired-of-this-day-and-this-life voice turns on, the one that turns every syllable into three. "I'm hungreeeeeee... and firsteeeeeee... and huuuuuuurt!"

I check his head for blood, more for the audience than for myself. I'm numb to head bumps these days. Then I pick him up to carry him back to the car, which just so happens to be parked on the other side of the stupid picnic table.

"We have an extra juice box, Mom," one of the Better Moms says as I walk past.

I look over at her. Cute blonde wearing a white baseball cap – probably not because she's having a shitty hair day. Probably because she had tennis lessons before the playdate.

She smiles at us and holds the juice box up. Her smile looks patient and genuine and not snooty and condescending like I was expecting.

Sam's eyes light up and he stops crying when he sees the drink.

The blonde scoots over and makes a space on the end of the bench.

"Sit with us," she says. She puts the straw in the juice box and sets it in front of the empty spot on the bench. Then she places a napkin on the table and uses her portable tongs (she really keeps tongs in her bag?) to put some meats and cheeses onto the napkin. "Here. We have plenty," she says, patting the spot.

I let Sam sit down and he must have been legitimately hungry because he cleans the napkin and polishes off the juice box.

I don't make excuses for myself or my playground inadequacies. I just say thank you.

"No problem!" she says, cheerfully. "We've all been there. I'm Genevieve, by the way. This is Lila."

I look at the other mom, with the big black

sunglasses, her dark hair in a smooth, low ponytail, not a single flyaway present.

"Lila? Like Lila Fowler?" I ask.

She looks surprised at first, then smiles. "You read *Sweet Valley?*"

"*Twins*, *High*, and *University*," I admit. "I'm Roxie. And this is Sam."

"I'm already in love with you," Lila says.

I realize two things then:

1. It's no wonder I can't have a second baby when I can't even take care of the first one.
2. I need to stop assuming the worst of other moms. Maybe *I'm* the one judging, not them.

Chapter Seventeen

July 2016

    I'm not sure how much longer I can sit here with this fake smile plastered on my face. This girl sitting in front of me has rubbed her pregnant belly no less than a dozen times in the fifteen minutes she's been in my office.
    I call her a girl because she's young, still in her twenties.
    P.S. That moment when I realized I was old enough to start thinking of people in their twenties as being young ... it sucked.
    "I definitely want to do a high tea party with a variety of loose leaf teas available for the guests. I'm going to request on the invites for everyone to wear hats, you know, like the kinds of hats Duchess Kate

wears? A very British type of party."

"Is your family British?" I ask. She doesn't have an accent, but her ancestors could have been from England. I'm all about celebrating your heritage.

"No," she says. "German, actually. I just like the idea of a tea party."

"Oh, are you a tea drinker then?" I ask.

"Well, no, but I think it's a unique idea for a shower."

It's not, but I'm not here to burst anyone's bubbles. I'm here to make money for the hotel by making her believe her guests are worthy of an expensive plated luncheon. So far, I'm doing a shit job because it seems all she wants to serve is tea and miniature cucumber sandwiches (three per person -- that's not even equal to a whole sandwich. These people are going to leave starving).

"We'll have cucumber sandwiches, a variety of loose-leaf tea, decaffeinated, if possible. If I can't have caffeine, they can't either," she says with a laugh.

Sigh. When did it become the norm for the mom-to-be to plan her own shower? It's the same thing with brides these days. Are they really so micro-managing? Or are their friends and families dropping the ball?

Maybe I'm just old school, but I always thought showers were thrown *for* you by someone else. Or maybe I'm just a bitch. And maybe this isn't the right job for me.

I write down *loose-leaf tea - decaf* on my notepad. It does sound like a nice shower. I'd love an excuse to wear a hat like Duchess Kate. But I'd need more than three-quarters of a sandwich.

"For the favors, I've ordered little teapots with the baby's monogram on them."

I absentmindedly chew on the end of my pen because I tend to zone out at the mention of babies. Defense mechanism.

"Then, for the souvenirs..." (Wait. What? There are favors *and* souvenirs? Souvenirs?! This is a baby shower! Not a trip to Vegas for fuck's sake!) "I've ordered picture frames. I'm going to put the baby's ultrasound photo in each one for them to take home."

Chew.

"I've also ordered custom sugar cookies with the baby's name on them. They aren't to be eaten at the shower, though. There will be a cake for dessert. The cookies are more like their thank you gift."

There are favors, souvenirs, *and* thank you gifts? Is she really this generous? Or does she just like to throw money around? And if she's going to throw money around, why not throw some over to the food? I'm over here waving my arms and ready to catch it.

"Now," she says, and I feel like she's about to say something *important,* so I set my pen down and give her my undivided attention. "I feel like it would be tacky for my guests to try to shove a teapot, a picture frame, *and* cookies into their purses. So I'm going to need a wrapping table set up. I'm going to get tissue paper and gift bags so that during the shower, each guest can go over to the table, wrap up all their goodies, and carry them home in a cute bag. The bags will also have the baby's monogram."

I write down *wrapping station.* "Okay, what I have so far is a gift table, cake table, wrapping table."

"Oh! I almost forgot! I also need an area set up for the photographer. He's going to have professional lighting, you know those umbrella things? And a custom backdrop made just for the shower."

Oh wow. I had no idea Jake was missing out on the baby shower scene. "Lemme guess, with the baby's monogram on the backdrop?"

"Yes!" she says excitedly.

She's not catching on to my sarcasm, which is a good thing because she is a paying guest of the hotel of which I earn my paycheck. Instead of being catty, I should be rolling out the red carpet for her. Wait. *Should* I get her a red carpet? I feel like she would love it. Should I ask? Or would that be going overboard? Nah. The red would clash with the pink. That's only acceptable in February.

"Now, is there some kind of diagram we can work on so that I can tell you where these tables need to go?" she asks.

I hate my job. Like, I really hate my job.

Once the princess leaves my office, I Google her name to see if she really is some type of royalty or celebrity, or if her baby daddy is, or what the hell they do for a living that they can afford to spend this much money on a baby shower. I mean, they could go to Amazon and buy everything they need for a baby about five times and still not have spent as much money as this shower is costing.

Speaking of registries, I look hers up because I always buy my moms and brides a gift from their registries to thank them for using our hotel.

Most of the silliness I am used to by now.

Wipe warmer. (Eye roll).

Bottle warmer. (Eye roll).

Diaper Genie. (A roll of poop? Can't you just put it in a plastic bag from the grocery store and take the trash out every day like a normal person?)

Baby Memory Book. (Moms-to-be are so ambitious).

Cloth diapers. (I give it 5 days - max - before Huggies end up in the shopping cart).

An expensive (but cute) crib bedding set that the baby can't even use because babies aren't allowed to sleep with blankets or bumpers.

Four various kinds of diaper rash cream. (Why are pregnant women made to believe they need diaper rash cream? Diaper rash isn't really a common thing. Sam had diaper rash only once, and it was when he had a stomach virus.)

A baby spa bath tub with a shower head. Hmm.

A thermometer for bath water ... because you can't tell that the water is too hot by using your own hand.

The Baby Bullet for baby food making. This one makes me laugh every time. Once you cook the foods, most of them can be mashed up with a fork. For those that don't mash easily, you can just use a regular blender. Although those little plastic containers with the smiley faces *are* adorable.

A formula maker? Huh? It's called measure, pour, and shake. It does not require a machine.

Whoa. A $400 dresser.

But this is one I haven't seen before -- Alcohol testing strips for breast milk?!? (I mean, not that she won't need the alcohol, but is that really something you would buy someone as a gift? Who am I kidding? Hope would totally buy me that, along with a fifth of tequila.)

As ridiculous as some of these things are, I'll still buy them for my friends, because all first-time moms deserve the right to be showered with a bunch of things they don't need. It's part of the excitement of having a baby.

I add the stuffed animal that plays lullabies and womb sounds to my shopping cart and make the purchase – that is one legit baby item right there. Then I go to my company's website to look for job openings.

♥

"Guess what, Mommy!" Sam says when he comes to the dinner table.

"What, honey?" I ask, as I set plates on the table.

"Me and Daddy were watching a movie today and the people in the movie took a bath in POOP! And then someone drew a giant PENIS on their car!"

Poop and penises. His two favorite subjects. *But what the hell was he watching?* I raise my eyebrows at Jake.

He holds his hands up in defense. "I didn't even realize he was paying attention."

"Yeah," Sam agrees. "They drew a giant PENIS on the car! It was so funny, Mommy!"

"What the hell, Jake?" I ask as I set a piece of chicken on each plate.

"Yeah, what the hell, Daddy?" Sam repeats.

Jake sits down at the table and shrugs. "I mean, you're teaching him swear words, so I don't think a little crude poop humor is that big of a deal. You know what he told me earlier?"

Do I want to know?

"He told me that some asshole at the gym parked over the yellow line yesterday."

He's right. No argument here.

"Baby?" I ask, changing the subject while I cut Sam's chicken and broccoli into bite-size pieces. "What would you say if I told you I hate my job?"

He doesn't appear to be surprised. "I would tell you to get a new one?"

"The hotel is looking for a sous chef."

He looks up from his plate, his whole face lit up. "That would be great!"

"You think?" I ask uncertainly. "I would love to work in the kitchen instead of with the public."

"What do you mean, do I think? It's what you went to school for. You would love it and you'd be great at it. What is there to think about?"

"I know," I say, finally done cutting up Sam's food. I squirt some barbeque sauce on his plate for him to dunk his chicken in. "It's just that, in sales, I work days mostly. As a sous chef, I'd have to put in some nights, maybe a lot of them. *Probably* a lot of them."

He shrugs. "So? What are you worried about?"

"I'm worried about child care. You have weddings every Saturday, and I'd be expected to work some Saturday nights. Your mom works Saturdays, too. Who would watch Sam? Obviously your job is the breadwinner here, so I don't want to apply for a job that might clash with yours. But I decided today that I legitimately hate my job. Something has to change."

"Babe, don't say I'm the breadwinner like you're less important. We get all of our benefits from your job. It's just as important as mine. And we'd need a babysitter for some Friday and Saturday nights? Big deal. I can ask Natalie. Or my brother. Or Adam and Emelia. Maybe they can rotate? They also have Friday and Saturday night childcare events at places like the Y. Go after what makes you happy. We will figure out the rest."

I sigh. "I love you," I say quietly.

"I love you, too."

"Family kiss!" Sam yells. "Time for family kiss."

The three of us lean in together for our three-way kiss.

"WUV YOU!" Sam yells before he gets back to his dinner.

I feel a huge sense of pride while I watch Sam shovel broccoli into his mouth like it's the best thing he's ever eaten. I might not do a lot of things right, but I got my kid to love vegetables, so at least I've got that.

"So what movie were you guys watching?" I ask. "I'd really like to see it."

"*Vacation*," Jake answers with a smug grin.

I start my period the next day. It's now been an entire year of fertility drugs, plus fifteen months of trying on our own. That's 27 straight cycles of trying to conceive without conceiving. I've looked at the stats. Over 90% of couples conceive within 24 months. How did we get so unlucky to end up in the other percent?

Are we being punished because we aren't married? Is there something wrong with me physically, and my body is not able to carry another baby? Maybe I would die carrying another baby, and I'm tempting fate when fate has actually been on my side this whole time. Should we stop? Keep going?

The next step is IVF. I never imagined it would come this far. I have done everything else. On top of drugs and IUIs, I have cut a pineapple core and eaten it for five days after ovulation. I've drank pomegranate juice for a healthy lining and eaten African yams to produce more eggs. I've taken CoQ10 for egg quality. Used a lubricant that's supposed to "nurture" the sperm and help carry it to the egg, like sperm Uber.

I've soaked my stomach in castor oil, carried fertility stones in my pocket close to my womb, avoided ibuprofen, worn two pairs of socks to keep my feet warm because supposedly if your body uses less energy to keep your feet warm, it'll have more energy to give to your uterus.

We've had sex every day, every other day, every three days. I've used a cervical cap to keep the sperm from coming out. I've held my legs up on the wall to let it settle in. I've been on the top, on the bottom, on the side, even upside down. And this is all in addition to medications and IUIs! I mean, what the fuck do I have to do to get pregnant?

Chapter Eighteen

September 2016

I come home from work to find Jake setting the table for dinner. I usually do the cooking when I come home, because after being on Daddy duty all day, I like to give him a chance to relax before bed. Also, because I'm better at it.

"This is a surprise," I say, setting my purse on the table in our foyer. I notice it's quiet in here. "Where's Sam?"

"My mom took him to the movies. She's gonna take him for a Happy Meal after. It's just us for dinner tonight."

I give him a kiss like I do every day when I get home. Hope's orders.

I see Jake has been having fun with the letterboard I bought at Kohl's over the weekend. I thought it would be cute to leave funny or sexy messages back and forth to each other. But I don't think I'm very good at it. Last night I spelled out "Can you kill the spider in the bathroom?" Tonight the board says, "Spider dead. Can I touch your boobs now?"

He pulls a glass pitcher filled with fruit slices and wine out of the refrigerator and sets it on the counter.

"I made sangria," he tells me as he pours me a glass and sets it on the table. "Here, sit down," he says.

I take a drink and I swear it's the best thing I've ever tasted. Have I mentioned how wonderful it is to live with a bartender?

He sets a plate in front of me. Filet, baked potato, steamed broccoli.

"This looks awesome!" I say, impressed.

"Cut into your steak before you get too excited. I had to Google how to cook a filet. I cooked it on the stove a little first, then the oven."

"And you let it rest?"

"Yes, dear," he says with that grin I can't get enough of.

I cut into a perfect medium steak and give him a thumbs up.

He sits down across from me with his own plate and lifts his glass of sangria.

"Here's to being satisfied," he says. "I wanted another baby, too, but I hope you know I'm completely happy with you and Sam. I'm ready to throw in the towel if you are. I just wish you could feel satisfied, too, because I hate to see you suffer so much every day."

I clink my glass to his and take a sip. Believe me, no one hates the suffering more than I do. I wish I could feel satisfied, too. When I pray at night, I don't pray for a baby anymore. I pray to stop *wanting* a baby. And since my prayers haven't been answered yet, I feel I need to keep trying.

"To patience," I say. "Thank you for putting up with me and these treatments for so long just to make me happy."

It's nice to hear that he's content with just one child. Sometimes I've worried that if I can't have another baby, he might decide to leave me for someone who can.

But Jake has been nothing but reassuring.

"I appreciate you so much," I tell him. "In fact, you've been a little too perfect lately. I think it might be time for you to throw an awful proposal at me to remind me that you're not too good to be true."

"You mean you didn't see the diamond in your sangria? I hope you didn't swallow it!"

I laugh, enjoying this time alone with him. Sometimes I get lost in my own head and concentrate so much on Sam, work, and TTC, that I forget that Jake and I are da bomb.

After dinner he suggests we go get some frozen custard before the shop closes up for the season. Everyone else must have had the same idea because the outdoor custard shack is packed. There's at least twenty-five people in line before us. But I don't mind because Jake holds my hand and makes me feel like a teenager on a date with my high school boyfriend.

Once we finally have our cones, we choose to take our frozen custard back to the car and eat it in the parking lot because it's a little chilly. After a few moments he turns the radio down. I hear him sigh and the sound puts me on edge immediately.

"Babe, I have to tell you something," he says nervously. His expression looks pained. "But before I do, I want you to know that I never intended to hurt you. That has never, and will never, be an intention."

I stop licking my custard and instantly feel like I'm going to throw up. My heart starts racing, my body starts shivering. What did he do? Why do I have a feeling my heart is about to be broken?

"You remember Tori, the DJ whose wedding I did after Sam was born?"

I remember Tori. Her wedding photos put Jake on the map. He'd been booked solid since, with at least one wedding each weekend and sometimes two. All this time I'd considered her a blessing, someone who came into his life at just the right time, and changed it forever.

But I thought she'd changed it for the best. Was I wrong?

"So the radio station she works at-" he tries to say.

I interrupt him, wanting the bandage pulled off quickly. "Did you have sex with Tori?"

He looks shocked. "Jesus! Roxie! No! Why do you jump to the worst-case scenario every time?"

"I don't know. Why do you start off a conversation saying you never meant to hurt me, unless you're about to say something that's going to hurt me? And then get surprised when I jump to worst-case?"

"Baby, look at me," he says gently.

I turn to look at him. I feel tears welling up in my eyes, and my bottom lip starts to quiver. I feel the kind of giant lump in my throat I haven't felt since the day my mom had to have emergency surgery. I've said so many times that Jake has never done a single thing to make me mistrust him. But I've also said so many times that our love is too good to be true. One day I'm sure I'll prove right about that. But I hope not today. I'm not ready.

He reaches across the car and takes my bottom lip between his thumb and forefinger to keep it steady. "You are killing me with this look. You never have to worry about me going somewhere else. I promise you that."

I turn my face away from his fingers and look out the window.

"Go on then," I say, bracing myself.

"You know Tori really loved her wedding photos, and you know she's always trying to give me a boost on social media."

I nod.

"When she found out that *Metro* magazine was doing a feature on small business entrepreneurs, she nominated me for a spot."

This doesn't sound like bad news. I'm confused.

"I didn't tell you at the time because I wanted to surprise you. They emailed me a questionnaire. I just had to fill it out and send a picture of myself and a picture I'd taken. And I was concentrating so much on sending them the right photos, that I didn't even realize what was missing on the questionnaire."

He reaches into the backseat and pulls a copy of the magazine from the pocket behind my seat. He opens it to the page of his feature and hands it to me. I balance the magazine on my knees and hold it open with one hand and hold my cone of coconut custard in the other.

Jake Odom was a twenty-three-year-old college dropout when he signed up for a summer photography class back in

2005. What started off as a hobby quickly became a successful side job for this full-time bartender/restaurant manager in Ann Arbor. Starting with high school seniors, he quickly moved to babies and families, and grew a large fan base on his Facebook page. Knowing he didn't want to be a bartender for the rest of his career, he took a risk and launched a boudoir campaign in the summer of 2012 that took the area by storm. He took a genre of photography once seen as risqué, and turned it into a mainstream art form in the Metro area. His business has since expanded to include weddings, thanks to the stunning photos he took at the nuptials of popular Detroit DJ, Tori McAdams. Now one of the hottest photographers on the scene, Jake Odom Photography is a one-stop shop for couples and families all over Southeast Michigan. Jake is a single father living in Ann Arbor with his three-year-old son. He is currently booking into next year and can be reached at his website or email listed below.

It's annoying, but not absolutely brutal. I mean, I *did* say he was too perfect lately.

I look at Jake for an explanation.

"They sent me this questionnaire that simply asked me, marital status, and I checked the not married option, which is true. It wasn't until I saw the article that I realized they didn't leave me an option to choose something else, like domestic partnership or something like that. I would have added a disclaimer in the email if I had thought about it."

I cringe at the term domestic partnership. Some people don't like the word moist. I don't like the words domestic partnership. I don't know why. I just don't.

I toss the article into the backseat and finish my custard quickly as it had started to melt down my fingers.

"Is there anything you want to say?" he asks.

"Not really," I reply.

"Are you upset?"

I shrug. "I'm happy that you were featured in a magazine. I'm happy you're not having an affair. I mean, you say you didn't do it intentionally, so what else can I say about it?"

"I'm glad you're not mad."

I stare straight ahead.

"You're not mad, right? Or you *are* mad, and I'm not going to hear about it until three weeks from now?"

"I'm not happy about it. But, like I said, what can I do? It's not like they're going to reprint it with a correction. And there's no way I want them adding a pathetic disclaimer to the front of a future issue. Correction: Jake Odom was inaccurately portrayed as single in the last issue. He actually has a girlfriend. Sorry for the mistake. That would be even worse. Besides, it wouldn't have ever happened if I said yes to any of your proposals, so it's my fault anyway. Now let's go get our kid. I need cuddles."

♥

A brides-to-be convention? The first thought I have as I read over the work order is *Thank God I'm not the catering manager anymore.* It's not just one bride to deal with. It's 150! I shudder.

I hear the click of Naomi's heels coming toward my office in the back of the kitchen. I'm guessing there's a last-minute issue with the order. Lemme guess, they want all organic? Not enough farro on the menu?

"Hello," says my replacement as she pokes her head around the corner.

I turn in my swivel chair. "What's up?"

Naomi is cute, blonde, and a recent college grad who makes me feel old and fat.

"I was just talking with the organizer of the luncheon," she says, "and I guess there's been a last-minute allergy added. She said one of the brides is allergic to mushrooms, and she can only have small particles or traces of mushrooms, and not large chunks. She's wondering if the risotto is going to have large chunks of mushrooms. And if so, if we can sub for a different side."

I pause. "Naomi," I say.

"Yeah?" she asks innocently.

"You do realize this person does not have a mushroom allergy, right?"

She shrugs. "I'm just telling you what she told me."

"This person does not have an allergy to mushrooms. She just doesn't like mushrooms. You do know that, right?"

She rolls her eyes. "Yes, Miss Condensation," she says. "I know what an allergy is. Can you sub the side, or not?"

She just called me Miss Condensation, when I'm sure she meant to say, "Miss Condescension." It would probably be condescending of me if I called her out on it right after calling her out on the fake mushroom allergy, huh?

I ignore it. I don't want to come across as *too* bitchy.

"I'll get her another side," I tell her. "But Naomi, in the future, don't let these people push you over. You just spent fifteen minutes of your time waiting for the service elevator to come down here to get a side subbed just because one person out of a hundred and fifty doesn't like mushrooms. You don't have time to accommodate every single person's idiosyncrasies at the last minute, and neither do we. Start putting your foot down when you need to, okay? It'll make you crazy otherwise."

I'm honestly just trying to be helpful, but I get the idea I've pissed her off. She stands up and smooths the front of her skirt, probably a nervous habit. Or maybe she's checking to make sure her stomach hasn't already bloated from the carbs she had at lunch.

"Thank you, Roxie," she says, with her nose pointed firmly in the air.

I get the feeling her intentional smugness is a defense mechanism that she puts up to avoid being seen as a dumb blonde. But what do I know? I'm no psychologist. And she did just call me Miss Condensation ... so ... maybe it's a good thing she puts up that front.

She is about to leave the office when she puts her hand on the doorframe and backs up.

"Hey, Chef?"

"Yes?" I ask, looking up again.

"Jake Odom, the wedding photographer, that's your boyfriend, right?"

"Yes."

"I thought so. I saw his name on the vendor list of the Taylor-Christianson wedding."

"Yeah. You'll see him often. He books a lot of downtown weddings."

"Oh, I know exactly who he is. He's totally hot. When someone said he was your boyfriend, I thought for sure they were talking about a different Jake Odom, especially since I just saw an article about him in a magazine and it said he was a single father."

Dammit. I had enough of a warning about the stupid article. I should have a rebuttal prepared for comments like this. Truth is, I've got nothing. I sit in my chair feeling like Princess Fiona as an ogre.

Telling her it was an editorial mistake makes me look pathetic.

Telling her it's true, that's he's technically an unmarried father and, to some people that is the same as single, makes it sound like I'm offering him up to the next bidder.

If I tell her it's *my* decision that we are unmarried, she'll think I'm putting up my own defense mechanism to make up for my own self-esteem issues.

I stare at my empty ring finger for a moment in silence before I shrug my shoulders.

"Yep. That's my Jake Odom. The hot one."

"I'm looking forward to meeting him. See you later, Chef."

I guess that was her passive-aggressive attempt at making me feel paranoid and insecure. She could have been implying that there's no way I'm good enough for him. She could have also been implying that, since he's "single," she intends to try to woo him with her fake eyelashes and that accident on her face she calls eyebrows.

Nice try, twat, but it's not going to work. I'm not going to be the uber-paranoid psycho girlfriend who shows up at any events the two of them are working and starts going through his phone and emails. This bitch will not get under my skin.

I'm a duck, I remind myself. Calm on the surface. Kicking like hell underneath.

After she leaves, I set my phone to the OneRepublic station on Spotify and get to work on the lunch plates. This is my favorite part of my job. Cooking and plating an entrée that I created, nobody in my face, no phones ringing, no emails to check. One hundred fifty peppercorn chicken breasts with buttered cabbage and mushroom risotto (one sub jasmine rice). When the plates are covered and in the hot box, my job is over for the day. I peel off my gloves, toss them in the trash, and head out the door.

♥

You wouldn't think a trip to the bathroom would be such an event. Just ask anyone who is trying to conceive, and she will tell you how many times she has analyzed the toilet paper looking for signs of ovulation, pregnancy, or periods. It's like an illness. A mental illness.

Some women stick their fingers up there to check the position and firmness of their cervixes. Some even stick Q-tips in to swab it and analyze their cervical mucus. Not me though. I'm not *that* crazy. I have no idea what my cervix is supposed to feel like, or how far up there it's supposed to be, so sticking my finger up there wouldn't do me a lot of good anyway. And as for Q-tips, um, no. Just no.

But when I see something on the toilet paper, I can't help but scrutinize it, and wonder if my body is going to ovulate on its own. With fertility meds, you don't need to analyze anything because you know from your ultrasounds exactly how many eggs you have and how big they are. And you know exactly when you're going to ovulate based on when you take your trigger shot.

But this is our first month off meds in over a year.

We decided to take some time off from TTC and stop throwing money down the drain while we decide whether to proceed with IVF. Our medicated IUIs were costing us $900 a month and that was *after* our insurance was applied. We have pretty good fertility coverage with our insurance company, but we still need to come up with about $6,000 for one IVF cycle, plus there will be monthly storage fees to keep our frozen embryos (should we be lucky enough to have any).

But maybe we won't need IVF after all, the hopelessly hopeful part of me thinks, as I stare at the toilet paper. It could be leftover sperm from sex, but it might be egg white cervical mucus, which would mean my body might be gearing up to ovulate without meds!

Everyone has heard the stories about the miracle babies that are made between treatments. Seriously, it happens all the time. There's no reason to think it won't happen to us.

I sit on the toilet and pick up my phone from the sink. I quickly type into the search bar, *how to tell the difference between ewcm and sperm*. Someone has obviously searched this before because it comes up before I'm even done typing. I'm not the only nut around here.

I quickly find the answer I'm looking for. If it dissolves in water, it's sperm. If it doesn't, it's ewcm.

Okay. Now, how do I find out if it dissolves?

Another Google search and I'm feeling like a scientist -- a mad scientist. Definitely mad.

After my experiment yields the results I was

hoping for, I clean up my mess and run out to the living room where Jake and Sam are building a Duplo Batman set on his play table in the corner.

"Jake! Guess what!"

He looks up from the Legos.

"I'm going to ovulate without meds!"

"Did you use an ovulation strip?"

"Um, that would have been much easier, but no. I didn't order any because I wasn't expecting to ovulate this month. But I just wiped, and it was slippery. So I put it in a cup of water to see if it dissolved, and it didn't, which means it's egg white cervical mucus!"

Jake stands up from the table and walks over to me slowly. He turns back to look at Sam.

"Hey kiddo," he tells Sam, "me and Mommy are going outside for a second. See if you can put some pieces together yourself, and I'll be back in a few minutes."

Jake slides open the patio door and uses his hand to gesture for me to step out.

I oblige and walk out into the night.

Jake closes the door gently. I can still see Sam kneeling at his table playing with his blocks.

It's a little chilly this evening even though it was warm earlier today. I rub my arms while I wait for Jake to tell me why he brought me outside.

"Honey," he says carefully. "This is getting out of hand. You just took a fluid that came out of your body and used our bathroom as some kind of lab for a science experiment. Does that not seem abnormal to you?"

I deflate. My heart hurts. I thought he'd be excited.

He crosses his arms in front of his chest. "Why did I see a bunch of plastic bottles in the trash today?" he asks.

What is wrong with him? He's supposed to be *with* me, not against me.

"I read that certain chemicals can be damaging to my eggs, so I thought this should be a chemical-free household."

"Roxie, don't you see? You've gone too far! You don't think of anything but getting pregnant, twenty-four hours a day! You have a three-year-old who wants to play monster trucks with you, but you're too busy with all of this hocus pocus bullshit to care! You have a boyfriend who feels more like a husband lately, because every single time we have sex there is a purpose other than wanting each other. Everything must be timed perfectly. You plan our sex at the beginning of the month the way people plan when to pay their bills! Like it's a fucking chore! Oh, look, it's time for a release, the sperm might be getting old. We need to keep them fresh so they're perfect for ovulation. Oh, and don't even think about having sex after ovulation. Orgasms aren't good for implantation, right? It's all bullshit, Roxie! All of it! The pineapples and pomegranate juice, now you're throwing our things away! Look at all the teenagers who got pregnant by accident! You think they only had sex on specific cycle days? You think they threw all their shampoos and deodorants in the trash? No! They got pregnant while surrounded by chemicals, cigarette smoke, and probably Boone's Farm!"

Do teenagers still drink Boone's Farm? Does it even exist anymore?

"I could probably handle all of those quirks, Roxie, if that was where it ended. I'd be okay letting you turn us into a chemical-free household. But what really aggravates me is that I'm starting to feel used. I'm beginning to feel like I'm nothing but a sperm machine to you."

"Look," he continues, "in the beginning we said to each other that we were going to try to have another baby, but if it didn't work, that was okay because we were happy with what we had. Remember?"

I nod.

"What happened to that? Why did this go from, another baby would be nice, to baby or bust?"

"I just, the more time, and money, and effort we spend on it, the harder it is to stop. If we stop now, then these last two years were all for nothing. I don't want to have done all of this for nothing. I feel like as long as we keep trying, we have to get there eventually."

"But at what cost? Are you willing to sacrifice your relationship with the child you have right here, just for a chance to have another? A small chance at that?"

I feel the tears rushing to my eyes. "So, I'm a bad mom, and that's why I can't get pregnant? Is that what you're saying?"

"No! Did you hear me say a single word of that? No! I'm saying pay attention to the kid you already have instead of obsessing about the one you don't have and may never have!"

"You're saying I don't pay attention to my kid. That's the same thing as saying I'm a bad mom!"

"I'm not! I would never say that! I'm saying I don't want you to look back on this time years from now and have regrets about the time you spent obsessing over having a baby that could have been spent doing other things. I feel like you need an intervention because this has gotten out of hand. We're supposed to be on a break, and you're still in the bathroom conducting science experiments!"

"Jake, I'm doing all of this *for* him! Because we want him to have a sibling. He deserves a sibling! Why does everyone else get one and he doesn't? It's not fair. Why does everyone else get pregnant whenever they want, but we don't? All of it is so unfair and it makes me frustrated and makes me crazy."

"Clearly."

"I've thought of so many reasons why we can't get pregnant. Like what if we aren't meant to be together, and that's why we can't have another baby? Maybe God wants us to be with other people."

He snorts. "That's the dumbest shit I've ever heard. Is that why women who abuse their kids can get pregnant? Because God thinks the kids deserve to be beaten?"

I cross my arms and look at the ground. "Well, no. Not exactly. Maybe we can't get pregnant because we're unmarried and living in sin."

He scoffs. "Oh, don't even think about it. You can't change your mind about getting married all of a sudden just to see if we miraculously get pregnant."

"You're saying you don't want to marry me anymore?"

"Stop putting words in my mouth! That's not what I said!"

"Do you want to marry me, or not?"

"I don't think this is the right time to talk about this."

"The day after I had a baby wasn't the right time to talk about it either, but we did. I think this is the perfect time to talk about it."

"Look, there are a lot of people in this world who

don't deserve kids, but have them. And a lot of people who do deserve kids, and don't have them. Don't forget how many couples out there are still waiting for their first babies. This obsession has got to stop. We are lucky. We have Sam. We have each other. We both have jobs. We have a house. Two pretty nice cars. Our bills are paid. Life is supposed to be good for us. Why can't you just let our life be good for a little while? Is that possible? Or do you have some deep-rooted intense need to always find the one thing that is missing and put all of your focus on *that*?"

I don't have an answer for him. He's right. Our life together is so perfect except for one thing. I've been letting that one thing take the joy away from everything else that's good. Sometimes he tries to talk to me, and I don't even hear him because my mind is on my egg quality and his sperm counts. Sometimes Sam talks to me and I don't hear him, because all I can think about is how sad he must be to be an only child. And maybe he's not sad at all. If he is, maybe he's only sad because his mommy didn't hear what he just said.

"Look. I have done everything you have asked of me," he continues. "I have taken the vitamins. I have come in a cup more times than I can count. I have shot you up with hormones. I have rose to the occasion and performed my duties as sperm machine every single time it's been requested of me. Now I'm asking you for something. Can you stop?" he asks me. "Can you please take the break we are supposed to be taking?"

I nod.

He finally uncrosses his arms, and I feel a sense of relief that he's opening up, maybe putting his defenses down, not being in combat mode. I don't like mad Jake. Even though I find myself more turned on right now than I've been in ... a long time. I feel wet. And without my special sperm-Uber lube. Imagine that.

He takes a step toward me.

"Good. Because I want my girlfriend back."

I nod again and try to remember the last time we had sex when I wasn't completely consumed with where his sperm was going, and not at all concerned with how I managed to get it out of there.

He steps closer to me and puts his palms on the wall behind me. When he leans his head in and I feel his breath on my ear, I gasp, surprised. Is he trying to seduce me during a fight? This wasn't even on the sex schedule.

"What do you think, Rox?" he says into my ear. "Can I fuck my girlfriend without trying to make a baby? Maybe even pull out and come all over your tits or your ass like I used to?"

I hardly remember a time when I wasn't desperate for every drop of his semen to go in the right place. Looking back, I don't even remember the last time I went down on him until he came because I thought of it as a waste of potential babies. Damn, I really do suck.

I reach down to his jeans and unbutton them. I look at both of our neighbors' houses. The lights are off in the upstairs windows. And we have a privacy fence. And who cares anyway?

"Can you see Sam?" I ask.

He glances through the glass doors over my shoulder. "Yes. He's playing just fine," he tells me.

I try to drop down to my knees, but he presses my hips into the wall with his hands to keeps me in place. His lips touch mine and he parts them with his tongue. Seriously, I don't even remember the last time we've kissed during sex. For the last six months or so it's been like, insert tab A into slot B. Remember how much I hated that shit with Caleb? How did I let it get this way?

He tries to pull his mouth away, but I suck on his bottom lip to keep him close. When he finally breaks free, he says, "I would push you up against the wall right now, but I don't think brick would be too comfortable."

"Throw me on the patio table," I whisper.

He picks me up, carries me over to the patio table, and sets me down a little more gently than my liking. But hey, we don't want to break the table.

He pulls off my yoga pants, pushes my knees up, and slams into me. It feels like the first time in a long time. Maybe because it's the first time in a long time that I've focused on how good he feels inside of me, instead of thinking about how soon I can get him to come so I can mark the day with a heart in my fertility app. I turned Jake into another check mark on a list. I'm so shitty. But he feels too good to think about that right now.

I love this position because I get to look at him. He's so freaking hot. How could I forget how hot he is and how badly I want him?

"Baby," I say. I arch my back to unclasp my bra and pull my shirt up. "Make sure you come all over me when you're ready. Don't let any get inside of me, okay?"

Just speaking about it seems to take him to the edge because I close my eyes just in time, and feel it across my chest and my stomach, some on my face even.

"Shit," he says, as he pulls up his pants and zips them. "Sorry, baby, I didn't mean to get your face."

I lean up onto one of my elbows and use my free hand to swipe a drop off my nipple with my finger. I lick it off. "It's okay. Just promise me next time it goes in my mouth."

He pulls off his T-shirt and hands it to me to clean myself off.

"By next time, you mean after Sam goes to bed?"

"It's a date."

He tosses me my yoga pants and underwear and I start to put myself back together.

"I better get back in. I'll see you inside," he says.

"Okay."

"Wait." He turns around and comes back. He puts a finger under my chin, so I am forced to meet his eyes. "I love you."

Good. He still loves me. Jake wouldn't say it if it wasn't true.

"I love you, too."

He heads back toward the sliding door.

I chew on my thumb nail. "Jake?" I whisper.

"Yeah?" he asks, turning around.

"Thanks for reeling me back from the ledge."

He shrugs. "Hey, that's what I'm here for. I'll follow you all the way off the damn ledge if I have to." He walks back, kisses me quickly, and heads back inside.

I won't be able to mark this as a successful day in my fertility app, but it was a successful day for our relationship, and that matters more. If I had to choose between having another baby and losing the family I have now, I would obviously choose them. Now I need to show them I choose them, prove to them that they are enough. I need to delete my app for a few months and let us live a good life. With him by my side, and that cute little monster-truck loving boy, that shouldn't be a problem.

Chapter Nineteen

Fall 2016

A few days before Halloween, Jake's mom is diagnosed with breast cancer. Her prognosis is pretty good since they caught it early (yay for October), but it's always scary to hear the C-word.

Jake's mom struggled a lot when he was growing up. As a single parent she fought to take care of the two of them. She needed one job to pay the bills, and a second job to help pay for the child care that was needed for her to go to her first job. They weren't starving, but the two of them weren't the kind of family that went out to dinner once a week and took a vacation once a year. It wasn't easy for Jake to be the kid without the latest brand name sneakers that everyone wanted, or the only kid without a tan after

Spring Break.

Looking through the eyes of a child, he thought he had it rough. And I thought so, too, back then. His mom was hardly ever home, and when she was, she was usually grouchy and/or drinking. Jake spent so much time at our house while he was growing up because he couldn't stand to be at home by himself, or at home with an angry exhausted mom.

Now we are adults with a child of our own. We have our own worries about bills, interest rates, child care, credit scores, health insurance, and all the other stuff adults worry about. We now see her with a completely differently set of eyes. The woman is strong as hell.

I am lucky to have a partner in this life, where she had no one. I have a full-time dad to our child, where Jake saw his father only a handful of times a year. Because Jake does most of his work from home, we rarely need to worry about childcare, and when we do, we have family. We are a two-income household, we go out to eat more than we should, and take at least one vacation a year. We even have enough money left over at the end of the month to pay for stupid fertility treatments. We're not the Kardashians, but compared to the life Jake grew up with, we do pretty well. And look how often *I* need a drink when I come home! I have nothing but respect for Sam's nana.

Now that her job as a mother is less demanding, as a grandma, she rocks! She's only one call away to help us with Sam when we need it, and she comes every single time. Sam has a boo-boo, she's on her way with the antibiotic cream and bandages. Sam's got a fever, she's on her way with extra Tylenol. Sam is bored, they're on their way to the movies. Sam's shoes look too tight, here's a new pair.

Knowing we could lose her to this is something I can't even think about because it hurts too much. Her grandchild has given her a new purpose in life. To have her taken away now, to have that new life cut short, would be brutal.

No matter how optimistic the doctors are, there is still a nagging fear in our minds as we get the holiday season in gear, a few less smiles while we put up the tree.

Speaking of the holiday season, Jake and Sam believe it begins the day after Halloween. Every year now since we've moved in, Jake has taken the Halloween decorations down and replaced them with Christmas decorations in a matter of days. I don't agree with it, but the look of joy on their faces as they carry the holiday decorations up from the basement while wearing their silly Santa hats, is enough for me to keep my opinion to myself. I choose my battles wisely, and trying to tear down their happiness with negativity just doesn't seem wise. So if you happen to drive past our house and see our tree twinkling in the window on say, November 4th, well, that's why.

♥

We remortgage the house in November. Jake wants to make sure we have some extra money around, if his mom needs it for anything her insurance won't cover, or if she needs help with bills if she has to take some time off work. I think it's an awesome idea. Of course we'll help his mom if she needs us to!

We are hosting Thanksgiving for both of our families today and I'm a nervous wreck. Not about the food. (A Thanksgiving feast for fifteen. Please. I could do that with my eyes closed.)

I'm not nervous about the cancer. Laura's been feeling very positive about her predicament. The doctors removed the lump, and are pretty sure they got it all out. Time will tell more, but today the outlook is good.

I'm not nervous about the company either. Even though this will be the first time we've ever invited both Jake's mom and his dad's family over for a holiday, I'm sure everyone will act like the adults they are.

I am a nervous wreck because Adam and Emelia are newlyweds, just married over the summer, and I am terrified they are going to announce a pregnancy at dinner. I haven't heard them mention any plans of trying for a baby, so this might be one of those times Jake would claim my worries are irrational. But hey, I never claimed to be anything else.

Adam and Emelia don't know about our fertility problems. Nobody does, except our doctors. The family will expect me to squeal in delight if such an announcement is made, as any aunt-to-be should do. And I will. I *will* be thrilled to welcome a new baby into the family, even if it isn't mine. I *will* love for Sam to have a cousin to grow up with, especially since he's an only child. There's not a whole lot in life that would make me happier than being an aunt.

But I know my *first* reaction will not be to squeal in delight. My first reaction, while hopefully quick, will likely be devastation. My second reaction will be to try to hide the devastation on my face before anyone sees it. My third reaction will be to blink back the tears.

If my brother and sister-in-law have an announcement to make, my joy will come. But it won't come fast. Not fast enough. The vulnerability of going through a barrage of painful emotions in a room full of people will be dreadful. I'm so nervous about it happening that I nearly make myself physically ill.

All morning, as I prepare the food and set the table with the hand-turkey name cards Sam made, I wonder how they'll do it. Will it be a nonchalant comment during grace...? "And we thank you for the extra blessing coming in about six months..." Or will they play a cute game? Wear announcement T-shirts? Have my parents open a grandparents' gift? Display the ultrasound photo on the dessert table?

I'm on edge all day. They arrive without announcement T-shirts, but I am looking over my shoulder, waiting for the attack throughout the entire football game. Twice I slip away to the bathroom thinking I'm about to throw up.

I don't tell Jake how edgy I am today. Sometimes (most times) he doesn't understand. He'd probably be annoyed that I can't just "get over it already." I agreed that I would stop trying, and I would take a break. And I have been. Absolutely. Check my phone. My fertility app is gone.

But not *trying* is not equal to not *wanting*.

I can't just unwant something on command. Unwant is not even a real word, because it can't be done. I still ache for another child. And seeing someone else get instantly what I haven't gotten after years of trying won't be easy. Neither will getting Jake to understand my anxiety. So I don't tell him. I just practically bite my bottom lip off instead.

We make it through the football game. No announcement made.
We have dinner. No announcement made.
We have dessert. No announcement made.
As I stand at the door hugging everyone goodbye, I feel a sense of relief. I won't have to worry about any pregnancy announcements until Christmas now. Unless they sucker punch me on a random Tuesday.

I close the door and kick the beanbag roll that keeps the chilly air out (what are those things called?) back into place. Thanksgiving dinner is over. The holiday season has now officially started and I'm going all-in.

I get Sam comfy in his new Santa jammies. I find *The Santa Clause* on TV. I sit down with a glass of wine and just one more mound of Cool Whip with a sliver of pumpkin pie hiding underneath.

That's when I receive a Happy Thanksgiving text from Allison, followed by a picture of Allison's oldest daughter, Kayla, and her high school boyfriend. In the photo, Kayla is standing in front of an open oven, pointing at the turkey cooking inside, and her boyfriend is standing with his hand covering his gaping mouth in mock surprise. The caption says, "Looks like there's another turkey in the oven."

What I text back is: Wow.

What I want to text back is: Are you fucking kidding me?

Here I am, still trying to have another baby, and my best friend is going to be a grandmother! Her daughter is seventeen for fuck's sake! My friend is going to be a grandma at thirty-four. That's incredibly young to be a grandma, and not at all typical. It's likely that Allison was devastated to find out her teenage daughter was pregnant. It must be hard to be in that position, to see your child repeat the mistakes you made at her age, to not want to see your child struggle the way you did, to want more for her, more opportunities, bigger plans, better options – but also, at the same time, she must feel guilt for being angry about her own grandchild. Yeah, I can feel it all. I can put myself in her shoes and feel the way her mind and heart must be twisting right now. I should be a good friend and call her, or show up with wine. I should reassure her that it's okay for her to be disappointed and excited at the same time, and make sure she knows I'm going to start calling her "granny" immediately. I need to let her know that her smartass best-friend is still here to make light of a tricky situation and make her laugh about it until she chokes on her wine.

But I don't. I run to the bathroom and throw up instead.

A few hours later Kayla posts her first official baby bump photo on Facebook – who posts a baby bump photo at six weeks, you ask? A seventeen-year-old, that's who.

This is when I have more pie.

♥

Our elf arrives on Black Friday. Santa sent him to our house from the North Pole! He is supposed to hang out around the house to keep an eye on Sam and make sure he is being good. Sam is instantly fascinated and names him Crunch a Munch, but we will call him Crunch for short.

I thought those elves were creepy little suckers. But my opinion changed when I realized their purpose was to get children to behave. Genius! I would like to extend my sincerest thank you to whoever invented the Elf on the Shelf. My kid has been an absolute angel all day while I've done my Black Friday shopping online. I overheard him talking to Crunch, being very polite. He even took the annual Toys "R" Us catalog over to the bookshelf where Crunch was sitting for the day, opened the book, and pointed out a few things he hopes Santa will bring him.

This is the first year Sam's really understood what was going on at Christmas. He knows who Santa is, and he knows that Santa brings toys, and he hopes Santa brings him some Rescue Bots that actually transform, and a garbage truck with lifters.

I remember seeing a meme going around Facebook that said, "I used to think being a kid on Christmas was the best thing ever. Now I know that having kids on Christmas is the best thing ever." I have learned that it's most definitely true.

The year Sam was born we started our first family tradition – Bronner's. Bronner's is the biggest Christmas store in the world, and only about an hour away from home. The three of us go the Monday after Thanksgiving every year and spend hours, seriously hours, getting lost in the store and picking out new ornaments. We each get to pick one ornament that represents our year. This year Sam picks out a garbage truck because the highlight of his week is every Tuesday when he can watch the garbage truck come by and lift all the trash cans up in the air. Jake picks out a Harry Potter ornament because he had finally gotten Sam to sit and watch the first movie with him. I wouldn't think a three-year-old would be able to comprehend all that magic and wizardry. But when I think Sam doesn't understand something, I'm usually wrong.

I have trouble finding an ornament for *my* year though. I don't see any syringes, needles, pills, or ultrasound wands in ornament form. Looking back over my year, that's all it was. Where were all the special moments that *I* spent with Sam this year? What were *my* highlights?

I know I shouldn't be so down on myself. Sam and I did a ton of stuff this year. We saw *Ghostbusters* and *Finding Dory* at the theater. We went to the beach, the carnival, the zoo, the cider mill. I know I'm not a bad mom. Deep down, I do know that. But I've talked to some other moms on Instagram, and a common side effect of secondary infertility is the guilt we feel for putting so much time toward having another baby when that time could have been spent with the ones we already have. It's a common emotion, and I acknowledge that I'm normal for feeling it, and then push it out of my mind. I am determined to have the best Christmas season ever, and I won't let fertility shit ruin this for me or my family.

I end up finding a cute pineapple ornament for all the stupid pineapple cores I ate this past year. Right now, it still hurts me. But year after year, when I pull out this pineapple to put on the tree, I hope I don't remember how much it hurt, but how hard I tried. I bet the pain will be less and less each year, and hopefully it will be replaced with pride, not regret. I can think of it as my own "nevertheless, she persisted" story. Someday, it may even be a symbol of hope. Because you can call me a lot of things, but you can't call me hopeless. My hope, my faith, my belief in miracles, is the only thing that keeps me going. It may be more of a hindrance than it is a help, because it would be much easier to give up if it wasn't there. But it *is* there. Unfortunately. And I hope someday to be proud of it rather than embarrassed or ashamed.

Somehow, I make a wrong turn in the gigantic store and we end up in the section of family ornaments. Rows and rows of ornaments showing families of various creatures – snowmen, Santas, elves, penguins – all arranged in families of three, four, and five, with spaces for everyone in the family's name to be written. We bought one of these on our first visit. We have an elf family – a mommy elf, a daddy elf, and a little baby elf. The nice ladies at the counter wrote our names on the elves' hats. Mommy, Daddy, Sam.

I remember hanging it on our tree back in 2013, our first family ornament. Jake and I decorated the tree together while little eight-month-old Sam played with a strand of twinkling lights on the living room rug. Jake took the best pictures of him with those lights that night.

I still remember the Christmas music in the background (Nsync), the Christmas Cottage scent in the Scentsy warmer, the cozy leg warmers I bought from Grace & Lace. I remember it all so well. But most of all, I remember how happy I was. For a moment in time, that moment, I had everything.

All I want is to feel that way again.

I remember coming back here a year later and walking past these walls and thinking to myself, maybe by next Christmas we'll be getting a family of four elves for our tree instead.

And the next year I thought for sure we'd need a new ornament before we were back in this store.

And here we are, still a family of three. Jake sees me glancing at the ornaments as we walk by them. I don't say anything, but I don't have to. He knows.

He takes my hand, pulls me close, and kisses me on my temple.

Sam notices and his face lights up.

"Family kiss time!"

♥

On December 15th we receive the best news – the cancer is gone! She will need periodic checkups to make sure, but the doctors believe it's a case closed. Even better, her insurance covered a great deal of the treatments and procedures, and she was able to work through with only a few days off. So, we are left with some money just sitting there in our bank account.

My mind immediately goes to IVF, but I don't bring it up to Jake. Being on a "break" from TTC is nice, even relaxing. I love being able to have spontaneous sex without making sure he has a certain amount of emissions every week. And a bonus – we are both getting more oral sex than we've had in years! High-five!

I surprise Jake with tickets to see *Elf: The Musical* at the Fox for our monthly childfree date night. Jake then surprises *me* by making reservations before the show at my favorite restaurant, *El Barzon*. Get this – It's Mexican Italian! You get bread and butter *and* chips and salsa!

Right around the time I'm nearly brought to tears because my asiago-stuffed gnocchi with chorizo cream sauce is that fucking good, Jake brings up the money in the bank and asks if I've thought about what we should do with it. I bring up the usual stuff – Invest, put some away for Sam's college, home renovations, take a vacation to Hawaii (natch). I even mention getting a pool put in the ground.

Jake mentions IVF.

Yes. You read that correctly. It was *his* idea.

"Why?" I ask. "I thought I was the only one who wanted to go that far for a baby."

He wipes a stripe down the condensation on his water glass. "Well, you *were*."

"What changed?"

"You know I overheard Sam talking to Santa the other day?"

"You did?"

I had seen the two of them whispering together like they were old friends, but I was too busy taking pictures to listen to what they were saying.

"Sam told Santa he would really like some Rescue Bots that actually transform. And then he said, 'If you've got room, can you bring me a brudder, too?'"

I put my hand to my mouth in surprise. I feel my eyes getting wet.

I have never talked to Sam about siblings. I didn't even know he knew what a brother or sister was. But with all the books he reads, and the movies he watches, I guess he would pick it up on his own.

"So there's that..." Jake says. "And I'd also like the opportunity to give my mom another grandbaby. I'm her only chance for grandkids. I figure with another baby, she will enjoy the rest of her life twice as much. And we will, too."

It's settled. I will call the RE on Monday and get us scheduled for IVF!

I'm totally buying a "Nevertheless, she persisted" T-shirt.

I can buy Jake one that says, "Nevertheless, he put up with her."

Chapter Twenty

Fuck Winter 2017

Jake goes all-in. There are days I start to believe he wants this to work even more than I do.

He Googles the crap out of it. Before I know it, he's started using acronyms like PGS, ICSI, and FET, like he's known about them for years.

He creates a medication calendar in our phones. He makes sure I take all the right shots on all the right days, plus my prenatals, coq10, baby aspirin, Vitamin D, and thyroid meds. He comes with me to my monitoring appointments, which he had never done in the past. He writes down the number of follicles and their sizes. He takes pictures of our follicles on the screen. He goes from nonchalant TTCer, to devoted IVF dad. He's probably days away from starting a Dad blog.

We are both ecstatic when the doctor retrieves 16 eggs! Those are substantial numbers! All the medications and supplements have done their jobs.

Being the delusional optimist that I am, I go home from my retrieval and imagine having at least ten blastocysts still going strong in five days. We could transfer two and freeze the other eight. We could easily get six months of transfers out of one IVF cycle. We could have all the babies we want! Our Christmas photos would be so adorable with all those kids! I'm thinking chambray shirts in a variety of blues with red checkered accents ... and pine trees in the background! I can see the canvas sitting on our mantle now...

But that isn't the way it works out. It never is, is it?

The embryologist emails the day after our retrieval to let us know that twelve have been fertilized. Okay, that is great. Looking good! Thumbs-up emoji!

She calls a day later to give us the sad news. Only four of our eggs are still thriving. I am disappointed, of course, but four eggs could mean four babies. And we are only asking for one. So we choose to believe we are still in decent shape.

The following day the doctor calls. All but one of our embryos have arrested. We have one three-day embryo left. One. Out of sixteen eggs.

Our plan was to do a fresh transfer on day five, but they want to transfer it right away rather than wait.

"Take a few minutes to talk it over with your husband," she tells me.

I don't correct her. But underneath my anxiety I do notice that her mistake is the only part of the conversation that brings me any kind of comfort. Interesting.

I don't need to explain it to Jake. He's done the

research. He knows they see the biggest drop-off between days four and five. He knows that whether we lose the embryo in the lab or in my body, we still lose it either way. Do we want to spend the money to transfer one egg that might not make it? Wait two more days and possibly have nothing left at all? Or regroup, wait a few months, take more supplements for egg and sperm quality, and pay another six grand to try this all over again?

We agree on option one. We did this for an embryo, so we want that embryo.

If the rest of my eggs were so shitty, it's unlikely this one will be any different, but I'd rather have two more weeks of hope than an extra two weeks of despair.

The transfer is easy. The waiting is not. There's an acronym for the wait. It's PUPO – Pregnant until proven otherwise. With all my IUIs, we never knew if any of my eggs fertilized, or if they disintegrated after ovulation.

After our embryo transfer, we *know* our egg is fertilized. We know we have a baby-to-be floating around in my womb looking for a place to attach itself. We are technically as pregnant as we can be at this time. Now I need to *stay* pregnant. Why is that so hard to do?

I do yoga. I meditate with orange stones. I get acupuncture. I avoid sex, baths, herbal teas, alcohol, caffeine, and exercise. I do everything I can to keep my little blastocyst safe in there.

But it isn't enough.

Finding out our only embryo didn't make it is the biggest blow we've been dealt thus far.

Jake takes Sam to Laura's when I tell him I started

my period. She didn't know what was going on because we hadn't told anyone we were doing IVF. But, like the awesome grandma she is, she doesn't ask for an explanation. She picks him up and heads off to the Ann Arbor Hands-On Museum.

And this little piggy stays home and has a temper tantrum.

"I'm done!" I tell Jake through my tears and hiccups. "I can't do this anymore! I can't go through this again! Please get all the meds out of the fridge. I don't want to see them again. Ever. Please get rid of all the pens and needles and alcohol swabs. Please."

I know he must be disappointed as well. And angry with the world in general, because this isn't fair. But he handles his feelings better than I do. Or maybe he hides them better.

He gets rid of the meds. I don't know where he puts them. I hope he didn't throw them away, because they are super expensive, and once I calm down, I will donate them to another woman struggling to conceive. But they aren't staring at me next to my Chobani Flips anymore. For that I am grateful.

He gets rid of the pregnancy tests, ovulation strips, and the special Hope Chest that contained a few cute baby items I'd picked up throughout the years. Three years! Three fucking years of my life – wasted!

Without a prompt from me, he starts removing the baby stuff from the basement. The crib. The swing. The Rock 'n Play. Boxes of baby clothes. As he loads our hopes and dreams and future and the family we'll never have into the SUV, I go upstairs to our bedroom and open the bottom drawer. I reach underneath a pile of my bathing suits and pull out the Big Brother shirt I'd bought for Sam so many years ago. That little size

12 Months T-shirt with the tag still hanging from under the arm. I still remember seeing it in Target that day. I remember the joy I felt when I put it in the cart thinking that all we needed to do to have a baby was decide we wanted a baby, and that was that. I am so stupid. So fucking stupid.

I take the shirt downstairs and throw it in with the rest of the baby clothes. Stupid, stupid fucking shirt!

I go over to the bookshelf in the living room and run my finger along the spines on Sam's shelf. I pull out a book I found at a yard sale a few years ago. It's called *Babies Don't Eat Pizza*. It's supposed to get older siblings ready for a new baby in the home. I throw the book into the box of clothes. Stupid, stupid fucking book.

Jake finishes loading up the SUV and takes it all ... somewhere. Maybe he donates it all to a thrift store. Maybe he takes everything to his mom's. I don't know. I'm just glad it's all gone.

That's it. Game over. We will be a family of three, and that is that.

After he drives away, I lie on the couch and cry. After thirty minutes or so, when it feels like I've gotten enough tears out, I absent-mindedly pick up my phone to distract myself.

I open Facebook. First I see a bunch of pictures of my "friends" celebrating St. Patrick's Day. Those without kids are celebrating with green beer, gold chains, and temporary shamrock tattoos. Those with kids are celebrating with green water in the toilet and green footprints leading to a basket of gold coin chocolates.

1. Is it St. Patrick's Day?

2. When did St. Patrick's Day become a bigger deal than Easter? Leprechauns never left me baskets of chocolate when I was a kid.
3. On a scale of 1 to 10, how crappy of a parent am I for not decorating the kitchen counter in green footprints?
4. Sam isn't even wearing green today. #momfail #whatelseisnew

In between the photos of green tomfoolery, there's Kayla complaining about her first stretchmark and adding a "feeling pregnant" to her status – as if anyone has forgotten. I press my finger to the unfollow button and throw the phone into the middle of the living room where I know I'll be too lazy to get up and get it next time I need a distraction.

I'm still sniffling on the couch when Jake gets home. He sits at the end of the couch near my feet, and puts his head in his hands for a moment.

I sit up, cross-legged, and take his hand from his head. I lie back and pull him on top of me, wrapping my arms around his chest as tight as I can.

"Thank you," I whisper. "Thank you for supporting me these last three years, even when I was close to falling off the edge. Thank you for letting me try everything I could to make this happen, even when it took time and money and effort that could have been spent in better ways. Thank you for not being mad at me about it. Thank you for giving me the kind of comfort I'm not very good at giving you."

Eventually we fall asleep, me wrapped up in Jake, and Jake wrapped up in me.

I have enough. This is enough. It has to be.

Chapter Twenty-one

April 2017

No. It can't be.
How can this be?
Thirty-six consecutive months of negative pregnancy tests.
Thirteen medicated cycles.
Six IUIs.
One egg retrieval.
One embryo transfer.
Too many injections, blood draws, and ultrasound wands to count.
Thirty-six months of praying and hoping and wishing so badly that the pregnancy test wasn't white as fuck.

But it was.
Every. Single. Time.
Until now.
When we stopped trying. When we agreed we were done.

I didn't just say we were done to pacify him, or myself. It was something I believed, something I could feel in my whole body. For the first time, I knew in my heart we were absolutely 100% <u>done</u>. And it brought the kind of peace to my mind that I hadn't felt in years.

So what kind of sick fucking joke is this? I wonder, as I stare at two pink lines on the test in front of me. No tilting required. No flashlight needed. There are two lines.

Well, what do ya know? All those annoying people who say, "Just relax and it'll happen." They might have been on to something.

All I can do is laugh.

I am terrible at keeping secrets from Jake, so I tell him that night. I put the announcement on the message board on the kitchen counter. "Roses are red. Violets are blue. We've finally been blessed with baby #2."

He thinks it's as hilarious as I do, but I can see in his face how happy he is. Or maybe it's not as much happiness as it is relief.

We should be reserved and cautious, but I choose to believe instead that there is no way we are not having this baby. There's no way we've been blessed with our greatest wish, just to have it taken from us. The world is not that cruel.

Chapter Twenty-two

June 2017

Oh, but the world *is* that cruel.

I am so stupid. I let myself get excited. I allowed myself to believe we were going to have this baby. I had no negative feelings about the pregnancy at all. Maybe that's why it hurts so much now – because the loss caught me off guard. Would it have hurt less if I would have worried every day for the last two months? Does being optimistic cause more pain when it turns out you were wrong? Does being pessimistic hurt less when you realize you were right?

I want to stay in bed and binge-watch TV shows on Netflix about fictional characters whose lives suck more than mine, while surrounded by crumpled up, tear-stained tissues, and Hostess cupcake wrappers, the chocolate ones with the white swirls on top.

But I can't do that. I have to care for my broken-hearted child and broken-hearted boyfriend. Jake would gladly take care of the household for a few days while I wallow in self-pity in my room, because that's the kind of guy he is. But I can't let him. He is hurting just as I am. And poor Sam ... he needs his parents to keep it together.

"I think we might need the support," Jake says, insisting that we tell our family about our loss.

He's right. We do need support. I'm not too proud to admit it.

But you don't tell people about miscarriages. You just *don't*.

I shake my head. "Absolutely not, Jake. That's selfish. Why tell them that a grandbaby they didn't even know about has died? What good will that do? All it will do is hurt them. It's bad enough we hurt Sam. We never should have told him."

I've been going through some major mood swings these last few days. Sometimes I'm mad at God. Why give us this blessing just to take it away? What are we supposed to learn from this? As soon as we decide we are ready to give up, you give us what we've been fighting for this whole time, and then use it to destroy us? *Why?* It makes no sense. There is absolutely no reason for this to have happened. And it makes me So. Fucking. Angry.

I'm angry at the situation, but also angry at myself. I did everything wrong. I did too much planning ahead when I should have waited until further into the pregnancy. I booked the three of us a babymoon in Siesta Key, so we could enjoy one more vacation as a family of three before we became a family of four. I booked it too early. I jinxed us. It's all my fault.

We had chosen our names. We'd agreed on a nursery theme and picked some things out on Amazon. It was all premature and shouldn't have happened.

But those things are forgivable. I was excited. I was a mom who wanted to celebrate our baby. I can't keep punishing myself for that.

But my biggest mistake, and the most unforgivable, was telling Sam. We waited until after our 8-week appointment when we heard the baby's heartbeat. Hearing the heartbeat is a huge milestone. They say once you hear the heartbeat, you're in the clear. At least, I *think* that's what they say. But did anyone really say that? Or was I just too excited to share the news with Sam that I couldn't wait any longer? I had been waiting to share that special moment with him for so long, and I honestly didn't believe the world was cruel enough to take our baby.

Jake and I bought him a Big Brother T-shirt and another book about getting a little sibling, since I'd sent the last one away. We let him tell stories to the baby and lie with his head on my belly to be closer to his little sister (or brudder). We showed him pictures every week of what the baby looked like. We wanted him to feel included. We wanted to grow our family *as* a family.

It was a selfish mistake – one I'll never forgive myself for making. I'm not going to make another mistake by telling our families.

Nothing good can come of it.

They might be hurt because they also lost a family member. This will then make my pain deeper. It's bad enough knowing I let down my son, my best friend, and my unborn baby. How much worse would it be to know I let down the rest of our family as well? I can't be responsible for anyone else's pain right now. Three broken hearts are enough.

Even if they aren't as devastated about the baby as we are (and it's likely they won't be, because they haven't had eight weeks to be excited about it), it will hurt them to know that *we* are hurting. Nobody wants to see someone they love in pain. We have plenty of pain between the three of us. There is no reason to go throwing it around like confetti. The thing about grief is that giving some to other people doesn't mean we'll have less of it left inside us. It means that shit will grow like mold on a loaf of bread until it smothers us all.

And maybe even worse than the idea of hurting them is the possibility that it won't hurt them at all. They have no idea how badly we've been trying for a baby. They might think a lost pregnancy is no big deal. They might say things like, *it just wasn't meant to be,* or *everything happens for a reason ... I'm sure you'll be pregnant again in a few months ... at least you lost the baby early instead of at birth ... next time just take more vitamins and don't exercise as much ... it was probably a blessing in disguise.*

"Honey, you don't deserve to go through this alone," he insists. "Stop punishing yourself. We kept our fertility treatments a secret from them because you wanted to be able to surprise them with a pregnancy instead of telling them every month that it failed. You didn't want them to be burdened by the constant disappointments the way we were. And I was okay with keeping it to ourselves, and waiting until we had happy news to share. But because we kept it to ourselves, that means we are asked at every family function when we are going to have another baby, or when Sam is going to be a big brother. Those questions have always hurt us. And now they are going to start hurting us more, especially once we get into the holidays when the baby was supposed to be born."

Ugh. I can't even imagine. I might skip the holidays this year, maybe plan a vacation to somewhere tropical and pretend it's not Christmas at all.

"Listen," he continues. "They will find out eventually, because four-year-olds don't keep secrets, nor should they have to. And when they do find out, they will feel like shit knowing they've been unintentionally sticking knives into our wounds for a long time. And honestly, call me selfish if you want, but I don't want knives in our wounds. And maybe I want to be able to talk to someone else about this."

"I'm not telling anyone anything," I finally tell Jake. "I don't want to talk to anyone. If you want to tell people, tell people. I *would* appreciate it if those questions at holidays would stop. But I don't want any phone calls, visitors, or frozen casseroles."

"Okay."

"But pizza is always welcome."

He smiles. The first smile I've seen from him in two days.

Sigh. That smile – keeping my shit together since 1994.

If I can keep *him* smiling, he can keep *me* smiling, and we can keep Sam smiling. We can somehow get through this. We can, and we will. We don't have any other choice.

Mom and Dad send flowers.
Adam and Emelia send a fruit bouquet.

Laura sends over a book for Sam called *We Were Gonna Have a Baby, But We Had an Angel Instead.*

It's a great idea, the book. I'm glad it exists, that there is help available for all the littles who lose their littles. But I would like it much better if the book read *itself* to Sam. I have a feeling his parents are expected to read it to him. And I can't.

I wake up on Friday morning and the first thing I think is *I would be thirteen weeks and two days pregnant today.* Baby should be the size of a hard-boiled egg, but is probably more like the size of a cotton ball by now. Did you know that babies start to shrink after their hearts stop beating? Yeah, I didn't either. I could have lived the rest of my life not knowing that. I bet you could have as well. I'm sorry.

I'm not ready to see anyone, so Jake says he's going to take Sam over to Laura's first, then comes back to pick me up.

I put Sam's shoes on and kneel to give him the biggest, tightest hug ever.

"Can I kiss the baby goodbye, Mommy?" he asks.

I swallow the gigantic lump in my throat that seems like it's taken up permanent residence. "Of course you can, honey."

Sam lifts the bottom of my Detroit Tigers T-shirt, exposing my tiny baby bump, and plants his lips softly just above my belly button.

"Goodbye, little baby," he whispers. "I love you. Have a safe trip to heaven."

I come to in the recovery room after my procedure, and I feel like one of the *Three Bears* when they discover Goldilocks has been in their home.

Someone's been in my porridge.

"Hi baby," Jake says gently from the chair beside the bed. "How are you feeling?"

Empty.

I lie on the couch when we get home. Sam is having a sleepover with his nana, so I'm free to be mopey and lazy for the rest of the day. I expected to have some cramps, but I didn't expect my throat to be this sore. It feels bruised on the inside. I guess from that thing they stuck in there to keep me breathing. I suppose it's not a terrible thing. It means I don't have to talk to anyone.

Jake makes me some tea with honey and lemon, brings me my favorite fuzzy blanket, and turns on *The Price is Right*.

When I was growing up, whenever I stayed home sick from school, I would lay on the couch and watch *The Price is Right*. Not because I liked it that much, but because it was on, and I was usually too sick to bother changing the channel. Back then changing the channel would have required me getting up and walking over to the TV. There was no Alexa. I don't even think we had a remote.

Now, as an adult, I've noticed the familiar sounds of the show bring me a kind of homey comfort, the same way a box of Kraft Mac 'n Cheese does. When I'm not feeling well, I want mac n' cheese, Vernor's, and *The Price is Right*.

"Wow. This is on late," I manage to scratch out.

"It's not," he tells me. "I recorded it for you. I remember you told me once that this show comforts you when you don't feel good. And I thought you might need some comfort. We could watch *Shameless* instead if you want, since Sam's not here."

It takes us about a year to watch one season of *Shameless* because it can't be on when Sam is home. I won't even watch it when he's sleeping in his room. If you've seen it, you understand why.

Because I wouldn't expect any less of him, at dinner Jake presents me with a bowl of perfectly cooked Kraft Mac 'n Cheese.

I'm not hungry, but I eat it anyway.

Chillin' on the couch watching TV all day is something that seems a lot more fun in my fantasies than it actually is. I'm already bored.

"Honey," I say when I finish my dinner. "Can Sam come home now? I really need a Snuggle Samwich."

Ever since Monday, when I found out the baby died, I've been extremely clingy with Sam. My paranoia about losing him began the day he was born. But these last few days it has increased, with good reason. He's slept with us every night since then, and I need my Samwich tonight, too.

"Mommy," he asks, while we're snuggled in bed that evening. "How far away is heaven?"

"It's very far," I whisper.

"More far than Cedar Point?" he asks.

"Yes."

"More far than Kings Island?"

"Yes, honey."

"Whoa! That's real far! It can't be more far than Grandma and Grandpa's house, though, right?"

"It is, honey."

"What? Heaven is even more far than Florida?"

He is quiet for a few minutes. And just as I'm about to fall asleep, he whispers, "You know what, Mommy? I don't care how far away heaven is. I'm gonna go there. And I'm gonna get our baby back."

Chapter Twenty-three

June 2017

Today I would be fourteen weeks pregnant. Baby would be the size of a Rubik's Cube. I suppose I'm expected to move along and get on with my life now and not wake up every morning remembering what we lost. And I suppose whoever expects that of me can fuck off.

We cancel our babymoon on Siesta Key and I add some vacation days to the end of my medical time off. It's not necessary physically. The doctor said I could return to work two days after the procedure if I wanted to. But I'd like to be able to enjoy a few days with my family this summer. "Enjoy" is probably the wrong word. Trying to get through it is more what it is.

Daddy is a little behind on his editing schedule. While he is working hard to catch up, Sam and I spend lots of quality time together. It's exactly what I need.

Hanging out with Sam reminds me of all the things that are so great about being a kid, things I would have forgotten about forever if I'd never had a child of my own.

<u>Awesome Things We Forget About When We Grow Up</u>
1. Peanut butter and jelly sandwiches cut into four pieces.
2. Sliding across the hardwood floors in our socks.
3. Doing cartwheels across the front yard.
4. Running through the neighbor's sprinkler.
5. Popsicles.
6. Squirt gun fights.
7. Cinnamon toast.
8. Laughing because there's a planet named Uranus. (Mommy, did you know that anus is another word for butthole?")

I take him to Belle Isle for a day to give Jake some quiet time. Shortly after we arrive, I scold myself for forgetting our beach gear and forgetting to check the weather report before we left the house. Here we are on an island in the middle of a river on a sunny 89° day, with no bathing suits!

Sam seems not to mind the heat and humidity – he never seems to mind the weather much at all. He plays happily on the ziplines for hours, runs through the giant playground while looking for Pokémon, and after it all, he convinces me to walk to the lighthouse to get a better view.

"Come on, Mommy," he says, waving me toward the long, shade-less path to the lighthouse. "YOLO."

I have no idea where he heard that expression (probably YouTube), but it's too cute for me to deny his request.

The lighthouse ends up being farther away than it looks. It's probably a little over a half mile each way, but today it feels like 12 miles ... through the desert. The heat doesn't slow him down a bit. He skips his way along the path like he doesn't even know it's hot out.

Meanwhile, I'm a nervous wreck trying to keep myself in check. Did I bring enough water to get us there and back? Did I put enough sunblock on us? The sun is so hot I feel like the skin is melting off my bones! Has there been some kind of chemical attack on the city? I try to load the news on my phone, but there's no service. What if we get heat stroke and can't get back to the car, and no one else comes out toward the lighthouse all day, and we end up dying right here on the gravel because of this shitty cell signal? Oh God, why did I ever agree to this? This is going straight to the top of Roxie's List of Worst Ideas Ever!

We do eventually make it to the lighthouse, which is surrounded by a fence and anticlimactic if you ask me. But Sam is excited, and I get some cute pictures of him, and some selfies of the two of us together. I look like a normal mom in the pictures. I don't look as crazy as I feel inside sometimes.

I swear I've never been as happy to see my car as I am when we make it back to the parking lot. Dead? No. Heat stroke? As yet undetermined.

"That's it," I tell Sam when we get in, blast the AC, and buckle up. That's a wrap. "Time to head home."

"But Mommy, we haven't even gone swimming yet."

"I forgot our beach bag, remember? No swimming today. Maybe we can have a water balloon fight with

Daddy tonight."

I bought this contraption at Walmart that's supposed to make 100 water balloons in one minute. I don't know if it works, but if it does – game changer.

As we pass the beach on our way back to the bridge, I look at the families having fun in the water and give myself another mental kick in the shin.

Why is it that I don't ever, just for one day of my freaking life, have my shit together? No matter how much I try to be the prepared mom, I always fall short. Sometimes I have drinks but no snacks. Suits but no towels. Sunblock but no hats. Hand sanitizer but no wipes.

"Why can't we just swim in our clothes?" he asks, as we drive past.

"We don't have your floaties."

"So what?" he asks again. "Just hold onto me."

I bite my bottom lip and think about it. One day Sam's childhood will exist only in our memories. When we look back on these days, years from now, what will we remember? Will we remember how prepared I was? Or how many things we had in our beach bag? Will Sam remember how comfortable he was driving home from the beach in dry clothes?

I put the car in reverse.

Sam claps in the backseat.

We stand on the sand holding hands and watching the families jump from the floating boat ramp. The water is crystal clear, almost like we've found a little bit of paradise in the most unlikeliest of places.

I look down at him and he's looking at me with pleading eyes. I know how he feels. I have some kind of intense need to be in water. It's practically painful for me to see water that I can't swim in. Sam is a water baby like his mommy and probably feels the same pain.

Being Paranoid Mom all the time is draining me. I am so effing exhausted from worrying all the time. Sometimes I want to be the carefree Mom. "Sure, swim in your underwear for all I care! Eat gummy bears for lunch! Your teeth will fall out anyway. Stay up watching *Ryan's Toy Review* on YouTube until eleven o'clock if you want!"

But we don't have any towels. We'll have to drive home wet.

I bite my lip. This is so hard. *Why* is this so hard?

I ask my inner Jonathan Larson, WWJD? And he answers the same way he always does – "No Day But Today."

"I'm going to have to hold you the whole time," I tell Sam.

He nods his head in approval and pulls his sandals and shirt off in two seconds.

I kick off my flipflops and set down my backpack. For a second I worry that someone might steal it, but I push the fear out of my mind. We lost a baby. I think we can handle a stolen backpack should the situation occur.

I take his hand in mine.

"Let's go, Mommy!"

Like a scene from a greeting card, we take off for the water. Since Sam doesn't have his puddle jumper, we practice swimming without it. I try teaching him to go under without breathing. He does well three times in a row, but on the fourth time he panics and gets a little water in his nose. I mean, a little. He was only bothered for a few seconds and went right back to swimming. I act like it's no big deal because I don't want to scare him. Believe me, it takes everything I've got. On the outside I look calm as ever. On the inside my mind is flashing red warning signs: Dry drowning! Brain-eating amoeba! Death! Caskets! Funerals! Headstones!

After swimming, Sam asks if we can walk over to the ice cream truck parked near the beach.

The normal mom response would be no, we haven't had dinner yet. But I'm trying hard to be carefree, and the irony of the idea is not lost on me.

"Sure. Let's have ice cream."

Sam gets a Spiderman ice cream – the kind with two gumballs for eyes.

In this insane heat, the ice cream bar quickly turns into a clusterfuck. The blue and red are melting so fast, down his hands, his arms ... the one pathetic napkin I find in my bag is no match for the melting superhero. Of course I don't have baby wipes in my bag today. Every other mom would have baby wipes. Of this I am sure.

All I can do is watch helplessly as Sam is covered in a red, blue, purple mess nearly all the way to his elbows.

He keeps licking his ice cream like nothing is wrong. He even laughs at the mess he's making. I grit my teeth together to keep from snapping at him out of frustration. It's not his fault his mom is dumb.

By the time the ice cream has been cleaned off at the sink in the bathroom, our clothes are dry. I call it a win and head home, stopping to pick up a Little Caesar's deep dish on the way.

Jake greets us in the driveway and happily takes the warm pizza from my hands. We follow him to the backyard where he has lit the citronella tiki torches and

Good Things Come

set the patio table for dinner. He has set out plates, napkins, two bottles of beer from Short's, and a Capri Sun.

Sam tells Daddy all about our day while we eat. There is nothing less than happiness in his story. There's no mention of the heat, the burning sun, dehydration, bad cell signals, missing towels, wet clothes, or water up his nose.

"And when I asked if we could get ice cweam, she said yes! Can you buhwieve that, Daddy? She said yes! *Before* dinner!"

"No, I can't believe that," he replies before giving me a smartass smirk.

"And then my Spiderman ice cream was melting all over my hands and arms, and it was so cool because it was like I was *literally* turning into Spiderman, Daddy!"

He literally just said literally. Except he said it like he was a British child. *Lit-willy.* I have no idea. None.

When we're done eating, I crawl onto Jake's lap to watch the sunset. Sam plays on the swing set and chases fireflies around the yard.

"Baby?" he asks.

"Yeah?"

"Did you notice in Sam's stories today he never mentioned any of the disasters you texted me about earlier?"

"I did."

"I think there's probably something we're supposed to learn from this."

"You mean something like ... what we see as a disaster, they might see as one of the best days of their lives?"

"Exactly. You have to stop beating yourself up,

babe. One of our jobs as parents is to do his worrying for him, and keep him safe, so he can live without that weight on his shoulders. You do that, and you do it well. You've got the paranoid worrying part down. But sometimes, maybe you could try to see things from his perspective. Maybe someday you could *both* have one of the best days of your lives ... together. At the same time."

He's right. Always.

He pushes my ponytail out of the way and kisses the back of my neck.

I sigh. Whether we have the best day or the worst day, there's still no one else I'd rather come home to at the end of it.

When he wraps his arms around my waist from behind, I'm surprised to see he's holding a black square box. I recognize the gold writing across the top. Alex and Ani.

"What's this for?" I ask. I take the box from his hand. I'm not used to getting surprise gifts from Jake. Surprise compliments, yes. Surprise adventures, yes. Surprise presents? Not really his thing.

"It's June 29th, one of our hundred and seventy-four anniversaries," he says. I can tell he's smirking behind me, even though I can't see his face.

Shit. *I* was the one who told *him* when our anniversaries were, and now *I'm* the one forgetting to celebrate them.

I look down at the box ashamed. "Jake ... I wasn't thinking ... I –"

"Stop. I was going to buy it for you anyway. It just happened to be a perfect day to give it to you."

I lift the lid on the box and pull out a classic Alex and Ani bracelet with a round turquoise gem dangling

Good Things Come

from the silver band. I know what it is. And it's perfect.

He uses his fingers to wipe a little dampness from under my eyes.

"I love you," I whisper.

"Love you back."

Maybe Sam was right. This just might have been one of the best days of my life. Maybe next time I can realize I'm having a great day while I'm *still* having the great day. Goals. Steps.

I fall asleep in Jake's arms, relieved to know that happiness can and does exist inside us, even without our baby.

♥

I return to work Wednesday morning. Sunshine isn't there. Sunshine always works Wednesdays, and is never late.

I make my own coffee with a shot of regular espresso and a helluva lot of hazelnut syrup because I don't care about caffeine or carbs today, or maybe any day, ever, for the rest of my life.

I drink my coffee and get to work while singing "Ain't No Sunshine" to myself.

I check reviews on Trip Advisor. Looks like they kept everything running smoothly while I was gone.

I check the 86 board to see what we ran out of.

I check the boxes that were delivered this morning to make sure we got everything we ordered.

When there is a lull in the breakfast rush, my line cook, Tyson, pokes his head in my door.

"Welcome back, Boss."

I fake a smile. I'll probably be doing that more often than not for the next few weeks. "Thanks, Ty."

"Did you hear about Sunshine?"

"No. I haven't heard anything," I say, alarmed. "What's going on with Sunshine?"

He steps into the office and pats me on the back gently. "I'm sorry to have to tell you this, Chef. I know how much she meant to you. But Sunshine has gone to a better place."

"What? Sunshine died?" *Oh my God.*

"No, no no!" he says quickly. "Sorry, I didn't mean she went to a better place like *heaven.* I mean she moved to a better position at a better hotel. She's at the Westin now. Banquet manager!"

Whew. I'm glad she's not dead. And I'm happy for her for scoring such a big job. I just wish she had told me she was looking. She was my wingman, my Girl Friday. Why would she leave without telling me? Without even saying goodbye?

I don't have a lot of time to dwell on it because we get hit with an obscene and unexpected lunch rush. The restaurant fills up with a crowd on break from the convention center. There are over thirty tickets on the line. I am so busy expediting, grabbing salad dressings, plating fries, that I don't have time to think at all, and that is exactly what I need right now – a break from my head.

"Shit!" I hear Tyson yell as I squirt rows of ranch dressing into ramekins across the back counter the way Jake used to pour shots at The Bar. "Why is there a chicken marsala on this ticket? We don't serve it until dinner!"

"Trust the server, Ty," I answer as I keep squirting. "There must be a reason. Just get it done."

"Chef, I haven't worked a dinner shift in six months! Chicken Marsala wasn't on our menu back then!"

I turn from my ramekins. "Are you saying you don't know how to make it?"

"Yes! That's what I'm saying!"

"Fuck! Shit." I run behind the line. There's at least twenty tickets on the screen with timers ranging from nine to thirteen minutes – way too long a wait time for lunch. "Okay, I need flour! Sunshine! I mean, shit." I look around for help. "Randy!" I ask the server assistant, "Can you please run to dry storage and grab a bag of flour?"

"Got it," he says.

He takes off running while I grab a handful of mushrooms and toss them into a frying pan. I pound out a chicken breast on the counter and quickly chop up some garlic.

When I see Randy heading toward me with a bag of flour, I hold my arms up toward him. "Throw it!" I yell.

He throws it from about eight feet away. It's heading right toward my hands – a perfect throw about to be a perfect catch – except the way the bag hits my thumbs tears the bag in half and I'm suddenly covered in flour. From my head to my slip resistant shoes. In my ears, in my eyes.

Yes, this *is* what I signed up for. The rush, the adrenaline, putting out figurative and sometimes literal fires, running behind the line to save the day while covered in so much flour I can't even breathe through my nose. This is why I love my job. You wouldn't think I would see being covered in flour as a blessing, but on my first day back to work, it is exactly what I need.

Six minutes later the chicken marsala is plated and gorgeous enough that I'll probably find it on Instagram tonight.

When the tickets are gone and the lunch crowd is eating happily, I have Ty spray me down with the dishwasher hose.

"You know," he tells me as I'm drying myself off with a towel he stole from housekeeping, "that is the funniest shit to happen in this kitchen since the day you found out black people don't eat green bean casserole on Thanksgiving."

I laugh until I cry and cry until I laugh again.

I get home from work to find my little boy on the couch looking miserable. I put my hand to his forehead. He's burning up. My mental stability takes a huge metaphorical step back and I nearly collapse.

I can't even describe the fear I feel in that moment. The dread is enough to eat me from the inside out.

"JAKE!" I scream. The tears show up without hesitation. They never seem to be far away anymore.

Jake calmly gets the thermometer from the bathroom. He calmly takes Sam's temperature. It's 103. Jake calmly gives him Tylenol and checks his body for other symptoms, like spots or rashes.

There is nothing about me that could be confused for calm. Sam has been sick a ton of times in his four years of life. Colds, ear infections, stomach viruses, bronchitis, pink eye, and the awful, dreadful Hand, Foot, and Mouth. He's a kid. He's loaded in germs. We take care of it and move on.

Not this time. No. My nightmares have convinced me that I'm going to lose him, too. He's my only child. My whole world in one little helpless body. Without Sam, I have nothing. I *am* nothing. I wouldn't even be a mom anymore!

I panic. It's the I-might-need-to-breathe-into-a-paper-bag kind of panic. This is it! This is how I lose him!

It's brain-eating amoeba! I just know it! When he got water in his nose at Belle Isle, he contacted a brain-eating amoeba! His chances of survival are like 5%!

I've Googled it. I've read articles about families who have lost their children to this freak occurrence. I've cried for those families. I've lost sleep over it. I've stayed up at night staring at his sweet face, looking for any signs of brain damage, feeling his forehead for the fever.

I've been waiting for the fever.

The fever is here, right on schedule.

"We need to get him to the hospital right away," I say to Jake, quickly gathering our phone chargers and throwing them into my bag. "The sooner we get him there, the better his chances of survival!"

I throw Sam's shoes into the bag. I'll carry him to the car. Or should we call 911 instead?

"Honey, honey, honey," Jake says, gripping my shoulders tightly, probably hoping I'll get a grip on myself. "Calm down! You're gonna scare the poor kid. He's fine! His fever should be down within ten minutes."

I just want to scream. *Don't tell me to calm down! Do you have any idea the amount of dread I hide inside me every day? Do you have any idea how hard I work to do that?*

I pick my little man off the couch and run to the car. Jake follows with the keys and drives us toward the nearest Urgent Care.

"No," I argue. "We need the hospital. We need specialists and a lot of machines." *Seriously. I need a paper bag. Does anyone have a paper bag?*

"If there is a problem that serious," he says calmly, while watching the road and driving like a normal person whose only child isn't in the backseat moments from death, "they will send us to the hospital. If we go to the hospital now, we will sit there for three hours before even seeing a doctor. His brain will be eaten alive by then."

He thinks this is funny! What part about your kid dying is funny? What in the actual fuck, Jake?

I shake my head furiously. "No. If I tell them he got water up his nose at the beach, they will see him sooner."

He turns the radio off. "Roxie," he says. Why is he calling me that? He hardly ever calls me by my name.

"What kind of water are these bacteria usually found in?" he asks in a voice that lets me know he already knows the answer. I suppose when your baby mama is as paranoid as I am, you've got to arm yourself with info.

"Shallow, warm, stagnant water," I answer off the top of my head. I'm a Wikipedia article in human form.

"Uh huh," he says. "And you were swimming in the Detroit River – a cold, deep, fast-moving body of water."

"We weren't swimming in a deep, fast-moving *part* of the river. It just happened to someone last week while white water rafting! That's fast moving! How do you explain that?"

This is one time I hope Jake is right and I'm overreacting. I know the chances of Sam catching a brain-eating amoeba are like one in forty million, but try telling that to my racing heart.

Dude. I need to get a grip.

I reach into my bag for my pill case. I open it and

pull out a little white pill. My doctor gave me a prescription for my anxiety right after Sam was born, but I am very careful to only take it when I'm having a well-being emergency. Sometimes my anxiety is merely a nuisance. Other times, like today, it feels harmful to my health.

My thoughts are out of control.

I don't even know who I am anymore.

I don't like living inside this head.

Less than an hour later the nurse tells us his Strep test came back positive. He has Strep throat. His brain is not being eaten by bacteria. He's not dying.

We stop at the pharmacy to get his antibiotic. When we get home, Jake takes Sam up to bed and makes me a Paloma.

I just want it to stop.

Chapter Twenty-four

July 2017

Today I would be 15 weeks and three days pregnant. Baby would be the size of a lightbulb. Instead of a baby the size of a lightbulb, I have a four-year-old with a fever. Again. 101. I'm not freaking out – yet – but I'm perplexed. Two days after our trip to Urgent Care, Sam was acting good as new. He was his usual bouncy, happy self. He said his throat didn't hurt anymore.

I kept giving him the antibiotic, because everyone knows you're supposed to finish the meds even when you feel better. But he has a fever again. While he's *still* taking the antibiotic. If he has a new infection, wouldn't the antibiotic he's already on have taken care of it? I'm confused.

Oh shit. Insert hand-smacking-forehead emoji. I

remember an article I read on the internet somewhere about the dangers of frequent hand sanitizer use. The article said it can cause immunity to antibiotics. Is that what's happened? Is he getting immune to antibiotics? Is this how I lose him?

I give him some Tylenol for his fever and get him settled on the couch watching a Disney Christmas cartoon on Netflix. Sam would watch Christmas movies all year if I let him. But I don't want an overuse of holiday movies to make him immune to the magic of Christmas.

But he's not feeling well ... and it *is* July after all. So why not enjoy a little Christmas in July? I could even put up some decorations to surprise Jake when he comes out of his office. *If* he ever comes out of his office. He's been in there a lot lately. He's probably hiding from me and my anxiety. I don't blame him. If I had an office where I could hide from my paranoia, I totally would.

I'm in the kitchen making hot chocolate to go with our theme when I get a phone call. I look at the screen. It's Hope Facetiming me.

Why, people?

Why is Facetime a thing? I'm at home on my day off. It's 10AM and I'm wearing giant sweatpants and a tank top I've had since high school. I have no makeup on, and my hair is in a messy topknot. To tell you the truth, I'd probably look the same way if she called at 2PM, or 7PM. By 10PM I'd probably have showered and changed into a different pair of gigantic sweatpants, but I'd still look like shit. It's my day off and my kid is sick. I'm allowed to look like shit.

I think about not answering it, but Hope hardly ever calls me. I better see what's up.

"Hello," I say as I wave at the screen.

"Hey, doll! What's going on?" She looks perfectly made up. Her blonde hair is tinted with a turquoise Ombre on the ends and is curled into loose Victoria's Secret Angel waves. Her brows are expertly arched. Her skin looks airbrushed, and her nude matte lipstick looks like it could withstand a nuclear bomb. Of course she looks good. I don't think anyone would initiate a Facetime if they didn't.

I sit down at the dining room table and sigh. "Not too much. Sam's got a fever, so I'm trying to decide if I should call the doctor or if I'm just being paranoid. What's going on with you?"

"Are you sitting down?" she asks.

"You can see that I am," I reply.

"You're not gonna believe this."

"What's that?"

She holds a picture in front of the camera. It's the kind of grainy black and white picture I know well, the kind that feels like a punch to the gut every time I see one.

"Twelve weeks!" she says excitedly.

Oh.

I feel pieces crumble from what's left of my heart.

I don't even know what to say. I was not expecting this. Hope never showed any interest in having kids. She doesn't even have a boyfriend. Not that she has to. I'm in no place to judge.

"I. Oh. Wow. Congratulations?"

She's three weeks behind me. I mean, she *would* have been three weeks behind me.

Now she's ahead of me.

Her baby will keep growing. Her belly will keep growing.

And I'll have to watch it.

Her baby will be born, and I'll have to remember mine wasn't.

Every year her baby will have a birthday party, and I will have to remember that my baby would be having a birthday party, too.

Jeez. And I didn't think the world was cruel enough to take my baby. Ha! What a joke. The world *is* cruel, and is not done with me yet.

"Thanks," she says. "It's crazy, right? They say your eggs decline once you hit thirty-five, so I figured it was now or never."

She doesn't know about the baby. I don't know what difference it would have made if she did.

"Um, yeah. Now or never," I agree.

Never. Never. Never.

I don't ask who the father is, because that would be rude. But I don't know what else to say. I think about "accidentally" knocking over my coffee and telling her I have to go.

"I've got an announcement going on Instagram later, but I wanted to make sure I told my closest friends before they saw it on their feed."

Okay. I appreciate that much I guess, but I'm not sure it would have hurt any more seeing it on Instagram. At least on Instagram I wouldn't have to sit here and smile when I feel like crying.

"Well, I'm happy for you!" I say in the perkiest voice I can manage. It's not a lie. I *am* happy for her. It is possible to be happy for someone else, but sad for yourself.

I hang up with Hope. The plastic bottle of Sam's liquid antibiotic is sitting on the table. He's always had pink bubblegum-flavored antibiotics in the past. This one is different. It's white and tastes so bad that Sam requests a chaser after he takes it. I think the fact that my four-year-old knows what the term "chaser" means is a pretty good verification that I'm a shit mom.

I pick up the bottle of meds and absent-mindedly start playing with the flap on the label. There's so much stuff printed on the label that the label was too long for the bottle. The person at the pharmacy had to fold it to get it all to fit. I wiggle the folded part of the label. I flick it with my fingernail.

Wait. What?

I pick it up and bring it closer to my face.

Keep refrigerated.

Fuck me.

Sam comes in to the kitchen looking for his hot chocolate. The hot chocolate I forgot I was making. I stand up and press the minute button on the microwave again.

Sam sits down at the table and waits, his tiny legs dangling under the chair.

"Hey Mommy," he says with a smirk. He looks to be feeling somewhat better. "What's the seal's favorite subject in school?"

"I don't know. What?"

He covers a giggle with his hand before he delivers the punchline. "Art, art, art!"

I laugh. A real laugh, the kind that comes all the way from the belly. This kid. I am so lucky to have him. But do I deserve him?

When the microwave beeps, I mix in a packet of hot cocoa without marshmallows because we don't like the ones that come in the packet. We like the real stuff.

I set the mug of cocoa in front of Sam and hand

him the bag of mini marshmallows. He likes to put them in the mug himself and watch them melt.

He drops a few marshmallows into the mug and watches intently, his eyes pretty much level with the top of the mug.

"Mommy?" he asks without taking his eyes off his marshmallows.

"Yeah, bud?"

"Were you crying because you miss the baby?"

I chew on the inside of my lip and focus on not crying again. I didn't mean for him to see that. Regardless of how I feel inside, I believe my kid should always feel like his parents have their shit together – even when we don't – which is pretty much always.

"Yes," I answer when I'm sure I'm composed. "But I was also crying because you're still sick."

"Remember in *Big Hero 6*," he asks, "when Hiro's brother dies, and he says he still feels his brother in his heart?"

"Yes." Effing Disney. Breaking hearts since 1937.

"I can still feel the baby in my heart, too," Sam says.

I slide off my seat and kneel on the floor so I'm at his level.

I hug him tightly. Then I tell him, "I'm glad the baby has such a special place to live, sweetie."

I get back on my chair as he takes a sip of his cocoa. The melting marshmallow leaves a mustache on his upper lip.

"What about Furricane?" I ask about Laura's dog who was put down about a year ago. "Remember Nana's dog, Furricane?"

"Yeah."

"Can you feel him in your heart, too?"

He looks curious for a few moments while he processes what I'm saying.

"Wait. Furricane DIED?" he asks with wide eyes.

"Yes," I say, surprised that he is surprised. "What did you think happened to him?"

He frowns. "I thought we donated him to a family that needed a dog!"

"Oh, honey, what made you think that?"

"Because that's what you told me!"

He bursts into tears, pushes his chair out from the table, and runs from the room.

I follow him and cuddle him on the couch until he falls asleep.

Did I really tell him that? I don't even remember. Furricane died last summer, right around my 11th or 12th medicated cycle. I was probably a legit basket case at that time, if a basket case is something that can be legit.

An entire year has gone by. I remember back then feeling like I was a wreck and thinking that any day now it would change, and everything would get better. I thought our future was nothing but good things. It's been a year, and instead of getting my head on straight, I feel like it completely fell off somewhere along the way.

Jake finds me slumped over the kitchen table in tears when he finally comes out of his office.

"What the hell is going on?"

The tone of his question makes it sound more like, *what the hell is your problem now? What is wrong with you this time?*

Jake is mad at me.

I just need him to hug me and tell me I'm not a bad

mom, that all moms make silly mistakes like this, that it's not my fault the baby died, that it's not my fault the pharmacy tech folded over the part about the refrigeration, that it could have happened to anyone.

Instead, he acts exasperated, like dealing with me is a pain in the ass.

I'm not sure I blame him.

Dealing with me *is* a pain in the ass. And I don't know how much longer I can do it.

I wonder how much longer can he?

Chapter Twenty-five
* Jake *

July 2017

"What the hell is going on?" I ask impatiently. I'm not mad at her. I don't mean to sound like I'm getting impatient. I know she's trying. I think the problem is that I have so much anger over the loss of our baby and don't know where to put it. I know she doesn't deserve it, but sometimes a little bit comes out in her direction anyway, no matter how hard I try to keep it reeled in.

She lifts her head up from the table, sniffling. "Hope," she manages to choke out, "is."

"Hope is what?"

Not pregnant. Please, please, please not pregnant. No, it's not that. Why would Hope be pregnant?

"Pregnant!"

There's no choking the word out. It comes out loud and clear.

Shit.

Fuck.

Why?

Fuck. Fuck. Fuck.

I kneel on the ground by her chair and wrap my arms around her.

"Shit, baby," I say while she sobs on my shoulder. "I'm sorry."

Damn. Hearing that one of her best friend's is pregnant while her other best friend's daughter is about to give birth, shortly after losing our baby, it must be heart-breaking. I imagine I would feel just as heart-broken to see my own friends having babies right now. I don't understand either why it happens to other people, but not us. It's a bitter pill. If Adam and Emelia announce a pregnancy anytime soon, we are both fucked.

She lifts her head and looks at me with her red, runny eyes. Her eyes are usually blue, but for some reason they always look green when she cries. I used to love that. I used to think it was something that only I knew, because she doesn't cry in front of anyone else. But damn, I'm getting tired of it. I want my blue-eyed baby back.

"And!" she continues. "Look at this!"

She shows me the bottle of liquid antibiotics we've been giving Sam three times a day for Strep. The label has a little flap on it that was folded over. She lifts the flap and I see that on the underside it says to keep the medication in the refrigerator.

"Sam had a fever this morning before he fell

asleep! His Strep is back! And it's my fault for not seeing this!"

I didn't see it either. It's just as much my fault as hers. But shit, it's nothing to cry over. I'm sure we're not the first parents in the history of mankind to not put the meds in the fridge.

"It's fine. We'll call the doctor and explain what happened and she can send over a refill."

"I already did that. We need to pick up the new script in an hour."

"Okay. So, you realized we had a problem, and you did what you needed to do to fix it. You took care of it. That's all you can do. There's no reason to cry all day over it, babe."

Every time I look at her she is either crying, about to cry, trying not to cry, or just finishing crying. And I have no idea what to do about it. I don't know how to make it better. She's falling apart right in front of me and I don't know how to put her back together. I'm supposed to be the one with the answers. I've always been the one with the answers.

Until now.

I stand up and grab my car keys.

"You're leaving?"

"Someone has to get the prescription."

I need space. I need air. I need a break from this ... brokenness.

It's probably a dick move, leaving her crumpled on the table with a sick child.

But what good does it do if I stay?

♥

"Have you tried telling her it's not her fault?" my

mom asks.

"That what's not her fault?" I ask as I cut into my Coney dog. Which part isn't her fault? There's so much on her plate right now I don't know which one to tackle first.

"Any of it," my mom answers. "She probably feels a lot of guilt. Have you told her it wasn't her fault the baby didn't make it?"

"The doctor did."

My mom tilts her head and frowns. "Jake. Don't you think she might need to hear it from you? Regardless of what the doctor said, if she doesn't hear it from you, she might think *you* blame her. Lord knows the girl already blames herself."

I chew my Coney to avoid answering.

The answer is no, I have not told her that it wasn't her fault. And the reason I haven't told her that is because if I'm completely honest about it, I don't know that for sure. Maybe it *is* somewhat her fault. I know she didn't do anything to hurt our baby intentionally. But maybe she drank too much caffeine, or picked up Sam too many times, or worried too much. I hate it that the thoughts are in my head. I wish they would go away, leave me alone, and let me take care of my girlfriend. But I'm just as clueless as she is. The doctor said it wasn't her fault. Whether she believes that, whether I believe that, the only thing we can do is move on. We can't change anything. And blaming her for it is absolutely not the answer. Blame is a tough emotion to feel. The worst part is knowing she feels it, too. I can't take hers away when I have some inside me as well.

"That would be a good place to start, Jake," Mom continues. "Make sure she knows that *you* know it wasn't her fault. And once you get that out of the way, maybe she needs a distraction. You know how much Roxie likes to plan things. Maybe plan a vacation. You guys have always wanted to go to Hawaii. Maybe a honeymoon! Have you thought about getting married? Maybe it's time you proposed. That will definitely distract her."

I almost choke on my french fry.

"What?" she asks innocently.

"Mom, I've proposed to her several times. She said no every time. Plus, she hates weddings."

"You proposed without talking to me first?" She looks hurt. "When?"

"I asked her to marry me shortly after we got pregnant with Sam," I tell her. "Well, I didn't exactly ask her to marry me. I asked her if we were *supposed* to get married."

"How romantic," she says sarcastically.

"Ha. I know. That's what *she* said. And then the second time was the day after we had Sam. But she said it was the wrong time."

"Absolutely the wrong time," she says, nodding in agreement. "I could have told you that."

Maybe I *should* have talked to her first.

"And the third time was when she said she wanted to try for another baby. I said we should probably get married before we have another baby. And she said if it's not broke, don't fix it."

"Jake Nathanial Odom."

Shit.

"*Supposed* to get married? Should *probably* get married? None of those sound like proposals to me. I wish you would have talked to me. Not because you need my permission, but because I am your mother, and you are my only child, and I have been waiting for this day for years."

I shrug. "Sorry, Mom. I didn't realize. But, like you said, none of them were real proposals. It was more like I was feeling out the idea before I put a lot of effort into it, dipping my toe in the water."

"Honey, nobody wants to marry someone who is feeling out the idea! Nobody wants to become a wife by default, or because circumstances pushed you in that direction. Don't you remember how upset you were in fifth grade when you entered that awesome project into the science fair and ended up with an Honorable Mention ribbon?"

I do remember that. I really thought my biodegradable foods experiment was a First-Place contender. I worked so hard on that project. The Honorable Mention ribbon made me feel like a puppy at the shelter who kept getting overlooked.

"Roxie doesn't want an Honorable Mention proposal, Jake. She needs to know she's in First Place."

"Huh," I say, thoughtfully. "Valid point, Mom. Maybe I'm just not sure about us anymore. She was never an honorable mention when we were younger. She was a prize. She was a blessing. She was someone who made me feel lucky every second of the day. But it's different lately."

"It's different, why? Because she's not the perky teenager you fell in love with anymore? Because she's a woman with a family who has been through a loss that she's struggling with? Because she's afraid of losing anything else and maybe she doesn't know how to handle the fear? Because she's all of a sudden not your personal cheerleader? Jake, relationships aren't always fifty-fifty. Sometimes one person only puts in twenty and the other person needs to put in eighty to make up for it. And sometimes that person will only be giving thirty and the other person has to put in seventy. It goes back and forth."

I look up from my fries and smirk at her. "Where'd you see that, Mom? A meme on Facebook?"

She laughs. "Actually, I think I did see that on Facebook. But the point is, Jake, that marriage is for better or for worse. If you don't want to support her at her worst, it's a good thing she said no to your semi-proposals."

I don't know what to say to that. But I do know that the though of giving up on her makes me sick to my stomach.

"I need you to come inside for a minute when you drop me off," she adds.

"Okay. I'm gonna order her a salad to go. I kind of left her collapsed on the table in tears."

"Jake!"

"Mom! She's been in tears for weeks. If I waited for a better moment to leave the house, I'd be a hermit."

I go inside mom's house when I drop her off. She says she'll be right back and heads toward her bedroom in the back of the house.

I stand in the foyer until she returns and hands me a little grey box.

"What's this?"

"Open it," she says.

I open the box to see a wedding band set. The engagement ring is a braided rose gold band with a large round solitaire in the center. It looks vintage, but brand new at the same time. Roxie would die over this ring.

"Is this yours?" I ask. My parents were never married. They had me when they were in high school. I didn't know of my mom ever being engaged to anyone.

"They were grandma's. They were recovered at the accident."

Wow.

"I saved them for you. I thought you would love to be able to share something this special with your future bride. And I know your grandparents would be honored for you to pass them on and keep them in the family. I've just been waiting for you to mention it."

Speechless.

My mom struggled hard bringing me up as a single mom. I can't count how many times I saw shut-off notices in the mailbox, or how many times she walked to work because her car needed repairs and she was saving money to fix it.

Through many years of struggles, she never pawned these rings.

I can't believe it. I've never known my mom was so strong.

I would never say that to her. She would be insulted. But I know how hard it was for her to hold onto these for me all those years, and it means the world to me that she did.

Now that the set is in my care, I need to make sure my mom's sacrifice was worth it. I need to make sure I give these rings to the right person.

My mom has given me a lot to think about. *Is* Roxie my Honorable Mention? Or my First-Place ribbon? Are we still together because we are crazy about each other? Or is it because circumstances pushed us here, and we're too comfortable to move?

I've got Roxie's lunch in the car, and Sam's medicine to pick up, so I can't hang out. I hug my mom and tell her thank you before I head out the door.

I get in the car and Imagine Dragons comes from the speakers. I turn the volume up real loud. I need the noise to distract me from where my thoughts are trying to go.

It doesn't work.

Three blocks from our house I pull over to the curb. I'm not ready to go home. I need to process my feelings before I have to deal with hers again.

I open the box and look at the rings one more time. I feel the pressure building behind my eyes.

When my mom said the rings were my grandma's, I was hit so hard with a truth that I almost fell over. My mom must really, really *love me*. And I didn't know that until today. But the crazy part is that I didn't realize I didn't know it, until I finally knew it. Then it all became clear at once.

There were many times as I was growing up when I felt like a nuisance. I was this kid who she needed to find childcare for. This kid who needed food and clothes and shoes and haircuts. I felt like her life would be better without me. And I felt like she would probably agree to that, though not to my face. I always thought she merely tolerated me, because it was what moms were supposed to do. I figured she loved me *just enough*.

Now, knowing how many times her car broke down, how many times our phone was shut off, how many times they threatened to turn off our electricity and water. And she kept the rings because she knew how happy I would be to have them one day.

I finally realize, a month shy of thirty-six years,

that my mother doesn't love me *just enough*. I realize she loves me more than herself.

Moms are *supposed* to love their babies more than themselves.

All Roxie did was love our baby. She loved our baby like she was supposed to. And now I'm acting annoyed with her for caring so much.

I can't keep being exasperated by her sorrow. I can't keep thinking this would be easier if she would just get over it already. Would I want someone who got over it so quickly to be the mother of my children? Don't I want someone who loves as hard as she does to be the one who loves *me*? And our babies?

I've been an asshole, avoiding her because looking at her was too painful for me. Because seeing her so broken was making *me* feel broken. I wanted to pretend nothing was wrong. There have been moments these last few weeks when I've been angry with her and wondered *Why can't she be stronger?*

But maybe I was wrong about her the whole time, just like I was wrong about my mom. Maybe Roxie is stronger than I think. She's not afraid to show her pain or vulnerability. She's not afraid to tell me when she feels crazy and hopeless or when she feels like a rotten mom.

I *am* afraid to show my pain and vulnerability. Maybe she wouldn't always see me as the strong one if I didn't pretend to be strong all the time.

I don't feel very strong now, crying on the side of the road in front of someone's garbage cans at the curb. But keeping it inside isn't working anymore. Roxie might have the right idea. Feel the pain. Get through it. Eventually we'll come out the other side.

Hopefully together.

Chapter Twenty-six
* Roxie *

July 2017

Today my baby would be the size of a Gameboy. Does this ever go away? I hope one day I can wake up and make it through an entire day without thinking about what could have been.

I wish I had someone to talk to about this. One out of four women, where are you guys? I wish I knew who you were, so I could ask you these questions. How long until I stop remembering how far along I'd be in my pregnancy? How long until I stop thinking of how big the baby would be? Will it magically go away after the due date, when I would no longer be pregnant? Or will I then move on to "my baby would be one-week old today?" I fucking hope not.

♥

After many long months of constant morning sickness, exhaustion, heartburn, and stretchmarks, Pregnancy-Sucks-Kayla finally has her baby.

I'm guessing there were about twenty-seven updates on Facebook throughout the last day, updating her devoted followers about her mucous plug, cervical diameter, water breaking, and exactly how many stitches it took to sew up her vagina after the birth. But luckily, I missed them all because I unfollowed her months ago.

I'm sure Allison also posted updates, though not as graphic. Maybe a picture of the tiny bed with the warmer light on. And probably a picture of Kayla's "pregnancy sucks" scowl from her hospital bed.

But I don't see those either because I unfollowed Allison, too.

Yes, you read that right. I unfollowed my own best friend. And that is why I don't know the baby is coming, and I'm blindsided by a newborn pic texted to my phone.

It's a Girl! (No shit. We've known that for six months.)
Ryleigh Paytyn
8lbs 9oz

Good God. Why? Why all the superfluous fucking Ys? I couldn't even make this shit up.

When I get the text I decide, against my better judgement, to open Facebook and check out Allison's page.

I see the same picture I was texted. It's been liked and loved by 71 others, with 32 congratulations comments. I see other friends of ours congratulating her on the birth of her first grandchild. I see a lot of balloon emojis and exclamation points.

I should type congratulations. It doesn't take a lot of effort. Just press a few buttons and log out. It's not like I have to call her and squeal into the phone. It's not like I have to show up at the hospital with flowers and balloons. Just type in a couple of letters, an exclamation point, and be done with it.

Just do it!

I don't do it.

I put my phone down on the kitchen counter and walk away.

I get in the shower.

I blow dry my hair.

I hate blow-drying my hair. This is how badly I want to avoid Allison.

I sit at my vanity and watch a YouTube tutorial for my new Anastasia eyeshadow palette.

"Hey, Mommy," Sam says from the doorway of my bedroom. "Knock knock."

I turn around in my vanity seat to look at him. "Who's there?"

"Little old lady," he says with a smirk, like he can't wait to start laughing at his own joke.

"Little old lady who?" I ask.

He bursts into laughter. "I didn't know you could yodel, Mommy!"

I burst into laughter, too. I laugh so hard that tears fall down my face and ruin my concealer. Then more tears fall, and I'm not even sure if I'm still laughing or if I've somehow segued into crying.

"Oh! Makeup! Can I put some on you?" he asks.

"Sure," I tell him.

I dry my tears and put the Anastasia palette away because it's too expensive for amateurs. I pull out an e.l.f. palette and hand him a brush. "Go for it, boo."

He gets to work, biting his lip intently as he carefully brushes layers of colors on my eyelids. He colors in my eyebrows with a pencil, then finishes the look with some hot pink blush on each cheek. I look in the mirror and find I don't look too bad. I would never be bold enough to wear hot pink blush on my own. But it's different when it's your kid's artwork. That somehow makes it okay.

"How's it look?" I ask him.

"You look beautiful. Like a princess."

He's such a charmer.

He holds out his hand for me. I take his little hand in mine and stand up from my vanity.

"I am a king," he tells me, "and this is my castle. The king would like to dance with his princess."

He twirls me around my bedroom a few times while I try not to cry again and ruin his masterpiece on my face. When we finish the dance, I pick him up and hold him like a baby. I squeeze him tightly and kiss his pink cheeks, then his nose, then each eyelid. "You're my best."

"You're *my* best, Mommy."

I open Facebook on my phone a few hours later and check out Ryleigh's newborn picture again. It now has 164 likes and 71 comments. I click open the comment box on the photo and my fingertips hover. There is no reason for me not to type congratulations on the photo. Not saying congratulations does nothing. It doesn't bring my baby back. It doesn't make me feel better. I think it even makes me feel worse. I mean, what kind of person have I become?

I spell out congratulations. Period. No exclamation point. No emoji balloons. I'm savage as fuck.

I knock on the door of Jake's office and poke my head in. "Hey."

He turns in his swivel chair to look at me. "Hi, baby. What's up?"

His voice sounds softer than it has the last few weeks. The sound feels good to my ears.

"Sam's napping on the couch. I'm gonna run up to the hospital real quick. Kayla had her baby this morning."

He slants his eyebrows in my direction. "You really want to go to the hospital? Can't you just send a congratulations text? Or send her something from Etsy?"

I shrug. "I've done a lot of thinking about it. Allison doesn't know about our baby, so it will seem strange that she hasn't heard from me. I'll look like a shitty friend and I'll feel like a shitty friend. And I decided that, even if it sucks, I'd rather feel like a good friend for doing something that might be hard on me, than feel like a shitty friend, because I've been feeling shitty enough."

This would be a wonderful time for him to tell me I have no reason to feel shitty, that the way I have dealt with our loss has been perfectly reasonable, and I am not shitty, nor crazy, and that none of it was my fault.

I hear crickets chirping instead.

"Okay."

"I'll just run in, say hello, tell them I don't want to hold the baby because I haven't had my D-TAP booster, and get the hell out of there. Fifteen minutes or less. Then maybe we can have tacos."

"You didn't get your booster? I thought you did."

"Jake. Who are you talking to right now? Of course, I did. But it's the fastest way to get out of a newborn's way."

He laughs out loud for the first time in ... I don't know when. Awhile.

"Okay. Don't let the baby catch ya. Go be a good friend. I'll have the tacos ready when you get home."

"Thanks."

I close the door and head down the hallway.

Then I go back, open the door again slightly, and stick my head in.

"I love you," I whisper.

"I love you, too," he says without turning around. I hope he means it. Because lately, I've been wondering.

"Are you sure?" I ask quietly.

I instantly regret asking the question and wish I could take it back. What if he says no? I shouldn't ask questions I don't want answered.

He does turn around then, only to give me a funny look.

"Never mind," I say quickly, and close the door before he can break my heart.

One might wonder if a heart can be broken if it's already broken. The five seconds between when I asked the question and when I closed the door were long enough to tell me that yes, a heart *can* be broken twice.

I get to the hospital and everything goes exactly as

I planned. I hug Allison. I congratulate the whole family. I use my vaccine excuse to get out of the room as quickly as possible.

I head toward the elevator feeling accomplished. I'm proud of myself for celebrating my friend's good news instead of acting like a whiny. I realize we all have our own lives, and what works for some families might not work for us. Most families have more than one child, but there are still a lot of families who don't. Maybe we are just meant to be one of those families. Maybe there's even a reason for it that I'm not able to see yet.

I feel good. I feel like I'm almost through the other side of this tunnel of hell.

Until the elevator opens.

A little boy steps out in front of his dad. He's wearing a Big Brother shirt and carrying flowers in his arm. He's holding a blue "It's a Boy" balloon in his other hand. The part that hurts the most is the look on his face. He's so proud. So happy.

I wanted to see that look on my baby's face so badly. And I'm beginning to accept that I never will.

It hurts.

Jake has the tacos ready when I get home. The counter is lined with little bowls filled with toppings. As I stand there loading up my shells, I notice the letterboard on the kitchen counter has been changed.

It now says, "Yes. I'm sure I love you."

I turn around where Jake is sitting at the table helping Sam roll up his soft taco shell. When he sees me watching, he smiles and shakes his head a little, as if to say, "What were you thinking, you noodle?"

He gets up from the table and takes a quick step

toward me at the counter. Before I have time to react, he places his hand behind my head, brings my face to his, and kisses me harder than he usually does in front of Sam. Maybe harder than he does ever lately.

When he pulls away, he says quietly, "I'm sorry I made you think you needed to ask that question. I'm even sorrier that I made you think you didn't want to hear the answer."

Chapter Twenty-seven
* Jake *

August 2017

It's almost midnight when I get in from a wedding reception held at Roxie's hotel. I don't usually work this late, but the wedding party had been friends since high school, and I was capturing interesting memories for them. I love that part of my job – knowing that this picture I'm taking is special, and that it might come up on someone's #throwbackthursday post ten years from now and make that person experience the same joy they were feeling in that moment. When I feel those kinds of vibes at an event, I stay later than usual. It's been worth it every time.

Roxie got off work hours ago, right after the dinner

rush cleared. I expect her to be sleeping when I come in.

She isn't.

I walk into the dining room to set down my camera and see the white envelope sitting on the table. Saturdays are the only days Roxie gets the mail first. I've been the one to intercept and destroy the advertisements, baby registry coupons, and formula samples. I wasn't there to intercept this.

A lot of times our dining room table is cluttered with crap – coupons, crayons, books, batteries, phone chargers. The table is empty now, except for this one envelope, this one piece of mail. I know what's inside. I also know why Roxie is still awake.

The doctor told us it would be coming. She'd suggested we bring it in and go over the results together in case we had any questions. Roxie said she would rather we opened it on our own. Between Google, Alexa, and Siri, we can find answers without paying a $30 copay.

She walks into the dining room quietly. "Hi, boyfriend."

I look up at her, feeling uneasy. I don't know what's going to set her off these days. She can be happy one minute, sad the next, and happy again the minute after that. I try to think of it as if I'm paddle-boarding into the surf – don't fight the waves, let the waves carry you out to calmer waters. The calmer waters are out there. Just stay afloat and we'll eventually find them.

"You stayed late," she says, more like an observation and not an accusation.

I give my girl credit for that. The catering manager who took her place, Naomi, is real flirty with me. I don't know if she's like that with all the vendors, or all guys, or if she is trying to get under Roxie's skin for some reason. But Roxie has definitely noticed, has mentioned it, but has never accused me of being interested, or acted like a psycho jealous possessive insecure girlfriend. I'm sure she's thought about it, and worried about it, because, well, I know her. But she hasn't said anything out loud, and I admire her discipline.

She's been a handful these last few months, without a doubt. But I know she still has somewhat of a clear head if I'm coming in late after working with Naomi all night, and she's not flipping out.

I kiss her forehead quickly.

"Mmmm. You smell good. Yeah. They were a great group. It was a fun reception."

She opens the fridge, grabs two beer bottles, and uses the bottom of her T-shirt to help her twist off the caps. Once opened, she hands the second bottle to me.

"Who is going to open it?" she asks.

"Do you want to? Or do you want me to read it first? And tell you if I don't think you should read it?"

She shakes her head. "Don't pretend I'm the only one who cares," she says quietly. "Maybe *I* should read it and let *you* know if it's something *you* want to know. Just because I'm the only one crying doesn't mean you don't care. Right? It just means you're better at not showing it. And if you *were* to feel upset, you probably wouldn't tell me anyway. You feel like you have to be the strong one to keep our shit together, right?"

Nail ... head. Has she been talking to my mom?

I nod.

"I will open it," she says. "I can take one for the team, too."

"Okay."

She takes a drink of her beer, and then sets it down to pick up the envelope. I watch her face while she pulls out the piece of paper, unfolds it, and scans it for the two most important pieces of the letter. She shows nothing on her face. If she feels anything, she makes sure I don't see it.

"Do you want to know the sex?" she asks.

"Do I *want* to know? Honestly? Not really."

"Okay," she says gently. "Then I guess our positions are reversed this time. I won't tell you if you don't want to know. I promise."

"Do I *need* to know?" I ask. "Yes. We're in this together, babe. I kept Sam's sex from you for a few *months*. I can't expect you to carry this around for the rest of our lives. I appreciate that you're willing to. But I won't let you. Go ahead. Give it to me."

Her bottom lip quivers, but she manages to choke it out. "I'm still a boy mom."

He was a boy. Sam had a little brother. We were going to name him Noel. Not No-el like the Christmas song. That was our girl's name. Our boy would be Noel, one syllable, like the character on *Felicity*.

"Noel," she whispers.

"Do you feel better knowing?" I ask.

She pauses for a few beats and then slowly nods. "Yeah. I do. Now we can refer to him by his name. Now we know our hearts are broken because we lost a real baby, a real part of our family. What about you? Do *you* feel better?"

I also nod slowly. "Yes. I like knowing exactly who we are missing."

"Me too. They found a reason for the loss. Do you want to know what it was?"

"As long as it wasn't something that was our fault."

She shakes her head. "No. It was triploidy."

"What is that?"

"The baby, Noel, had three sets of chromosomes instead of two. If he had somehow made it to birth, he never would have made it home. It wasn't our fault."

I pull my phone out of my back pocket and quickly type triploidy into the search bar.

After scanning the Wikipedia article quickly, I see that she is right. It wasn't our fault. Even before Roxie took that pregnancy test, before we heard the heartbeat, our baby never had a chance. We unknowingly picked out names for a baby who was never coming home with us.

Losing the pregnancy before we knew about it would have been the best outcome. Losing the baby after he was born would have been worse. But the Wikipedia article also mentions that carrying a baby with triploidy to full-term is dangerous for the mother. So losing both of them would have been the worst outcome. I think, all things considered, losing him at thirteen weeks was actually a blessing. It's a different perspective to have.

I take the piece of paper from her fingers gently, set it on the table, and hug her tightly. I wrap my arm around her head and pull her close to my chest.

"I'm sorry," I whisper. "I'm so sorry, baby."

All this time, I'd had that little bit of blame for her. And all this time it had never been her fault. No matter how much coffee she drank, how many squats she did at the gym, how many busy nights she'd had at work. Noel was never going to make it.

"I know," she says. She doesn't ask what I'm sorry

for. She knows. Somewhere, some way, she has always known. "It's okay. I blamed me, too."

Chapter Twenty-eight
* Roxie *

August 2017

Today I would be twenty-three weeks pregnant. We would probably be planning a cute gender reveal right about now, to let the world know about our baby boy.

I've finally stopped crying myself to sleep at night. Not because it hurts less, but because I know Jake is growing frustrated. I now go to the garage when I need to cry, usually in the afternoon when Sam is chilling on the couch after lunch, and Jake is in his office. And on a side note, is it weird that I have a crying schedule?

Jake changed the message board on the counter last night. It says, "I love you more than yesterday.

Yesterday you got on my nerves."

It makes me laugh out loud, and that's something I really need this morning.

Sam is starting school tomorrow, *real school*. They call it Young 5s. It's a full-day public preschool for kids who will turn five this year. I try to be excited about it for his sake. But inside I feel like I'm being choked. I can barely breathe.

My phone rings. I lean against the kitchen counter and put it to my ear.

"Hi, Mom."

A regular phone call. My mom doesn't do Facetime. I appreciate it.

"Hi, honey. How are you holding up?"

"Okay." Lie.

"How's my Sweet Pea? Is he excited? Scared? Does he like the backpack I sent?"

"He's a little nervous, I think. But he's excited to be able to play with the other kids. And yes, he loves his new backpack. It's packed and ready to go."

I lean against the counter and take a sip of my Almond Joy coffee.

"Okay, good. Tell him I wish I could be there. I'll call tomorrow so I can send him off with a phone kiss. Hey, did you see Christina is having a boy?"

I wince. "No, Mom. I don't see Christina's posts."

"Why not?"

"I unfollowed her when she announced her pregnancy."

Christina was a little girl who lived next door to us when I was growing up. I used to babysit her. She had her first child *after* we started trying for our *second*. Now she's having a second baby in less time than it's taken us to have, well, zero.

"Why'd you do that?" she asks.

I inspect my silly yellow school bus manicure. Fake it til ya make it.

"I unfollow pregnant people, Mom. It's nothing personal. I don't need to be reminded of what I can't have every time I look at my phone."

"Roxie..."

"At least I typed congratulations first. At least I did that."

"Honey, I don't think this is normal."

"How many babies did you lose, Mom?"

"None. I was lucky."

"Exactly. So how do you know what normal is?"

"I just don't think after all this time, you should still be-"

I open the fridge and take out the eggs and bacon. "All this time?" I repeat. "Mom, it's been two months. I am still supposed to be pregnant. Don't expect me to get over this while I'm still supposed to be pregnant. Maybe after the due date, but not before that. It's not fair for you to expect that."

"I just think maybe you should talk to someone, a counselor, or someone who has been through it. It's not the end of the world. You can still have another baby someday. It just wasn't the right time for this one."

I feel like I'm going to choke, like my throat is actually closing on me. My own mother! I expect this kind of cruelty from random people. But my own mother?

It wasn't the right time for our baby? Homeless people have babies. Prisoners have babies. Addicts have babies. People have babies after they've lost their jobs, after they've lost their spouses, after they've found out they were terminally ill. There are so, so many couples who have babies at the wrong time, at the worst possible times. Their babies live! But it just wasn't the right time for ours. It's such a simple answer. Why didn't I think of that a long time ago?

I leave the phone on the counter, leave the burner on for the bacon, and sit down on the kitchen floor. I don't even know if I hit the end button on the phone first.

I lean back against the cupboard and cry so hard I choke and sputter and hiccup and gasp for breath. All the crying I've done the past two months seems to cumulate for some kind of epic grand finale of heartbreak. At least I hope it's the finale. Maybe I need to get it out before I can begin to get over it.

Jake comes in a moment later. I don't look at him, and he doesn't say anything. I see his feet next to me in front of the stove. I hear him tear open the bacon and start cracking eggs.

When he's finished with breakfast, he takes the food outside the French doors to the patio. When he comes back in the house, he goes upstairs to get Sam. But he takes Sam outside through the front door instead of the back, I'm assuming so they won't have to step over my weaknesses on the kitchen floor.

After about forty minutes of nonstop tears, I feel some kind of peace come over me, like a blanket wrapping me in comfort. My gasps turn to deep, slow breaths. My cries turn to quiet whimpers.

When I finally get up, I stop in the bathroom to wash my face, make myself another cup of coffee, and head outside. Jake is sitting at the patio table with his laptop. Sam is playing on his swing set.

I sit down.

"Good morning," he says, like it's the first he's

seen me today.

"Morning," I say quietly, somewhat embarrassed. "Did you put sunblock on him?"

"I've done this a few times before," he says lightly, with a smile.

"Thank you," I say.

He sticks his fist toward me and I bump it with my own.

"I got you," he says. "Always."

Chapter Twenty-nine
* Jake *

September 2017

"You know," I say to Sam as we walk home from school hand in hand, "your mom and I, we used to walk home from school together when we were little."

"Really? When you were as little as me?"

"No. Not as little as you. Your Uncle Adam and I were probably like eight or nine before our parents let us all walk home from school alone."

"Oh," he says thoughtfully. "Is that how old I need to be to walk home alone? Eight or nine?"

"Oh, I don't know, buddy. I haven't thought that far ahead yet. Maybe."

"How old do I have to be to drive a car?"

"Sixteen."

"And how old do I have to be to drink margaritas?"

My four-year-old knows what margaritas are. That might mean he has some shit parents. Or it might just mean his dad is a bartender.

"You have to be twenty-one to drink margaritas. But you only have to be eighteen to make them. That means I can teach you how to make some margaritas in fourteen years."

"And what about watching *Sausage Party* on Netflix? How old until I can watch that?"

I can't help but laugh. "Ummm ... seventy-five?"

"What? I have to wait until I'm seventy-five before I can watch *Sausage Party*? I might be dead by then! What about *Friday the 13th*? When can I watch that?" He then adds his own music to the conversation by huffing and puffing the theme sounds from the *Friday the 13th* series. "He he he, huh huh huh."

"Sounds to me like you've already seen it. Where'd you hear those creepy sounds?"

"YouTube," he answers matter-of-factly.

Figures.

"Hey, buddy," I say, changing the subject. "I have an idea. You wanna cut through this cemetery today? I heard there's a lot of Poke Stops in there."

"You wanna go through a cemetery? Where the dead people are planted?"

When Pokemon Go became popular and teenagers started running through cemeteries, everyone was in an uproar about our lack of respect for the dead. But I've given it some thought, and I feel like, as long as we are respectful and quiet, there isn't anything wrong with walking along the path. Hey, maybe the spirits will get a kick out of a four-year-old trying to catch some Pokemon.

"Yeah. There's like twelve Poke Stops in there. All we have to do is follow the path and go out the other side."

He shrugs, and we enter the old cemetery through the wrought-iron gate. I open the Pokemon Go app on my phone and the map is filled with Poke Stops, just like I'd heard it would be.

We walk along the path spinning the stops and collecting our balls as we go.

This is a great cemetery, an older one – the kind filled with giant statues and headstones of granite, concrete, marble. There's plenty to look at while we walk from stop to stop.

Sam keeps asking me, "How old was that person when they died, Daddy?"

Most of them were older, and everything is going well until he asks me why there is a statue of a baby angel over there.

Well, shit.

"Is that where the babies are, Daddy?"

"Um, yes, I think so."

"Oh."

He is quiet for a moment. We both are as we look at the baby area, The Angel Memorial Garden, with all of the sculptures of angels, babies, and teddy bears.

"Let's go visit them, Daddy," he says, taking my hand.

"Okay," I say, because I can't really think of a legit reason not to.

We walk from baby grave to baby grave. At each one I read their name and tell Sam how old they were. Most were under a year old. Some of them were only days old, and a few passed away the day they were born.

"This is Lillian Harper," I tell Sam as we stand at a headstone with a heart carved into the concrete. There is a pretty bouquet of fresh flowers sitting on the stone. I squat down to get a better look at the dates. The grave is old, and the script is fading. June 6, 1967 – June 9, 1967.

Baby Lillian lived for three days.

Fifty years ago.

And there are fresh flowers on her grave.

Somebody has been missing this baby for fifty years. Somebody is still thinking of this baby after *fifty years*. And I'm pretty sure I know who that person is – her mommy.

Again, I realize how wrong I have been about Rox.

I can't believe I ever thought, for a single second, that she was my honorable mention ribbon. No. She's not. She's had a hard time for a few months. But she's still the girl I fell in love with when I was twenty-three, the girl who isn't afraid to be the only one dancing at a concert, the girl who is likely to burst into showtunes at any moment, who sometimes snorts when she laughs, who swears more at baseball games than the coaches, and who knows about eighty different uses for balsamic reduction. She's still *that girl*. My girl. My first place.

Chapter Thirty
* Roxie *

September 26, 2017

    Remember back on Sam's birthday when I described parenting as living in a virtual comic strip – the disasters follow me from little square to little square while others point at me and laugh over their morning coffee?
    I really should have waited until Sam started school before I made such a claim. This proclamation of mine has proven true every day since. Getting him ready for school in the morning, sending a healthy snack and packing a lunch, sending in money for various fundraisers, school mascot gear, school pictures, RSVPing to birthday parties and playdates,

permission slips for field trips, trying to remember which "day" it is at school because it seems like no day is ever just a normal day, making sure he has tennis shoes on gym days, old clothes on art days, his library book on library days ... getting him to school is practically a third job! Seriously! Why does no one ever mention this?

And why is no day ever just a normal day? We've had blue day, red day, hat day, mismatch day, rainbow day, superhero day, 80s day.

Today is favorite book character day.

Thank God for Amazon Prime. I ordered a Pete the Cat T-shirt Friday when they sent the "schedule" home, and it was delivered yesterday afternoon, just in time.

We walk over to the school and I'm feeling pretty good. Even though this school thing is a lot of work and a lot to remember, I feel like I'm doing it and doing it and doing it well. Just like L.L.

Sam still lets me hold his hand on the way there. He hasn't reached that, "get away from me, Mom" stage yet. He still comes home every day to snuggle with me and tell me about school. Even though I was dreading the silence around the house, I admit it has been nice to have some time to do chores, grocery shop, get my nails done, without worrying about keeping Sam occupied.

Yep. Everything is just fine.

But, as seems to be the case more often than not, the next meltdown, whether mine or Sam's, is only one little square away.

Today, as seems to be the case more often than not, the meltdown is mine.

I feel proud of Sam's T-shirt until I get to school

and see no one else is in T-shirts. They're in elaborate costumes. It looks like an Etsy page exploded in the schoolyard. Putting a T-shirt over your kid's head and calling it a day is not enough for these parents. The one that sends me off the edge is little Dayja dressed as Cindy Lou Who from *The Grinch Who Stole Christmas*. She's not only wearing the costume, but someone, probably her Better Mom, has spent an awful lot of time getting her braids to stick out half a foot from her head on each side, and over a foot high on top. And makeup on her face, too. For crying out loud, how early did they get up?

Sam's T-shirt can't compete with this. I mean, not that it's a competition. At least, I wasn't *aware* that it was. Apparently, I was the only one unaware. Because who would put in this much intricate work and details if it wasn't?

My first thought is to take Sam's hand and walk in the other direction. I can't send him to school feeling inferior. What if he gets teased? What if they think his mom doesn't love him enough to get him a costume?

But just because I like to run away from my problems doesn't mean I need to teach Sam to do the same. I need to teach him to do the opposite.

I kiss him goodbye and send him into the school. He's oblivious that he's one of the only kids not in costume. I pray it stays that way.

Jake is awake when I walk in the door. He's at the kitchen counter making coffee in his gym shorts with no shirt on. Damn. He is hot. Another bonus about Sam being in school is morning sex. Lots of it.

I put my arms around his waist from behind and kiss the back of his shoulder because that's as tall, I mean, as *short* as I am.

"Morning, boyfriend."

He turns around, still inside my arms. "Good morning, baby mama." Then he narrows his eyes at me. "Why do you look so wounded?"

I let go of him, sit down at the table, and lazily rest the side of my face in my hand. "I feel like I'm not a very good mom today."

He sets a coffee on the table in front of me. "Oh shit. What now?" He doesn't sound annoyed. More like amused.

"You know today is Favorite Book Character Day at school, right? I ordered him a T-shirt on Amazon thinking that would cover it. But these kids are all dressed up in costumes! Like real costumes with clothes, hair, makeup. I feel like I failed him today. Should I go to Party City and get him a costume real quick? Or should I go get him and take him out of school today?"

He leans against the counter. "No. And no. And I'm proud of you for not already doing either of those things." He picks up my coffee mug and pours it into a portable cup with a lid. "We're taking our coffees to go."

"Where are we going?" I ask.

"It's a surprise."

"Oh. Do I have time to shower first?"

"Nope."

He grabs a T-shirt out of the basket of clean laundry that I folded and never put away. Story of my life.

Once he has a shirt on, he sticks his feet in his Nike slides, grabs the keys and both coffees, and heads to the door. "Come on, baby doll. We have an anniversary to celebrate."

Good Things Come

Fuck. Again? I forgot one of our anniversaries AGAIN?

I follow him out to his truck, wishing I'd had time for a shower. Or at least some dry shampoo and mascara.

I climb in, and he says, "Alexa, please play playlist Jake and Roxie."

"We have our own playlist? By the way, I love how polite you are to someone who isn't a real person."

"Shhh ... we've always had a playlist."

The first song is "Pon de Replay" by Rihanna.

"You know I get a hard-on every time I hear this song?" he asks as he backs out of the driveway. "It reminds me of our summer, and the way just a tiny touch or a secret smile at work made me crazy."

"It reminds *me* of our first night together, and how you almost ruined it by asking why I wanted to come over."

He looks at me and smiles, still so fucking sexy. "I needed confirmation," he explains. "I'd spent weeks wondering how to get you in my bed, and the last thing I expected was for *you* to be the initiator. I was like, is this for real? Is this really happening tonight? Am I really this lucky?"

I reach over to touch his hand on the gear shift. Then I run my finger over the tattoos on his forearm. "That's basically what I still think every day when I come home to you," I tell him.

"Same," he says.

The next song is Justin Timberlake's "Still on My Brain."

"This song is sad," I complain.

"Our story wasn't always happy," he explains. "This is the way I felt those seven years without you."

"Let's skip this one. I don't like thinking about

being without you. How do I get Alexa to fast forward?"

"You want to skip a JT song?"

"Shhh ... don't tell anyone. It would totally ruin my reputation."

"Your secrets are safe with me."

"The One That Got Away" by Katy Perry is next.

"This is definitely the summer of 2012," I say.

Then comes "Best Day of my Life" by American Authors. That song was released just before Sam was born. We used to sing it together to get Sam to sleep.

He drives past the house I grew up in, which is where Adam and Emelia currently live. I'm glad they bought it from my parents and kept it in the family. That's the living room where I found Jake crying in 1994. The porch we laughed on together after our first kiss in 1999. That's the kitchen island we had sex on in 2005. The bedroom door he pushed me up against in 2012. The same garage where he almost got busted with his head up my skirt when my parents pulled into the driveway. And most importantly, the kitchen we were standing in when he told me he loved me for the first time. People say nostalgia is important, and that we should put pictures up to remind us of where we came from. We do have a ton of pictures on our walls. But nothing reminds me of where we came from more than that house.

The next song on his playlist is "For the First Time" by The Script.

"I picked this one," he says, "because it's a song about a couple reconnecting when they thought they were falling apart. I feel like we do this several times a week."

"Is that okay?" I ask.

"Is what okay?"

"That we fall apart and reconnect several times a week? I mean, is that normal? Is that how it's supposed to be?"

"I don't know how things are supposed to be, babe. I only know how things are. And that's just us. It's what we do."

I sometimes think the way Jake and I fall apart is a sign of weakness in our relationship. But maybe I need a different perspective. Maybe our ability to put the pieces back together time and time again is a sign of our strength.

"Does it bother you?" I ask him.

"No. It means I get to fall in love with you over and over again. And I end up loving you more each time."

I feel my heart move then. Not just a regular heartbeat. It feels like it's growing, like the missing pieces Noel took with him are growing back, like the cracks are healing. I know that sounds super dramatic, even for me, but that's the only way I know how to describe it.

I've been hurting for so long. I felt alone, like no one understood, like I was exaggerating, like I was crazy. All I needed, all this time, was for him to love me, to let me be sad, to tell me it was okay. And he didn't.

But now, something has changed in him. He seems to be loving me again. And I can feel my broken pieces being put back together.

I wish it hadn't taken him so long. I wish I hadn't suffered by myself for so long. But I won't be resentful toward him for it. We both learned a little from these past few months. And the scar tissue that heals us, it also makes us stronger. At least, that's what I read on Instagram.

He turns down a residential street in the same neighborhood where we grew up. To my surprise, he pulls over to the curb, and puts the truck into park.

"True" by Ryan Cabrera begins to play. It was the last song we danced to before I left for school that summer. You'd think hearing it would make me feel a little sad, because that was the end of us for such a long time. But it makes me remember instead, how great it was to be loved. And how great it is to still be loved. The summer of 2005. That was twelve years ago. I still feel those butterflies. I still get goosebumps when he touches me. I still get dizzy when he kisses me. It's all real. It's all "True."

He unbuckles his seat belt and turns to his right to face me.

"Happy Anniversary," he says with a smirk.

I take a better look around and realize where we are. I laugh. "Happy Anniversary. You're a much better kisser now."

"Do you think maybe you'll want to kiss me for the rest of your life?"

"There's no maybe. I *will*. I *do*."

"I realized that all the other times I asked you to marry me, I was forgetting something pretty important."

I turn to look at him. *Wait. Is this another proposal?* But before I can ask him, I see what he's holding between his thumb and finger. It's a ring. It's so beautiful I feel like my breath gets caught in my throat, and I can't even open my mouth to say something sarcastic.

The rose gold band is braided and wraps around

the solitaire. The way the sun hits the diamond sends little rainbows across the inside of the truck. Rainbows on the seats, on the dash, on the steering wheel.

Have you ever heard someone use the term Rainbow Baby? It's a baby born after the loss of a previous baby. It's the rainbow that comes after the storm.

I never gave much thought to rainbow babies, because I knew I wasn't going to have one. But the sun coming in the truck at just the right angles to sprinkle us with rainbows, in the same spot Jake kissed me for the first time eighteen years earlier, it feels not like a coincidence – it feels like an answer. *This* is the rainbow after the storm. *We* are the rainbow.

"So…" he says, "do you want it, or not?"

I laugh and wipe tears from my eyes. "You're so fucking romantic."

He laughs, too, but I feel bad for saying it. He planned all of this. The playlist. The ring. The spot. On this day. He told me he falls in love with me over and over again. He's the perfect mix of sweet and sexy, funny and serious. And he's mine.

"I can't believe you would still want to marry me after these last few months. I've been so hard to put up with. I've been weak and whiny and dramatic. And you asked me to marry you on today of all days? When I haven't showered, my hair's a wreck, and I feel like a shit mom for sending our kid to school without a costume on book character day?"

"You *have* been difficult these last few months. That's true. You know what else is difficult for a few months every year? Winter. The cold. The snow. The shoveling. The defrosting. I hate that shit so much. But what happens a few months later? Spring, then summer, then fall. They're all amazing. They're so great that they make us forget how much it sucks to have our nostrils freeze together. And we would never, *ever* cancel summer because winter sucks, right?"

I sniffle and shake my head.

"Rox, do you remember when I asked you to marry me the day after Sam was born? And you said you didn't know what you did to deserve me?"

"Yes. I remember."

"Do you remember what I told you? That when people looked at me, they only saw me for everything I wasn't? And you were the one who always saw me for what I was?"

I nod.

"It's kind of the same thing now, but we've switched places. When you look at yourself, you only see everything you're not. Not thin enough. Not crafty enough. Not calm enough. Not organized enough. Baby, when I look at you, all I see is everything you are. You're brave, spontaneous, adventurous, and beautiful. Your freckles still make me dizzy after thirty years. You taught Sam to tie his shoes, ride his bike, and tell great jokes. With the exception of the last few months, you spend most of your days smiling, laughing, and making other people smile and laugh. And yes, I asked you to marry me right now, unshowered and post-mom-meltdown, because I want you to know I love you at your best *and* at your worst. Would you want to marry someone who didn't?"

I shake my head again.

"Are you gonna take this ring, or not?" he asks again.

I reach out my hand to take it from him, but he pulls it back, just out of my reach.

"What I mean to say is, are you ready to wear this ring? To be mine forever? To make that promise?"

I nod. "I am. Finally," I add.

He takes my left hand and slides the pink ring on my finger.

I flitter my hand around to watch it glisten and wish I'd had my nails done. "It fits perfectly," I say.

He shrugs. "I had it sized."

"I can't believe you picked out something so unique. I couldn't have picked a better ring myself."

"I hope you're not disappointed, but I didn't pick it out myself."

I peel my eyes away from the gorgeous ring to glance up at him and raise my eyebrows. "No? Who did?"

"My grandpa, actually. He picked this out for my grandma like sixty years ago."

If the sight of the ring had my words caught in my throat, hearing who it used to belong to leaves me breathless. I had no idea his grandma's wedding rings still existed. If I had known, I would have considered myself unworthy of them. I feel unworthy now.

And he knows it.

"And before you tell me you don't deserve it, I want you to know that I didn't decide to give you this ring on a whim. I've had it since July. I thought long and hard about it. And these last few months, you've given me a lot of long, hard things to think about. But in the end, it was still you, baby. I still choose you. I'm not *stuck* with you. I'm not *settling* for you. I'm *choosing* you. To wear this ring. To have the same last name as the rest of the family. To be mine. Forever. Because there isn't any other way I'd want it."

When I'm finally able to get words out, all I can

think to say is, "This is the part where I ask myself, 'Is this for real? Is this really happening? Am I really this lucky?'"

Chapter Thirty-one

October 2017

I place the toy in the paper gift bag, place the tissue paper on top of the toy, and step back to see how perfectly put-together the gift looks.

It looks like I set the tissue paper on top of the gift and walked away.

Damn.

How do other moms know how to do the tissue paper?

I bet there's a YouTube tutorial.

I pick up my phone and start furiously swiping into the search engine.

"Mommy! You said we were leaving at 2:45 and it's 2:48!"

"Okay, buddy. We're leaving."

I crinkle the tissue paper a little to see if it looks more natural that way. Nope. Now it looks like I crinkled the paper. Dammit.

I shrug my shoulders and grab the bag by the handles. The birthday boy is turning five. I guarantee he doesn't care about the tissue paper. And I'm not going to worry about what the other moms think. Maybe my gift presentation needs work, but my braised short ribs can bring a man to his knees.

We arrive at the party venue right at the 3:15 start time (so weird), and Sam quickly takes off his shoes and joins his classmates on the inflatables. We are new to this birthday party stuff, so I'm still not sure if I'm supposed to drop Sam off and leave, or stay and help supervise. Leaving him there alone doesn't seem right to me yet, and I'm glad there are other parents who have stayed as well. I sit down on a bench and pull a paperback out of my bag so I don't look too helicopter-ish.

When the kids are done playing, everyone is escorted into a room where the food is served. There are twenty little plates set at the long table with a slice of pizza on each. The kids sit down and dig in while the party host is still pouring drinks into paper Paw Patrol cups. Wait. Coke?

Sam isn't allowed to have pop. I figured that was a pretty normal rule for a four-year-old. Now I'm stuck with a dilemma. Do I stand up and take the drink from him, making a scene, embarrassing us both, and probably making whoever brought the Coke feel like crap? Do I let him drink it? Am I wrong if I don't let him drink it? Am I wrong if I do?

I don't have to fret about it for long. As the teenager working the room begins to pour Sam's Coke,

Sam says, loud and proud, "I don't drink pop. Can I please have water?"

I hide my tears behind my book.

I remember when I was a child, I read this quote – "Stand up for what you believe in, even if it means you're standing alone." I've never been a person to do that. I think I've been pretty open about the fact that I am insecure at times and often think too much of what others think of me. And the fact that my four-year-old son had the courage to speak up in a room full of his friends, that he wasn't afraid of being different, or being noticed, it's an amazing feeling. He stood up, even though he was standing alone. One of my proudest moments.

I'm not good with tissue paper, and I suck at self-esteem. But I've done something right with my kid.

"You see, babe?" Jake says when I tell him the story later. "You always thought we needed a second kid to get things right. But it's possible we got it right the first try."

"Ha," I reply while I load the dishwasher. "I wouldn't go that far. There were definitely mistakes made. Think of all the money we spent on expensive diapers and wipes when we could have been buying Amazon brand."

"And the nursery we decorated that he probably spent four nights in total."

"Ugh. All those stuffed animals and blankets babies aren't even allowed to have."

I finish loading the dishes, close the door to the dishwasher, and turn it on.

When Jake speaks again, I can hear in his voice that something is wrong. "Baby?" he says, carefully.

"Yeah?"

He holds his phone up so that the screen faces me. "Hope just posted funeral arrangements for her sister."

♥

Hope's sister was twenty-six. Nobody in the family had any idea she'd been using heroin. I spend the evening on her Instagram. She looks healthy and vibrant in her photos – a cute, happy blonde who just graduated magna cum laude in the spring with a BFA in Dance – not at all the way we see addicts portrayed on TV.

The picture that chokes me up the most is the one of Hope's sister happily holding up a tiny onesie that says, "My Aunt Becky loves me."

I don't have a sister. But I do have a brother. And a child. And I can't imagine having a child who never knew my brother, or a brother who never knew my child. How can Hope have a baby, the most important person in her life, who will never know the other most important person in her life?

There's nothing like a tragic, senseless death to knock us on our asses and really show us what it means to be grateful.

I get an early one-day flight to LaGuardia and take a Lyft straight to the funeral home. She doesn't notice me at first when I enter the room, so I have a chance to take her in for a moment while she greets family members near the casket.

Her short-sleeve, empire-waisted black maxi dress shows off the cutest, most perfect baby bump I've ever seen. And that makes me so sad for her, for that baby who will never know their aunt, for her parents who will never see their daughter be an aunt. There are so many rotten, horrible, unthinkably sad things about this tragedy. Yet somehow, she looks classy and remarkably composed.

It's hard to believe I spent the last few weeks avoiding her phone calls because I didn't want to hear about the baby, unfollowing her on Facebook so I wouldn't have to see her bump. I thought her pregnancy was going to be too difficult for me. As if seeing my friend's little sister in a casket isn't as difficult as it gets! As if she wouldn't trade my grief for hers in a second! What a fool I am. What a fool I *have been*. For years. So much time I wasted. So many moments with my family that went unappreciated because I was too busy thinking of everything I didn't have, instead of being thankful for what I did have. I am probably, legitimately one of the worst people on this planet.

I wish it didn't take death for me to learn the lesson I was supposed to have learned from this journey. But I know, standing there in that funeral home, that I won't waste another second of my life wishing for a baby.

Chapter Thirty-two

November 27, 2017

Twenty-seven. That's how many days I was able to hold Jake off on decorating for Christmas. He tried throwing that shit up as soon as the Halloween decorations came down. In the past, I've let him win that battle. This year it was a battle I chose.

I'm okay. Really. I'm much better than I was over the summer. Jake and I are in a great place. It feels like we're sharing the same breath. Sam is loving school and learning so much. It's all good.

But Noel was supposed to be here right before Christmas. I understand the day is going to come, whether we decorate for it or not. But I appreciated a few extra weeks of not having to sit inside a perpetual snow globe while watching my trashy reality shows on

MTV.

"It's the Monday after Thanksgiving, boo," he reminds me when we wake up in the morning.

"I know what day it is, babe," I tell him as I floss my teeth at the sink in our bathroom.

"We're still going to Bronner's right?"

I look at him in the mirror, but I don't say anything.

He doesn't wait for me to answer before he continues, "We always go to Bronner's today. It's our tradition – a tradition the three of us created together. And I think it's important that we keep the traditions we've created as a family. We need to have moments and events that are consistent, regardless of what else is happening in our lives. They keep us grounded. They bring us comfort. We always dye eggs at Easter. We always carve pumpkins at Halloween. And we always go to Bronner's to pick out a new ornament the Monday after Thanksgiving."

I toss the floss into the trash and sigh. He's clearly put some thought into this speech of his, and I can't argue with him about it. He's right. We need consistency. We need traditions. With so many things in life being out of our control, we need those moments we can depend on.

I shrug my shoulders. "Okay. Let's go."

"What?" He looks surprised. "I didn't even need to bribe you with the present I got you?"

"You got me a present?"

"Well, yeah, but it doesn't look like it's going to be necessary. I can return it."

I only need to give him a look before he takes my hand and pulls me back into our bedroom. He goes into the closet for a second and returns with a red gift bag, tissue paper perfectly presented.

"Although I do feel we need to keep traditions," he says, "that doesn't mean we can't have something new to make this year a little different. And, also, I thought maybe it would cheer you up a little."

I take the gift bag and pull out a grey oversized off-the-shoulder sweatshirt. The front says, "NSYNC Christmas album on repeat."

He's been way too good to me this year. Luckily, he's giving me the rest of our lives to make it up to him.

"Thank you, baby," I say sincerely. "I love it."

Traditions are important, yes. But he is right. New things are important, too. This is a new shirt. It's not a shirt I wore when I was pregnant or even *looked* at when I was pregnant. It has nothing at all to do with being pregnant, wanting to be pregnant, or waiting to be pregnant. And as silly and dramatic as some may see this, I have been known to collapse in grief just by seeing a shirt I wore when I was pregnant, cooking a meal I made when I was pregnant, hearing a song I listened to when I was pregnant. I can't even explain it. There is so much of my life that exists outside of those few months, outside of Noel. I don't think to myself, *I listened to this song 75,000 times in the last five years.* No. I only think, *I listened to this song when my baby was still alive.* It's like I have tunnel vision. If only I could find a new tunnel.

It's easy for me to find an ornament at Bronner's this year. I get a chef's hat that says "Bon Appetit" on it, because this was a year I finally spent doing something I love for a living.

Jake picks one out that says "She said yes!" Then

he has the personalization artist write "(finally)" underneath it.

But Sam has a hard time finding the right one. We look at trucks of all kinds, Transformers, aliens, sharks, ships ... all his favorite things. And he keeps shaking his head.

It isn't until we're walking by the nativity section when he finds one. An ornament of little baby Jesus in his cradle.

"This is the one I want," Sam says. "I want a baby ornament."

Oh dear. A baby? I say a silent plea that this isn't another request for a baby brother.

"A baby?" Jake asks. "Why do you want a baby ornament, bud?"

Sam looks at me and slays me right there in the store. "I wanna give it to Mommy so she won't be sad anymore."

Wow. I would have rather he asked for a brother.

Thank baby Jesus that Jake steps in to diffuse the situation so I don't have to.

"Mommy already has a baby, bud. She has you. You're her baby. And my baby. Even though you aren't a baby anymore, you're still our baby. And that's all Mommy and Daddy need. Just you."

"Okay," he says, not looking like he completely believes him. "If you promise me Mommy is happy already, I'll get the Optimus Prime."

When did my kid get so skeptical? And wise?

I kneel in front of him. "Mommy is happy. I promise. You know what I think we need?" I ask them both. "I think we need a new family of three."

We already have the elves, but I was just talking about how we need new things for our new life, the one where there are no more babies coming.

I lead us over to the dreaded family section of the store and find that it doesn't bother me as much as I thought it would. After some discussion, we decide on a family of peas. Three peas in a pod.

Once Sam picks out a real ornament, an Optimus Prime, and we have our names added to the peas, we head home to (finally) do our decorating.

I put the NSYNC Christmas album on and make us chili and hot chocolate while Sam and Jake put on their silly Santa hats and dig into the Christmas box. When the tree is decorated, I watch my future husband-slash-baby daddy-slash-love of my life pick up our son and hold him up to place the star on top. It's as if the moment happens in slow motion. And I remember the goofy Jake I knew as a kid, the trouble-maker I knew as a teenager, the horny 23-year-old who kissed me like no one else ever had, the intense 31-year-old who fucked me like no one else ever had, the 32-year-old dad who had no idea what he was doing, but was confident that we would figure it out, and the 36-year-old devoted daddy who seems to have everything figured out and still wants to marry me even though I'm sometimes a shitshow.

I see the huge smiles on their faces as they place that star on top, and I know that I have everything I need in this Game of Life. Just Jake and me, cruising across the board in our plastic car with that little baby blue peg in the backseat. Not only do I have everything I need, but my life is amazing. I'm proud of this family, of where we came from, and where we're going. There were delicate times hen I feared it might be over. But the sun shines the brightest after the darkest clouds. The three of us, we shine bright.

I said earlier I needed a new tunnel. In that moment, I know exactly the tunnel I want to fall down.

Chapter Thirty-three
* Jake *

December 22, 2017

I open my eyes to an empty bed. She's already awake, getting Sam ready for his last day of school before winter break. I'm apprehensive as I swing my feet to the hardwood floor. I have no idea what kind of mess I'm going to find when I leave the bedroom.

Today is the day we've been dreading for six months.

Today is Noel's due date.

I'm surprised when I get to the kitchen and find that it isn't an emotional disaster after all. She's not on the floor. Nothing is burning on the stove. Everything appears to be fine.

Christmas music plays from her phone on the counter – "Dance of the Sugar Plum Fairy." My future wife happily bobs her head to the music while she stands at the stove, Sam standing on a stool next to her. She watches as Sam gently shakes a few chocolate chips into a pot of oats and then stirs the pot with a wooden spoon. He gets excited watching them melt and she turns her head toward him and smiles. It's not a fake smile. It's real. She probably doesn't know it, but for the last few weeks she's been radiating some kind of joy from deep within her that I haven't seen in a long time.

"Morning, boyfriend," she says when she sees me.

"Morning, babies," I reply as I grab a coffee mug from the mug tree and pour myself a cup.

I don't know what to say next. Should I mention what today is? If she's not thinking about it, then I don't want to bring it up and remind her and ruin the vibe. But that kind of thinking is absurd. She *knows* what today is. She *remembers*. Nobody forgets their baby died. I bet twenty years from now she'll still think of Noel on this day. We both will.

If I don't mention it, she might think *I* forgot, that *I* don't care. And I don't want her to think that. Again.

She looks so happy right now. I don't want to ruin it.

I stand behind them at the stove. I kiss the top of Sam's head. Then I kiss the back of her neck.

"You look extra beautiful today," I tell her, honestly. "I kinda wish you didn't have to go to work this morning."

"How come?" she asks innocently.

I give her a smirk and a shrug.

She laughs. "It doesn't matter. You have to work

today, too."

"Not for hours."

She seems so ... normal. *This* seems normal.

"You're okay that I took this wedding tonight, right?" I ask. I knew when I took the job that it was on *this day*, and I thought about turning it down and making sure I was home to take care of her if she needed me. But January and February are slow months for this business and I can't really afford to turn down work if I don't need to.

"Yeah, of course, babe. It's your job."

I grab some bowls from the cupboard and set the table.

"I know. I just wanted to make sure you were okay with me not being home tonight."

She brings the pot over to the table and starts spooning the oatmeal into the bowls. "I'm okay. I promise."

She really does sound like she's okay.

"You know if anything changes, you can call me. I'll only be fifteen minutes away if you need me."

She puts a hand on my shoulder and leans over and kisses my cheek. "I appreciate you being concerned, but I'm honestly okay. Are *you* going to be okay?"

I nod. "Yes. If you're okay, I'm okay."

She shrugs. "Okay then. We're okay."

After breakfast we do the get-Sam-ready-for-school dance that we perform so well every morning you'd think it was professionally choreographed.

She packs his lunch while I get him dressed (today in snowflake pajamas for Pajama Day).

I get his water bottle and snack in his backpack while she does teeth and hair.

I help him into his shoes while she helps him into his mittens.

She zips up his coat while I put a hat on his head.

I get him strapped into his car seat, give them both a kiss goodbye, and they pull out of the driveway.

Some brides pay for an all-day photographer, meaning I'm there with her and her bridal party and family in the morning while they're drinking their mimosas and getting their hair and makeup done. The bride I'm working for today, someone named Jennifer, did not pay for a full day.

I'm not scheduled to arrive at the venue until 4PM.

I use my free time to go shopping for Roxie's stocking. As much as I get into the spirit of the season, stockings are always something I forget about until the last minute.

Roxie texts me at two.

ROXIE: Hi baby! I forgot to tell you. I bought you a new outfit to wear on Christmas. I left it hanging behind the closet door. You should wear it to the wedding you're doing tonight. You'll look hotter than the groom ;) Also, I can't wait to take it off you when you get home tonight.

Roxie doesn't usually buy me clothes. She trusts me to pick out my own shit, as she should. But I don't put too much thought into it. It's a rough day. If she needs to distract herself by micromanaging our wardrobes, I'll go with it. For now. Besides, she promised to strip me after work.

I find the outfit behind the closet door where she said it would be. Black dress pants, an Airforce Blue button-down with a small white dotted pattern on it, beige wool suspenders, and a beige wool bowtie. It's very hipster-ish, but I dig it.

She texts me again.

ROXIE: Check the pockets.

I check the pocket of the pants and find a folded piece of Roxie's stationary – because she still believes in stationary. I open it up and read it.

Go to the place where we had our first kiss.
Look in the tree for something you don't want to miss.

Is she sending me on a scavenger hunt before work? Why do I feel like she's pulling a Jake and trying to turn a bad day into a good one?

I go to the place where we had our first kiss, the place where she almost choked to death on a piece of gum. And also the place I parked the truck when I proposed.

I look up in the little tree on the piece of lawn between the sidewalk and the street and see a clear plastic Christmas ornament dangling from an empty branch. I pull it down. The ornament is similar to the plastic Easter eggs I used for the gender reveal. It's meant to be filled with something. I pop it open and remove another piece of folded stationary.

Best Things About Fall
New TV shows
Apple cider

Leaves
Friday night football games
Hoodies
Chili

Underneath the list is another clue.

If you remember making this list, go to the place where we talked about the kiss.

Easy. That's Adam's house. Adam's porch to be exact.

I've been on Adam's porch hundreds of times since that day in high school. Hell, I lived in that house for three years. But sometimes I can still see her standing there, teenage Roxie, with her fading freckles, her smirk, and her long sleeves pulled over her hands to keep warm.

I find another plastic ornament sitting on the porch swing. I pop it open to find another note.

Do you remember where we were the first time you told me you loved me?
Go there now. You already know where I hid the key.

Where did I tell her I loved her for the first time? It definitely wasn't high school. It couldn't have been our summer together in '05 either, because we were both pretending that was just a summer fling. It must have been after her divorce...

Got it! It was the summer of 2012. We had gotten into an argument. I don't remember about what. Probably just the normal let's-pretend-this-doesn't-mean-anything-even-though-it-does kind of fight. We were in the kitchen.

I go around back and find the key where it always is. Hopefully it's okay with Adam and Emilia that I sneak into their kitchen real quick.

I find the ornament on the kitchen island. Of course.

Remember when you threw me a Welcome Home party at the pool?
You'll find another clue there. Look on a stool.

I check my watch. It's 3:10. I have to be at the venue at 4:00. I have my equipment in the truck, so I should be able to make it to my old apartment complex and then head straight to the ceremony.

When I pull into my old apartment complex, I see a text from Jennifer, the bride.

JENNIFER: Hi Jake! There's been an incident at the venue. A pipe burst! A friend of mine is offering the use of his backyard. I'm on my way now to check it out, and I'll text you the address as soon as I get there. TTYS!

Oh damn. What a disaster. She seems to be taking it well. I just hope everyone is going to be warm enough. The high today is only thirty-four. *Brrr.*

I head over to the pool at the complex. In the summer, you need a key to get into the pool area. But I guess they don't care in the winter because the gate is unlocked. I walk in and find the clue on a stool just like she said it would be.

I know you have a wedding to make, but first you have

some dishes to break.

She's referring to the night I gave her a box of old dishes to slam on the patio at The Bar. It's not far from here. I check my watch again. 3:35. I check my phone. No text yet from the bride. I should be good.

The patio tables and chairs have been removed from the back of The Bar for winter, but I do see my next clue dangling from the mistletoe above the back door.

Working together that summer was just the start.
Do you remember where we were when I gave you my whole heart?

This bulb has a mini airplane bottle of Fireball inside it. I'm not sure if it's meant to keep me warm, or if it's part of the clue. Airplane bottle – airport.

Her whole heart. The keychain. We were in the back of my truck, parked at that field near the airport.

I check my watch and phone again. Still no update from Jennifer, so I feel safe heading toward the airport.

Throughout the years, the field has been home to several restaurants. As of now it is just an area of grass and pine trees off the side of the road.

At least, it *was*. Until someone turned it into ... this.

A magical winter wonderland lay before me.

The property has been decorated in blues and silvers with lace, burlap, and pine. A giant twinkling Christmas tree filled with blue and silver bulbs sits near a frozen pond. A few dozen chairs are set up in front of a makeshift altar made of lace and pine needles. There are electric heaters and portable gas fireplaces spread throughout the area. One of the fireplaces has a s'mores-making station – and not just the basics either. I see Reese's trees, berries, toasted coconut, and Nutella – because if there's one thing me and Roxie agree on, it's that Nutella makes everything better.

It takes a few minutes for me to acquaint myself with the area before I realize there is soft Christmas music playing ... *Oh, Holy Night*. From where, I'm not sure. Maybe a hidden speaker in one of the fireplaces?

Next to the wonderland is a giant insulated tent. The area is cozy, beautiful, and surprisingly warm thanks to the heaters and fireplaces. I feel like I'm inside a snow globe.

An empty snow globe. There's not another person in sight.

There's a black F-150 parked near the Christmas tree. Funny enough, it looks exactly like the one I used to drive when I was twenty-three, the one we hung out in all summer that year. In fact, we were in the bed of the truck when she gave me her whole heart.

I walk toward it, thinking maybe there's someone in the truck. But no. It's empty as well.

I'm so confused. Am I in the right place? It's been a very long time since I've been here, but I'm pretty sure this is where we used to park. I just don't understand why it looks like a wedding is happening here. Is this the wedding I'm covering tonight? Did Roxie contact the bride to get the location? There are no broken pipes around, and this is definitely not something that was thrown together at the last minute.

And what was the point of the scavenger hunt? Was she just entertaining me for a few hours before I started work? Maybe she wanted to distract me to keep me from thinking about Noel?

I'm trying to decide what to do next when I see a Hummer limo pull into the field. The tires make a dull crunching sound as they hit the snow.

I can't see who is inside because the windows are very heavily tinted. But once it comes to a complete stop, a back door opens.

I watch intently, intrigued to see what happens next.

A little boy steps out of the limo. *My* little boy. He's dressed in a suit with the same color suspenders and bowtie that I'm wearing, but with a white shirt instead of a blue one.

"Hey, buddy!" I call out to him.

"Hi, Daddy," he says when he reaches me. He hands me another plastic ornament.

I pop it open. This one has a note and a small blue box. I open the note.

Daddy, here comes your bride.

In the box, I find our wedding rings.

This is indeed a wedding. It's my wedding, *our* wedding.

Everything after that seems to happen in a blur. The officiant appears at the altar. I'm not even sure where he comes from. A photographer appears as well. I'm not familiar with her, but I trust that Roxie wouldn't have chosen someone who wasn't great.

Our mothers exit the limo and are escorted to their seats by Adam. My siblings, their boyfriends, and Emilia have a seat as well. Allison's husband, Brahm, joins them.

Once our small audience is seated, Adam joins me

and Sam at the altar. He is wearing the same outfit as Sam. He smacks me on the back.

"Happy Wedding Day, brother."

Allison comes out of the limo first and walks slowly down the aisle toward us.

When she reaches the altar, I hear the music change from "These Are The Special Times" by Christina Aguilera to "Love's in Our Hearts on Christmas Day" by NSYNC. Everyone stands up to turn around and I see Dr. Hum open the limo door.

I get a little choked up when my beautiful bride steps out. I barely hear the shutter sounds or the music. She's so darn beautiful that she drowns out the noise and all I see is her, coming down the aisle toward me, in her long-sleeve lace trumpet gown with the deep V-neck. (I only know these descriptions from working with so many brides ... and trust me when I say the dress is spectacular).

Once she arrives, the officiant asks, "Who supports this woman in her commitment to this man?"

"Her mother and I," Dr. Hum says, before giving her a quick kiss on the cheek and having a seat next to his wife in the front row.

I admit I don't pay much attention to how he begins the ceremony. My mind is still spinning from the surprise. When it's Roxie's turn to say her vows, my head spins again.

"When I was little," she begins, "I used to think love was what I saw in the movies. I thought it was kissing in the rain like in *Breakfast at Tiffany's*, climbing up a fire escape like at the end of *Pretty Woman*, or riding off into the sunset on a lawnmower like in *Can't Buy Me Love*. But as I've grown up, sometimes with you, and sometimes without you, as we've seen our credits roll several times, I've learned that love isn't always about grandiose gestures and romantic scenes. I've learned that love is the way we put our pieces back together when they're broken, love is a fist bump across the table when our son does something hilarious, love is the silly messages you write on our letterboard before dinner, and the way you always seem to know what I need before *I* know what I need. You've had my back since I was four years old. You're a part of my favorite memories, and now you're also the co-creator of our family. I look forward to high-fiving you for the rest of my life."

Wait. What?

No.

I'm supposed to be the one who says all the sweet shit. And she's supposed to be the one who laughs and says something sarcastic. I think she just beat me at my own game.

At the end of the ceremony, after the officiant says, "I now pronounce you partners for life," and "You may seal your promise with a kiss," it's time for my favorite part of every wedding – the photography.

We get into the back of the pickup truck for pictures (nice touch, Rox – high-five for this one), and she whispers, "Are you mad?"

"If by mad, you mean absolutely crazy about you? Yes," I whisper back.

"I mean, because I didn't let you plan the wedding."

"Are you kidding? I never cared about planning a wedding. I only cared about being your husband. And by the way, how did you get a marriage license without me?"

"I didn't," she says timidly. "This was actually a commitment ceremony. We will get our marriage license next week. When we get back from our honeymoon."

"There's a honeymoon?"

"Of course."

"Where are we going?"

"The three of us our going to Universal for Christmas to see the Harry Potter stuff…"

"I love this."

"After Christmas, Sam is staying with my parents, and we are going to Barbuda and Antigua."

"I love this, too."

"I hope you're not upset that I did all of this without you. You're always doing the sweetest, most thoughtful things, and I feel like I never really do anything nice for you."

"Roxie,"

"What?"

"Stop. Lemme kiss you."

"'K."

Good Things Come

Note from the Author:

Heyyyy, guys! It's me, Jodie. Remember those Choose Your Own Adventure books from the 80s? I've decided to let you guys choose your own ending for Jake and Roxie. Their story CAN end here. And it can end *happily*. They are at peace, satisfied with their life together, and happier than ever. There is really no reason at all for me to add anything else to this story.

But I did.

And I'm leaving it up to you to decide whether or not to read it. Should they live happily ever after as they are now? Or do you want more? Your choice.

And P.S. THANK YOU for reading!

Good Things Come

Epilogue
* Sam *

November 2018

Daddy pulls our SUV into a parking spot in the crowded lot.

"And he nails it!" I say proudly from the backseat.

I see Daddy look back at me in the rearview mirror. He shakes his head and laughs. I love making Daddy laugh. It's not that hard, really. He laughs all the time.

"I don't know where you came from, buddy," he tells me as he turns off the ignition.

"Silly!" I say. "I came from Mommy's belly. That's where babies come from. Everyone knows that!"

Daddy gets out and opens the door behind his.

Last night Daddy took me to the store and bought me a new car seat. A big boy car seat! It uses the regular seat belt instead of coming with its own.

My car seat has always been on the passenger side, my whole life. But this morning Daddy took out my old car seat and put it in our garage. Then he put my new seat on the driver's side. Being on this side is going to take some getting used to. Every time we drive over train tracks, the rule is that Daddy looks to the left for oncoming trains, and I look to the right. This morning we both looked to the left! That means there could have been a train coming from the right, and now we'll never know! I'll have to remember next time to tell Daddy to look right. We can't keep crossing the tracks blind on one side. We just can't live like that.

When Daddy opens my door, he leans in to unbuckle my seat belt.

"I got it!" I yell. "I can do this on my own now."

I lean over and press the red button to release the seat belt. Being able to get out of my car seat on my own is so cool. I can't wait to show my friends at school my new car seat. It even has a cup holder.

I slide out of my booster seat and get ready to climb from the car. Daddy puts his hands out, but I'm a big boy now. I can get out on my own.

I turn my back to him and lower my foot carefully until it reaches the ground.

"See, Daddy?" I tell him. "I got this."

"So you do," he says. I think he's proud of me.

He closes the back door and takes my hand. Even though I'm a big boy with a big boy car seat, I still have to hold hands in parking lots. Don't play on the stairs and always hold hands in parking lots. Those are Mommy's two biggest rules.

We take a few steps, hand in hand, while I look at our shadows on the ground.

"Daddy, look how tall your shadow is," I point out.

"Uh oh!" he says, stopping suddenly. "We forgot the picture."

Oh! Right! The picture I drew.

We walk back, and Daddy presses the button to unlock the doors. He opens the passenger seat and carefully picks up my drawing.

"Here ya go, bud," he says as he hands it to me.

"Thanks for remembering for me, Daddy," I say.

We take off again, hand in hand, careful to watch for cars.

When I see automatic revolving doors at the entrance to the building, I get really happy. Revolving doors are so fun! Especially the ones that move on their own. "Can I go in by myself, Daddy?" I ask. *Please say yes. Please say yes.*

"Sure you can," he says.

I jump up and throw my fist in the air. "Yes!"

"You go first," Daddy says while we wait for the right moment. When the time comes, I jump in quickly. Daddy gets in the one behind me.

I walk in pace with the door and hop out when I see an opening.

Daddy comes out behind me.

"Thanks for letting me go by myself," I tell him.

"That was really cool!"

"You did great!" he says, beaming. I think he's proud of me again. I love it when Mommy and Daddy are proud of me.

I look around at the gigantic lobby we've entered. There are hallways in every direction. "Where to now?" I ask Daddy.

He points straight ahead. "To the elevators."

Elevators! Wow, this day is just loaded with fun! A spinning door *and* an elevator! "Can I press the button?" I ask.

"Of course."

We walk toward the elevators. Well, Daddy walks. I skip.

"Up or down?" I ask.

"Up."

"Okay." I carefully push the Up button with my knuckle. Mommy taught me to press buttons with my knuckles whenever I can because buttons are so germy, and you can get sick if you press it with your fingertip, because your finger touches things more often than your knuckles. And sometimes I accidentally touch my mouth or my nose with my fingers and Mommy freaks out. One time, when we were at the zoo, we saw a sea lion that was lying on the bottom of the aquarium. He wasn't swimming like the other sea lions and he was breathing really fast. The person who worked at the zoo told us he was sick. I think the sea lion probably got sick because he forgot to use his knuckle for the elevator button. That's why I always remember to use mine. I don't want to get sick. Especially if it involves throwing up. That's the worst.

The elevator doors open, and we step inside.

"Which floor?" I ask.

"Five," Daddy tells me.

I look over the numbers carefully and press the number 5 with my knuckle. I know all of my numbers and all of my letters now.

The doors close, and I look up to watch the numbers go by on the digital display.

Two, three, four...

At the fourth floor the elevator stops and the doors open. A lady steps on with us. She is very pretty like my mommy. She wears navy blue pants and a navy blue shirt. A name badge hangs from a cord around her neck. I can read a lot of words now, but I'm not good at reading names.

"What floor?" I ask her.

She smiles at me, but it looks like a sad smile and not a happy one. I don't know why.

"Seven," she tells me.

I press the 7 with my knuckle.

"I like your shirt," she tells me. She blinks her eyes a few times quickly.

"Thank you," I say. I hold up my picture. "I drew a picture," I tell her.

She smiles again, that sad smile. I recognize it. My mommy used to smile like that, too.

"That's very nice," she tells me. "Is that your house?"

"Yup!" I say proudly. "That's our sidewalk and that's my bedroom window right there."

The elevator goes up to the fifth floor and the doors open. I step out and hold my arm in front of the elevator door to let my daddy out. Daddy used to do it all the time, but now he lets me do it.

"You're such a gentleman," the lady tells me.

I'm supposed to remove my arm now, so the door will close. But I reach into my pocket instead and pull out a rock. It's painted with a rainbow on it. I made it for my mommy a few months ago and it made her really happy. Maybe it can make someone else happy, too.

"Here," I reach out my hand and drop it into hers. "It's a rainbow. Rainbows are the brightness after a dark storm."

She looks up at Daddy and then back at me. "Oh, sweetie. I can't take your rock."

"Sure you can," I insist. "I have a lot of others."

"Thank you," she says. She looks up at Daddy. "What a special little boy."

Daddy nods but doesn't say anything.

I wave goodbye and the elevator doors close.

I look up at Daddy and I see him rubbing his eye. He might be sad. I hope I didn't make him sad because I gave the rock away.

"Daddy?" I say as we walk down a hallway filled with doors.

"Yeah?"

"Are you sad because I gave her the rock?"

Daddy stops walking. He kneels down and looks at me. Whenever Daddy kneels down, I know he's going to say something important. He puts a hand on each of my arms to make sure I look at him and don't squirm away. Oh no. He must be real mad.

"No, buddy. I'm not sad at all. I'm happy, because you're an amazing kid, and me and Mommy are lucky to have you. You make us so proud and so happy every single day."

I smile. I'm glad he's not mad.

"For the next couple of weeks," he continues, "the three of us will have a lot of adjusting to do. It's going to be busy and hectic. We'll all be tired and maybe frustrated. You know your mom, she'll probably even be crying. But promise me that no matter what is happening around us, you will never ever forget how much we adore you."

I nod. "Okay, Daddy. I promise."

He stands up and takes my hand again. "Are you ready for this?"

"I'm ready."

We walk toward a door that is partly open. Daddy taps on the door softly.

"Come on in," I hear Mommy's voice say from inside the room.

Daddy pushes open the door the rest of the way and we walk in.

I see Mommy in the bed. She smiles so big when she sees me. Maybe the biggest smile ever.

"Hi, baby!" she says. "Come here! Gosh, I missed you like crazy!"

We walk over to the bed, and Daddy picks me up and sets me down on Mommy's lap. I give her kisses all over her face before I see the little baby resting in

Mommy's arm. The baby is wrapped up in a blanket, and all I can see is its pink face. I look closely and see little white dots all over the nose and dark eyelashes resting on the baby's cheeks.

"Sam, are you ready to meet your little sister?"

I nod, eagerly.

"Let's see if we can wake her up."

"Skylar," I say, touching her cheek. "Wake up so you can meet your big brother. I finally got to wear my Big Brother shirt today. And I made you a picture of our house, so you'll recognize it when we bring you home."

I wipe my finger across her cheek again, and she finally opens her eyes.

Hello, baby sister. I've been waiting for you my whole life.

"So, Mommy," I say, once I've spent some time admiring my sister, "now that Skylar is here, I need to see exactly how big the hole is that she came out of."

THE END

HIGH-FIVES AND FIST BUMPS

First, I thank YOU, the readers. You guys have been so patient waiting for this story. I apologize for taking so long to write it. The truth is that I was having a hard time writing a happy ending for someone else when I was so desperately fighting for a happy ending of my own. You guys are still here cheering me on after five years, and there aren't enough thank yous in the world to express how much I truly appreciate that.

My parents, Mom, Dad, and John, and the rest of my family – you believe in me even when I don't believe in myself, you push me when I need you to, and you also know when it's best to leave it alone. Special fist bumps to my cousins, Chelsea and Lee, for being the sisters I never had.

My best friends – Lisa, Cas, Christine, Amy, Amanda, and Gen. You guys had been chillin' on the backburner for a decade, but as soon as I needed you, you were front and center. I promise I won't forget that. I hope none of you ever need me to repay the favor, but I promise to be there if you do.

My proofreaders and beta readers – Courtney, for making sure Jake wasn't doing all the work; Kelly, for noticing and correcting those annoying idiosyncrasies; and Jess, for being the wedding planner – All three of you, and your input and ideas, were incredible!

Tina Torrest, for helping me with the blurb. The

fossilized French fry is still my favorite part.

My editor, Madison Seidler, who, besides being a great editor, could be the best human I know. The world might one day be a better place if more people cared the way you do.

My cover designer, Michelle Preast of Indie Book Covers, for your hard work, kindness, sincerity, and patience. Oh, and book cover!

The bloggers, reviewers, and fellow authors for sharing your love, your thoughts, and my links.

Lots of love to my 600+ TTC Sisters on Instagram. I'm so happy that most of you are seeing your rainbows at the end of your storm. Thanks for being there for me during my most difficult times.

And lastly, thank you to my cover star, my best, my hashtagblessed, the little boy who turned my cup half full. When I was pregnant with you, I would sing that Michael Buble song, "Haven't Met You Yet." *I promise you kid, I'll give so much more than I get. I just haven't met you yet.*

But the thing is, Ian … I lied. It's been over seven years and I still can't figure out how to give so much more than I get from you. But I promise you, kid, that I won't stop trying. I love you, Munchie. I'm so glad that the rainbow at the end of my storm was you.

About the Author

After earning her Media Arts degree from Wayne State University in Detroit, Jodie moved to Wilmington, North Carolina with big dreams of writing for film and TV. But there was a beach. And she got distracted.

Now a waitress by day and writer by night, Jodie is again living in the Detroit area and killing it as a single mom to her 7-year-old son.

She loves to hear from readers and you can reach her at:

FB: **www.facebook.com/sweetbutsnarky**

Snap: jodie-beau

Instagram: jodie_beau

Email: **booksbyjodiebeau@gmail.com**

Other works by Jodie Beau

The Good Life

All Good Things

Lights Out

All available on Amazon for Kindle or paperback.

Made in the USA
Middletown, DE
02 February 2019